Girl Child

Bette L. Crosby

PublishAmerica
Baltimore

ISBN: 1-4241-7869-X
PUBLISHED BY PUBLISHAMERICA, LLLP
www.publishamerica.com
Baltimore

Printed in the United States of America

For my husband Richard,
who has given me a place to dream
and the inspiration to follow my heart.

Acknowledgments

I am deeply thankful to the following people, all of whom helped me breathe life into this story: Our dear friends, Bruce and Marie Libby, for time spent sharing their stories and the reams of background research they provided. Leon Goolsby, for sharing his extensive knowledge of the Shenandoah Valley and its people. Fellow author Sunny Serafino, for reading every word of the manuscript and helping to push the stumbling blocks aside. My sister, Geri Conway, for her continual support and encouragement. The Scripteasers Group, eight wonderfully talented women writers, whose critique sessions challenged me to grow beyond myself. Dan Grant, who allowed me to cut my baby teeth in his writing group. The ladies of the Analyze This Book Club, who month after month provide a wealth of warm stories and chilled wine. And, my Mother, whose delightful Southern voice still echoes in my ear and provides inspiration, although she is gone. But, most of all, I thank my husband, Richard, for reasons too numerous to name.

Abigail Lannigan

Born—August, 1912

was barely thirteen years old when Mama died and left me and Will in the care of Papa, a man who'd think nothing of shoving a dose of castor oil down my throat just so he could watch my face turn inside out. "It's good for what ails you," he'd say, yet I noticed he never gave Will the same big dose. Papa didn't say it in precise words, but he made it clear enough he wouldn't give two hoots if all the girl babies in Chestnut Ridge, Virginia were in the graveyard along with Mama. Of course, with him being a staunch Methodist, I don't believe Papa was capable of taking a butcher knife and slicing off heads or anything, but he surely knew how to destroy people from inside, a sliver of spirit, a piece of pride, a chunk of heart, until one day there's nothing left but a walking around shell to do the cooking and laundry.

It's a roundabout story but Papa's blind-sightedness is the very reason Destiny Fairchild may end up in the Women's Correctional Facility, which is a fancy way of saying penitentiary. Everybody's life could have been a whole lot different if Mama hadn't died before she got a chance to set things right. She was the one to tell Papa there were two sides to every story and he should have the fairness of mind to hear them all the way through. Will, bless his heart, wasn't the least bit like Papa but nonetheless we'd get to scrapping over something—who was smarter, who slacked on their chores, who said what and who didn't—that's when Mama stepped in. She'd make us sit at the kitchen table and tell both versions of how the tussle got started. After everything was all explained, she'd generally say we should be ashamed of ourselves, fussing over such a bit of nonsense when here we were twins, born of the same seed, a brother and sister, linked together for life. More often than not, she'd dole out a punishment that involved standing in opposite corners of the room and thinking things over for a while.

Unfortunately, Destiny didn't have Mama to see to the fairness of things before they got out of hand, besides in her case there were three sides, hers,

Elliott's and mine. Problem is, no one's ever heard mine—not even Judge Kensington.

The first time I laid eyes on Destiny was back in 1994, when she rented the old Meyerson place—it sat cattycorner from mine. By then, the house had been empty for four, maybe five years; the windows were near black and the grass so tall the front yard had the look of a wheat field from June till late October. It broke my heart to see the place in such a state—especially when I'd think back on dear Margaret Meyerson and the hours she spent squatted down by that flowerbed. She truly did love those flowers. The summer before she died, I caught sight of her picking aphids off the geraniums and shaking her head as if those little bitty bugs were the most worrisome thing she'd ever laid eyes on. Anyway, I'd begun to believe that poor house was on its way to ruin, when one morning I looked across and there was Destiny. She was perched on a wobbly kitchen stool, her yellow ponytail swishing back and forth as she scrubbed at those windows. I watched her for a good long while, watched as she'd wipe and shine one window then move on to the next. Dirty as those windows were, you've have figured it to be a full day's work, but when she finished the windows, she started in on the yard. She hauled out the old lawnmower Ben Meyerson kept in the shed and took to muscling her way through a tangle of knee-high grass. I must say, it was good to hear that lawnmower again, it brought to mind the way Ben took care of the place. His lawn wasn't much bigger than a picnic blanket, but twice a week he'd haul out that lawnmower and set to work. You knew without looking it was him, 'cause he'd be whistling some out-of-tune song you couldn't quite recognize. Back when Ben lived there, I'd find my morning paper brought right up to the doorstep and slipped inside the screen. Every time I mentioned something about how nice that was, a grin would slide across Ben's face but he never did take credit for doing it. After he went to live with his daughter in Schenectady, I'd find my paper over behind the bushes or at the far end of the drive.

Destiny lived in the Meyerson place for a good two months before we actually spoke in any sizeable measure. Oh, she was neighborly enough, toot the horn and wave as she drove by in her little red Pinto—it had the look of a piecework quilt, one green fender and a patch of blue tape on the side window—but once she'd rounded the corner, she was gone for the day. She left early in the morning and didn't get back till after dark. Whenever she was home she'd be working on the house—with the windows wide open and no curtains or shades, you could see her plain as day, scurrying up and down the ladder, painting and polishing. I'd heard tell she actually had a full time job in the bookstore downtown but it sure didn't stop her from scrubbing and cleaning the way she did. Anybody would have had to admire the girl's industriousness.

One Saturday morning in the early part of October, I went out to fetch my Middleboro Tribune and it was nowhere to be found. I'd gotten somewhat used to it being behind the wisteria, but this time it wasn't there. And, it wasn't up under the porch, where it had also landed on a number of previous occasions—those delivery boys could be fairly irresponsible at times. I started thinking maybe it hadn't come yet and was about to quit looking when I spotted the Cooper's paper on the far edge of their drive. It stood to reason that if their Tribune had been delivered, mine had also, so I poked and prodded my way through every bush along the walkway. Finally, I spotted the darn thing hanging off the edge of the roof, the plastic wrap snagged in the gutter—it was dangling there like it was right ready to drop. So, I got hold of a broom and took four or five jabs at it, but it wouldn't budge. By then, I was pretty well winded and about ready to give up, but Destiny came trotting over with that wobbly stool hooked under her arm. "I'll get your newspaper, Missus Lannigan," she called out.

That's me, Abigail Anne Lannigan.

I'd seen Destiny scamper on and off that stool fifty times or more, but this time she reached a bit too far and over the stool went. It toppled sideways and when I tried to catch hold of it so she wouldn't fall, we both ended up on the ground, flat on our back, with that blasted newspaper still stuck to the roof.

"Oh! I'm so sorry, Missus Lannigan," she sputtered. Before I could tell her it was my fault, she was back on her feet and tugging at my arm. "Can you get up?" she asked. "Here, let me help you. You hurt?"

"I'm fine," I answered. "Fine." The truth was that my knee was bothering me, but mostly because of the arthritis. I hadn't taken much of a fall. Destiny, however, had gone heels over head; she had a good size scrape and a sizeable welt rising up on her shinbone. I'd seen enough bumps and bruises in my day to know that ought to have ice on it, so I said, "Come inside and I'll patch you up." She was so pleased, you'd think offering to put a chunk of ice on her leg was the kindest thing in the world. I looked at her great big smile and right off noticed what a pretty little thing she was. Velvety green eyes, not bright like an emerald, not yellow either, a misty color so soft you'd wonder if there wasn't a touch of gray mixed in. Elliott can claim I don't have a speck of sense in my head, but I'm telling you, God Almighty would have trusted this girl if he'd caught sight of those eyes.

Once we were inside the house, I couldn't for the life of me remember where I'd put the ice pack but things like that didn't bother Destiny. She took an ice cube and slid it up and down her shinbone. "See," she said, "this works just fine."

That morning it was a bit on the cool side so I fixed us a pot of tea and, busy as she was, Destiny sat there talking to me for well over an hour. I said, "You must have better things to do than spend time with a clumsy old lady," but she smiled like she was having a real nice time and poured herself another cup of tea. She was a talker, Destiny, and when she got to telling a story, you'd lean in close to soak up every word that came out of her mouth. Her voice was so sweet; you'd think it impossible for a mean word to ever come from her mouth. Looking back, I can honestly say I can't remember a single hard-edged thing about the girl, she was little and delicate-boned, sweet as a summer strawberry.

Sitting at the kitchen table, babbling on like we'd been friends for a hundred years, I learned the God awful fact of how her mama run off and left her— sent the poor kid away to church camp one summer, then disappeared without a trace. Destiny was only nine years old when she came home and found her mama's stuff gone from the apartment. Weeks she was there, living on whatever was left in the cupboard, plain spaghetti, cereal with no milk, crackers—she figured her mama was sure to come back. She'd about run out of things to eat when the landlord came looking for rent money and discovered her living by herself. A neighbor lady took her in for a few months, then she was shuffled from one spot to another till she was old enough to get a job and make her own way. I knew she was a spunky little thing by the way she tackled that old house, but I sure never supposed she had all that sadness in her life. I came close to telling her about how my own papa had no use for girl babies, but I figured we'd had enough fretting about the past for one day.

Late that night, a rainstorm came up. In the springtime we get feathery rains, rain that sounds like an angel whispering, but this night it was a fall storm—wind knocking flower pots to the cement, raindrops the size of grapefruits banging against the window. The noise woke me and I opened my eyes but stayed in bed. I was thinking about what a nice visit I'd had with Destiny when I heard a noise in the bush outside my bedroom window. A few months back the house at the end of the block was burgled, so I wasn't about to take any chances. I jumped out of bed so fast you'd think my rear end was on fire, tiptoed down the hallway and into the kitchen. I knew not to turn on any lights 'cause it would give a burglar fair warning. Once I got hold of the big butcher knife, I slipped back into the bedroom and peeked through the venetian blind slats to see what was going on. Right there, on top of the wisteria bush, was that blasted newspaper. For a half-hour I laughed about what a silly old lady I'd gotten to be—but silly old lady, or not, I still handled the situation without hollering for the police.

The following day was Monday. Mondays and Fridays are when the county aide comes to lend a hand, although in this woman's case I'd say it was more like a finger. She does drive me to get groceries, which is something I truly appreciate, but other than that, she hardly budges—I usually have to fix her lunch and sometimes an afternoon snack if she stays a bit longer. "Oh, I *know* you want to watch *Oprah*," she'll say, then plop herself down to listen to advice from Doctor Phil. Anyway, it was Tuesday before I got around to making the cookies, chocolate chip with walnut chunks. That evening when I saw the lights in Destiny's window I headed over to her house. She had on paint-splattered dungarees and looked ready to start working. "I don't mean to barge in," I said, "just wanted to bring you some of my homemade cookies."

"Oh my, don't they look delicious!" A real glad smile brightened Destiny's face and she pulled the door wide open. "Come on in," she said, "we'll have some together."

She didn't have any tea but made instant coffee and set two cups on what was supposed to be her kitchen table—it was a small size piece of plywood stretched across some cinderblocks. There wasn't a stick of furniture in the living room or the dining room, just two tipsy-looking lamps without any shades. Destiny must have supposed I'd notice such a thing, 'cause she started apologizing.

"I'm sorry for the way this place looks," she said. "I've been working down at the book store and it doesn't pay much so I haven't bought any furniture yet. But, my luck's about to change…" She laughed and rubbed her hands together like a kid with a jolly good secret. "I got a job that's gonna pay real money," she said. "Waitress. The dinner shift. Good tips *and* more time to work on the house!"

She gave me the only chair and perched herself atop a step stool. I admired her being such a genuinely determined person who didn't feel the least bit sorry for herself. Elliott, who's nothing more than a twice removed nephew, always had some sad story and long before he got to the part where he said what he was wanting, I knew he was gonna ask for a loan. Destiny never wanted a thing from me, maybe that's why I was so inclined to do for her. "Why, I've got an old kitchen set downstairs in the basement," I told her. "You'd be more than welcome to that."

"Thanks, Missus Lannigan," she answered, "but, you might need that set someday. I can make do with this stuff for a while."

I wondered what *stuff* she was talking about; the only real furnishings she had was two broken lamps and one spindle back chair. "Nonsense," I said, "that furniture is just collecting dust. You'd be doing me a favor to haul it away." I had a number of things she could put to good use: a kitchen set with four perfectly fine chairs, some mahogany end tables, a bookcase and an overstuffed chair you'd have thought brand new if not for the burn hole Will made in the right arm. That happened before I knew about the pitiful state of his health, although I should have guessed something was wrong when he just sat there and let the cigarette between his fingers burn down to an ash. I told her, "Destiny, it would be a kindness to take those things off my hands, it's too much for an eighty-two year old woman to be burdened with."

"Oh, Missus Lannigan," she said, "I couldn't just *take* your perfectly good furniture, but I'd be real happy to pay you for the things."

"Pay me?" A blind man could see that child didn't have two spare quarters to rub together, let alone pay good money for some stuff that wasn't doing anything but dry-rotting in my basement. "Destiny," I said, "you don't need to pay a cent for that worthless old stuff. I'd get a lot pleasure out of giving it to you. If you don't take it, I'll have to call the Salvation Army to come get it."

"I think you're just being nice," she said with one eyebrow stretched up like a person who doubted my intention to give the stuff away. "How about if I don't pay you cash money, but pop over once or twice a week and lend a hand with the chores?"

"That would be right neighborly, honey. You don't have to do any chores though, just come and sit a spell, have some tea, that's enough."

We laughed and shook hands like two big-deal businessmen, then we got back to finishing up the cookies I'd brought over. I'd made those cookies dozens of times, but somehow they tasted better dunked in Destiny's instant coffee.

On Thursday, that was her day off, Destiny showed up on my doorstep at about eight-thirty in the morning. She was wearing those paint-spattered dungarees and had a Dunkin Donuts bag in her hand. "I've brought some muffins," she said. "We can have a nice snack together after I've finished the chores."

"Forget about that nonsense," I told her. "You just sit yourself down and I'll fix some tea." I was about to ask if she'd prefer to have coffee—I had some of those coffee bags that can make a single cup at a time, same almost as making tea—but by then she'd already latched onto my cleanser and bucket and was heading down the hallway toward the bathroom. "What do you think you're doing?" I called after her, but she laughed and reminded me that a deal was a deal. "You haven't seen the kitchen set yet," I said, but she didn't seem to care, just started in cleaning and scrubbing. In less than two hours that little devil had breezed through the entire house and had everything as polished up and sparkling as those windows of hers. Not that I would in any way compare Destiny to the county aide woman, but lazy old Lucille hadn't done that much work in the two years she'd been coming to help out.

I had a crock of leftover chicken soup in the refrigerator, so I heated some of that and we had ourselves an early lunch, then for dessert we ate the two blueberry muffins from Dunkin Donuts. There was something about Destiny's company that seemed to make ordinary food a lot tastier. When lunch was finished, she went down into the basement, cobwebs and all, and lugged up the table and chairs, all by her lone self. I helped a tiny bit once she got the stuff halfway up the stairs, mostly just by guiding the legs of the table around the corners as she heaved and hauled. If she told me once, she told me half a dozen times how happy she was to have such nice things for her house. Anybody else might have mentioned the burn hole in the arm of the chair, but not Destiny, she just went on and on about how lovely it would look in the corner of her living room. "It's the perfect place to sit and read," she said and that's when I fetched the floor lamp out of that back bedroom and handed it to her.

"No sense in you straining your eyes," I said. "Anyway, this lamp *belongs* with that chair." One by one she carted those things across the street and into her house. Everything except the overstuffed chair, it was too heavy for her to carry all that distance, so she wheeled it across the street on my trash-can dolly. Nothing more than a few scraps of furniture, but Destiny was happy and excited as a kid on Christmas morning. The odd thing was I had that same happy feeling—anybody might think it was something contagious and I'd caught this case of zippidy-do-da from her. As for me, I knew that's where I got it.

I never had any such feeling with Elliott, although he was supposed to be my blood relative. His great granddaddy was my papa, a fact which in and of itself would have been enough to turn me against the boy even if he didn't have such a pricklish personality. He sure wasn't related to Mama, she had a sweet disposition. Elliott's great grandma was Papa's first wife, a woman who died in 1881, almost thirty years before Papa married Mama. For the longest time, I never even knew Elliott existed and to this day I wish it had stayed that way.

He came nosing around after Will sold the farm, then after Will died and Elliott found out I'd gotten all of the inheritance money, he started coming to see me. He'd show up every once in a while, just often enough to remind me that he was a relative, someone who maybe ought to be in for a cut of the pie. Anybody with half an eyeball could see it was the money he was looking to latch onto; he sure didn't care a thing about me. Not once did Elliott offer to so much as wheel out the trash bins, let alone clean the toilet or take me for a Sunday afternoon drive. No, his visits usually lasted about fifteen or twenty minutes, then he'd have someplace else he had to dash off to. Well, it certainly didn't bother me; I can't say I enjoyed his company anyway. I never did watch out the window and hope he'd come by, the way I did with Destiny.

Judge Kensington didn't get to see that side of Elliott, all he heard was that slick-tongued story about an unfortunate nephew who had his inheritance swindled away. Nobody thought to tell Judge Kensington that Destiny was the one who'd call up and ask if I needed a quart of milk or loaf of bread when she was going to the store. He also never got to see the happy look in the girl's eyes whenever I gave her some little thing to brighten up that empty house of hers.

I sure as hell would tell him the truth, if I were able.

The Shenandoah Valley

Ninety Years Ago

n the spring of 1912, Livonia Lannigan's body grew round and firm. Her breasts became heavy and her stomach swelled to a great size. She took to leaving the waistband buttons of her dresses unhooked but even so could barely fit into the clothes she had worn just one year ago. The cotton bodices pressed tight against her tender breasts and she worried that it might stifle the milk flow needed for the baby so she loosened them whenever she was alone. Last summer, her ankles and feet had not swollen, now they throbbed and were thick and heavy as ham hocks. All of these discomforts were of no concern to Livonia as she was thankful for the size of her stomach, surely an indication that this baby was growing robust and healthy. When walking became painful, she sat on the front porch, rocking back and forth so slowly that at times she appeared motionless. For hours on end she would remain that way, waiting to feel movement from the baby that would come in September. Every night she crouched down with her knees pressing against the hardwood floor and her hands folded across the rise of her stomach. "Please God," she would pray, "help me to deliver a healthy son for William."

Her first baby boy had died, before he was christened or even named. The birth came two months early, on the second Wednesday in August—a day when William rode off to the Lexington Market long before the cock crowed. Livonia could blame no one but herself, for it was she who felt such a burning hunger for the cool breezes of the Rappahannock River. It had been a brutal summer, almost no rain, the earth so dry that gritty dust rose from nothing more than the flutter of a bird's wing, a dark red sand settled into Livonia's pores and stripped her hair of its luster. On that fateful day, her only intent was to cool herself, sit beneath a shady oak tree, and perhaps dangle her feet into the edge of the water. She saddled Whisper, a mare named for her gentleness, and rode out beyond the meadow. The animal moved along at an easy canter, slowing when she came to a dry stream bed or overgrown thicket, seemingly aware of the precious cargo she carried. No one could have known that a flock of wild turkeys would tear across the pathway and startle the poor mare so that without warning she'd rear up and throw the rider. Late that afternoon the animal returned home with an empty saddle; there, she stood alongside the barn and waited.

William did not return from Lexington until almost nightfall. The much needed rain had started that afternoon and on three different occasions he was forced to climb from the wagon and walk the skittish horse through a flooded gully in the road. He was wet and weary when he arrived home and it angered him that Livonia had not lit a lamp in the window. He did not see the still-saddled mare until he pulled close by the barn. Livonia would not be foolish enough to go riding in this weather, he thought as he guided both animals into the barn then hurried to the house calling out for his wife.

When William heard nothing but the sound of his own voice echoing back from the mountains, he took a lantern in his hand, folded an extra blanket beneath the mare's saddle, and started across the meadow in search of his wife. The rain had washed away any trail she might have left, so William had to rely solely upon his understanding of Livonia's nature to figure out which way she had traveled. He rode for three hours, calling her name out as he went, "Livonia, Livonia." He finally came upon her lying in the mud of the narrow pathway, near unconscious, a bloody baby locked in her arms. The baby's eyes were closed and its tiny fingers curled into fists. When William lifted the dead baby and saw it was a boy, he let out a wail so mournful that folks say it echoed up and down Massanutten Ridge for days afterward.

William Lannigan was a man who worked from sunup till sundown. He plowed and planted, harvested the crops and whatever produce he didn't use to feed his family, he carted off to market in the back of a horse drawn wagon. He single-handedly loaded his bushel baskets of apples onto the wagon and traveled twenty-three miles back and forth to the Lexington Market. Even in the drought years when many Shenandoah Valley farmers abandoned the fruitless land, he stayed, worked the farm, and eked out a living for his family. When the orchards failed, he planted corn and beans and tomatoes. His father before him had done the same, only his father had three stropping sons to help with the labor. William, being the eldest, had inherited the farm. A farm he would one day pass down to his own eldest son. But last November William turned fifty-six; he was feeling the weight of a man who had fathered seven girl babies and two boys, three if you include the dead child of his fourth wife Livonia. Not one of his boys had lived to see five years of age. William had already made his decision—if Livonia failed to produce a healthy baby boy this time, he would burn the crops and let the land lay fallow for all eternity.

In the last week of August, when the temperature in the valley was at an all time high, Livonia noticed a red stain on her panties and flew into a panic. Not again, she thought. It was too early. She had another three or four weeks before her time. *It can't happen to this baby, not this baby* she repeated over and over in her mind, all the while reminding herself how everything in the valley got dusted over with the gritty red sand that rose from the earth in the heat of summer. This time, she had done nothing to cause a miscarriage; she had weeded the garden and gathered eggs early in the morning then stayed indoors when the sun was at high noon, even rested twice a day. It was a healthy baby, she had felt him moving. She soothed his restlessness with the gentle stroke of her hand and a whispered lullaby. This time Livonia had done nothing wrong. *Nothing.* She went to the bedroom and checked her panties against the red discoloration on her white smock but it was not the same. The smock had splotches of a reddish brown color, the panties were the color of watered down pig's blood. Livonia went to the front porch and rang the large copper bell with a firm hand. The clang echoed through the mountains, loud and clear for almost five minutes, then Livonia sat down in the rocker and prayed.

That afternoon William rode across the valley and deep into Bear Trap Hollow. "Ruby, you've got to come now," he cried out as he pounded his fist against the cabin door.

A stoop shouldered woman with skin splotched and rutted by time and hardship pulled open the door. "Stop hollering," she said, "babies come in their own sweet time."

"This time it's different. Livonia is swelled up to the size of a cow and she's started to bleed. You've got to come stay with her till this baby is birthed." The midwife refused to leave before she had finished her chores, so William waited as she fed the chickens and two tiger striped cats, then wrote a note for her brother, who was out cutting timber. It seemed an eternity until the old woman tucked a package of herbs and potions inside the worn saddlebag and climbed astride an aging mule to follow him back down the mountainside.

It was almost dark when they reached the Lannigan farm but Livonia was still sitting in the rocker, kneading her stomach with circular strokes and singing a lullaby she remembered from childhood.

"Child, you need to come inside and lie down in the bed. Ruby's here now, you're gonna be just fine." A bony hand took hold of Livonia's arm and she rose from the rocker. "In no time at all, you'll have yourself a fine new baby."

The baby did not come that night, or the next day. Ruby brewed a tincture of loganberry tea and had Livonia drink three cups, then she sat her into a tub of warm water and rubbed juniper oil and mustard powder on the swollen stomach, to ease the pain. On three separate occasions Ruby felt the rise and fall of movement within Livonia and said, "There's more than one baby inside of you." The old woman even put her ear to Livonia's stomach and listened for the baby's heartbeat. "Two," she said. "Two heartbeats, two babies." But for three days there was no baby, only pain.

On the fourth day, a sudden rush of warm water ran down Livonia's legs and she called out for Ruby.

"This is it, honey," Ruby grinned an almost toothless smile. "That baby's coming. Before noontime he'll be suckling at your breast." But it was almost dinnertime before the first baby came. A boy, small in size but healthy and squalling. By dark a second baby had been born, this one a girl, smaller than the first baby, but healthy.

Ruby called out to the barn for William to come. "You got yourself a healthy boy," she said handing him the first baby. "Matter of fact, you got two babies."

"Both boys?"

"No. The second one's a girl. A mite small, but healthy enough."

"Oh," William answered, then walked away with the boy in his arms and did not turn back to see the second baby. "William," he said aloud. "I'll name him William after myself and my father, and his father before him. William Lannigan. The young master of what will one day be the finest farm in the Shenandoah Valley."

From her bed Livonia could see William holding the boy baby in his arms. She cuddled the girl closer to her breast and whispered, "Don't worry, sweetheart. Don't you worry. He's gonna love you too, he just needs time."

Livonia wanted to believe her own words, but thoughts of William's behavior kept her from sleep. Late that night, after both babies had been tucked into the same cradle, she heard someone moving about the parlor. She knew who it was by the shuffling clomp of heavy boots. The footsteps stopped for a moment then a flicker of light came from the doorway. The lamp had been lit. William never liked to sit in the parlor, so why would he do it in the middle of the night? Curious, Livonia climbed from the bed and tiptoed into the hallway, she hung back in the shadow where she could see but not be seen. She watched as William took a key from the top ledge of his grandfather's secretary, unlocked the cabinet door and removed a large black book. He then lowered the writing shelf and took a pen in his hand. For a long moment he sat there, leafing through the pages and shaking his head in the most sorrowful way. He paused for a moment, wiped his hand across his eyes and then started to write. After only a few strokes of his pen, he replaced the book and closed the cabinet door. Livonia slipped back into bed before she was discovered.

The next morning William rode off to the fields as he did every day and Ruby readied herself to leave. "You take care of that little girl," the old woman told Livonia. "The mister will see to the boy, but that sweet little thing is gonna have a hard time of it. I can feel it in my bones."

"He'll come to love her too," Livonia answered. "He just needs time."

"Mind my words, Missy, that little girl needs to know she's loved cause she's gonna walk a mighty rocky road. I *know* these things. I got me a sense of the future; I see things most people can't see." Ruby pulled a tiny leather pouch from her pocket; it was cracked and weathered, but wound tight with a yellow tie. "You put this under her pillow every night. She'll grow strong, able to get by no matter what meanness comes her way." She placed the gift in the palm of Livonia's hand. "Don't undo the tie and don't tell nobody you got it."

"What's inside?"

"Courage. Same as the heart of a she-wolf." Ruby hoisted herself astride the mule and started down the road. Only once did she stop and call back, "Mind my words, missy, mind my words." The old woman with her scrawny legs hooked around the belly of a gray mule then disappeared around the bend. For a few minutes Livonia stood there, letting Ruby's words take root in her heart, then before the trail of red dust settled, she started down the road after the old woman.

"Wait, Ruby!" she called out, but by time she reached the bend, the old woman was gone. "Please, please don't go ..." Livonia sobbed but her words were swallowed by the mountain mist and she was left with only the sound of a frail echo.

Livonia returned to the house and lifted the smallest baby from the cradle. "You're our precious baby girl," she cooed. "Of course your papa's gonna love you. He just had his mind set on a boy. Give him time, honey, just give him time."

During the laziest part of the afternoon, after William had eaten his mid-day meal and returned to the fields, after the babies were fed and sound asleep, Livonia's thoughts returned to the book she had seen William worrying over. She carried a kitchen chair into the parlor, climbed up on it and felt along the top ledge of the secretary. The key was on the back edge. She unlocked the cabinet doors and took a large black book from the top shelf. It was the

Lannigan Family Bible. On the first page was the handwritten notation: William Matthew Lannigan—born September 1824—died January 1879

Married to Hester Louise Dooley—March 1842

Sired three sons,

William John Lannigan—born August 1856

Joseph John Lannigan—born September 1857—died August 1883

Samuel John Lannigan—born July 1859—died October 1883

This was the Lannigan Family Bible. Why Livonia wondered, would William feel the need to lock it away? For a moment she was saddened by the thought that both of his brothers had died in the prime of their life. Neither of her babies would ever even know them. Why, Livonia herself was not yet born the year they died. She thanked the Lord God Almighty that her William had been spared, then she moved on to the next page.

William John Lannigan—June 1876 married Bertha Abernathy, mother of,

Margaret Louise—born April 1877

Two girl babies—born March 1878—one dead at birth

Two more girl babies—born June 1879

William Matthew—born August 1880, died Christmas Eve 1883

Girl baby—born September 1881

Bertha Abernathy Lannigan died in childbirth—September 1881

Livonia could hardly believe what she read. William had said nothing about this marriage, nor had he ever spoken a word about these children. *Girl babies. Not so much as a name for most of them.* Where were they now? What happened after their mother died? Livonia's hands trembled as she turned to the next page.

William John Lannigan—July 1882 married second wife Lucy Maude Perkins,

William Matthew—born November 1884, died February 1885

William Matthew? Livonia flipped back to the previous page and traced her finger along the line marked William Matthew. The first boy was dead; now here, a year later, William gave the second boy the exact same name. Good Lord, she thought, how he must have been hurting. She turned back to where she had left off.

Lucy Clare—born January 1886

Girl baby—born July 1888

Lucy Maude Lannigan died January 1, 1900

Livonia heard one of her babies whimpering and she went to pick it up. How could this be, she asked herself. So many children, so few of them named.

Where could they have gone to? She had lived in this house for the past three years and not once seen a trace of these children, no pictures or story books, no packed away baby clothes. Nothing. Then Livonia remembered how William had gone up into the hay loft and returned with a good sized cradle, a cradle made from the wood of apple trees that had grown right here on the Lannigan farm. She knew that for a fact, because William had told her so. Her own baby girl was sleeping quietly at the lower end of the cradle, where Ruby's gift was tucked under the quilted pad; it was the baby boy who was fussing. She picked the baby up and held him in her arms as she returned to the open page of the Lannigan Family Bible.

She sat down and counted up the children William had fathered, nine before he married her. Seven girls and two boys. Livonia went to the next page where there was only a sparse bit of writing at the very top of the page.

William John Lannigan—May 1903 married third wife Bessie Thurston
Bessie died childless August 1909

The remainder of the page was blank. Livonia's name was at the top of the following page.

William John Lannigan—April 1910 married fourth wife, Livonia Goodwin,
Boy baby—born August 1911, died at birth
William Matthew—born August 1912
Girl baby—born August 1912

Livonia tearfully turned her eyes away from the book. It angered her to have her boy child named after those other sons, babies that were no more. He was not a substitute child; he was a special gift from God. A strong and healthy boy. A child who would live to till the land as William did. Livonia knew she could do nothing about young William's name, but her precious girl deserved to have a name alongside that of the boy. A name written onto this page of their father's Family Bible, a girl's name penned in blue ink as was the boy's. Livonia picked up William's pen and dipped it into the inkwell. She scratched a line through the words 'girl baby' and wrote Abigail Anne, the name of her own mother. She would allow that the boy be named William Matthew, but the girl would be known as Abigail Anne Lannigan.

Livonia closed the Bible and replaced the key on top of the ledge, then she moved William Matthew to her breast. She thought back to Ruby's words, "The baby girl will walk a rocky road." No, Livonia vowed, as long as there is breath in my body, no harm will come to either of my precious babies.

William Matthew, she whispered, and sweet Abigail Anne.

Livonia Lannigan remained true to her vow and as the years passed she learned how to cast each of her eyes in a different direction, one always focused on Abigail as the other watched young Will trailing along behind his father. When the boy was barely three, she'd hear William saying, "You watch this, boy. You got to *know* how to fix a tractor. You listening up, Will?" Of course, the boy wasn't listening, Livonia could see that. Any fool ought to know a three year old boy just wants to romp and play. Other fools maybe, not William. He'd swing little Will up onto the back of the quarter-horse and never once take notice of how scared the boy was. Will had the thickset bones of his father, but a real timidness when it came to horses. Many a time Livonia heard the poor child crying to get off, but William was so fixed in his ways he'd keep right on circling that horse around and around the pen. "You *got* to learn to ride, boy," he'd say. "What kind of farmer don't know how to handle a horse!"

Abigail Anne was the one he should have been teaching, she was always hanging after her papa, trudging along behind him like a stray puppy. That child would have done handsprings if she thought she'd get a sliver of attention. Will would be begging to get down off the horse's back and there she'd be, standing at the gate with those tiny little arms stretched out, "Me, Papa, me," she'd say, but she got less notice than a gnat buzzing by her daddy's ear.

"Abigail Anne is every bit as capable as Will," Livonia told William time and again; but he'd generally turn off with some sort of sneer or pretend he hadn't heard a word of what she'd said. When he tired of hearing about how Abigail Anne could keep up with whatever her brother did, William would remind Livonia that running a farm was, and always would be, men's work.

"Cooking the supper and seeing to a man's needs, *that's* woman's work!" he'd say and usually it was the end of the discussion.

The more William ignored her, the more determined Abigail Anne became. Livonia saw this in the child, so she fussed and badgered until the girl was allowed to ride the gentlest of the horses, Whisper. By the time Abigail Anne was six years old she could ride as well as boys twice her age, even bareback. Little as she was, she'd take hold of the mane and dig those heels into the mare's side hollering "giddyap, giddyap." Of course by then, Whisper was well into years and the most the poor horse could do was a sluggish trot. "Let me ride Malvania," she'd say. "Please, Papa, please!" Of course, he wasn't about to, especially when Will had not yet sat astride that gelding's back.

"He's no horse for a girl!" William would answer.

"But I can do it Papa, I can, I can!"

William wouldn't even hear of it. "Stop pestering me, girl!" he'd say. "Get in the house and help your mama like *girls* are supposed to do. The good Lord didn't see fit to make you a boy, and I swear, by Jesus, you ain't gonna act like one!"

"But, Papa..." Abigail would whine and stand rooted in the spot as he turned his broad back and walked off. No matter how many times William turned away, Abigail didn't give up; she followed after him, pestering him first about one thing and then another. "I can fix the tractor," she'd say. "I *know* how to do it. I can tend cows too!"

When Livonia saw this happening, she would come to Abigail Anne's side and lead her off to some other interest, a new path that needed exploring, a new flower that needed planting, stories of women who, bold as brass, marched into Washington, DC and pestered congress to give them the right to vote. "Same as men!" Livonia would say, and a big smile would stretch across Abigail's face. The child's favorite was always stories of the fair-haired girl who lived in the glass snowball. When Livonia shook the ball, a flurry of flakes went flying, and as the snow drifted down she told tales of the girl's life—enchanting stories of friends and parties and far-flung adventures. But once the story ended and the snow settled, Abigail would be saddened because the little girl was still sitting there with her dog alongside a big Christmas tree.

"Why can't we *see* the parties?" she'd ask.

"Because they happen in our imagination," Livonia would answer. "Magic happens inside our heads, people can't *see* magic."

In the spring of 1923, when a number of the Valley's farmers moved off to places where there was work in factories and a man could make a decent living, the Lannigan family dug deeper into the parched earth. Livonia had a vegetable garden that for years had been plentiful, but this particular summer the string beans withered on the vine, the blackberries didn't grow at all and the yams were small as hen's eggs. William's patience was shorter than ever and at times even young Will's lack of attention would be enough to set him off. "Damn it, boy, you're gonna grow up stupider than a mule!" he'd shout and then tear into a God-awful rage over some piddling thing such as the proper way to pitch a forkful of hay.

"Fussing at the children won't make the crops grow better," Livonia would say but she could just as well have saved her breath.

It happened that summer, on a Tuesday morning when the air was so thick and heavy it clogged a person's nose just to breathe, the awful animosity between Abigail Anne and her papa got to be full blown. It was the same Tuesday two milk cows were laboring to birth calves. William had been out in the barn since suppertime the day before. One of the heifers had slid down the chute like greased lightning and was already suckling on its mama but William's best milker had a breech calf damned and determined not to make its way into the world. Right after breakfast, Livonia sent young Will to the barn, "Give your papa a hand," she'd told him; but when the second cow took to bellowing like her guts was being torn out of her, the boy got sick and came scurrying back to the house with his face green as early meadow grass.

"Please don't make me go back, Mama," he said. "That cow's suffering something awful. She's gonna die. I can't just stand there and watch."

"You're not supposed to watch. You're supposed to help."

"I can't. I just plain can't."

"I can, Mama!" Abigail Anne piped up.

"You'll do no such thing," Livonia told her. "You stay in this house and leave your papa alone. He's got troubles enough this morning."

"But, I know how! I seen a book on birthing calves."

"Book or no book, you leave your papa alone!"

For a few minutes it seemed as if Abigail had settled down and forgotten the notion of birthing a calf but as soon as Livonia's back was turned, the girl slipped out the screen door and made her way down to the barn. "I come to help you, Papa," she said. But William had both arms up inside the cow trying to turn the breech calf and didn't so much as nod. "Papa," Abigail repeated, "didn't you hear? I come to help. I know about birthing." She moved toward the stall.

"Get out of here, girl. Get back to the house."

"No. I come to help. I'm not scared of the cow. See." She stepped closer.

"You get your skinny little ass out of here, Abigail Anne, else you'll get the switching of your life."

Abigail didn't back off, just stood her ground and stayed right where she was. "I can help as much as Will," she said.

William didn't even answer, just kept pushing at the guts of that poor cow. A short time later he pulled a dead calf free of the bawling mother, then he turned to Abigail Anne and whacked her across the face, full force with the back of his hand. "No piss-ant girl's gonna sass me!" he roared. "Now, get outta here and stay outta here!"

His hand had come down so hard that Abigail Anne went sprawling clean across the barn and already had three red welts rising up on her right cheek. "I hate you, Papa!" she screamed, then turned and ran from the barn fast as those little legs could carry her.

Much as it might be something she'd never admit, Abigail Anne could be every bit as willful as her father. Halfway back to the house she spotted Malvania in the pen and, defiant as a headstrong bull, she scooted under the gate and climbed up on the gelding's back. For a few moments the horse pawed the dirt like he was going to buck but he didn't, just huffed and snorted. Three times the animal circled the pen, balking at first for he had never been ridden bareback. "Go, Malvania, go!" Abigail urged with her legs clasped tight to his belly, then the gelding suddenly took off at a run, jumped the fence and disappeared down the road with her still shouting "Giddyap, Malvania, giddyap, giddyap!"

By that time both Livonia and Will were out of the house and moving toward the pen. "Not Malvania!" Will screamed when the horse jumped the fence, then he took off running down the road behind a trail of rising dust. "Hang on, Abigail!" he called out, "hang on!" Of course there was no way he could keep pace with the gelding and before Livonia caught up to him, the boy had fallen in the road. "It's Papa's fault!" he screamed, "I know it's Papa's fault! He's never happy 'less he's beating up on Abigail! I hate him! I wish he'd never been born!"

Livonia lifted the boy from the dirt and brushed back his hair. "Will, don't say things like that about your papa," she told him. "He's a hard man to understand at times, because he's set in his ways, but he loves you. You and Abigail both. For a man like your papa, a man who's used to hard times and hard living, it's not easy to show you the love that's in his heart."

"Papa don't love nobody but this farm!" the boy answered angrily.

"Hush such talk. Why, there isn't a thing in the world your papa loves more than you children." Livonia took the hem of her dress and dabbed at a bloody scrape on Will's chin. "Now stop this foolishness and let's get on home, Abigail Anne will be back when she's cooled down a bit." As they walked along the road a festering seed settled into Livonia's heart, it was the grain of truth planted there by the boy's words—*Papa don't love nobody but this farm.*

Will kept glancing back across his shoulder, looking down the road for Abigail. "Suppose she rides off and never comes back?" he said. "Suppose she gets hurt?"

"Abigail's a bit high-spirited but she'll be back," Livonia put her arm around the boy's shoulders and smiled, remembering Ruby's gift, which was still beneath Abigail's pillow. "Don't you worry," she said, "your sister will be just fine."

Livonia spent the afternoon trying to busy herself and keep her mind from thinking the unthinkable. Twice she walked into the bedroom and checked that the leather sack was still beneath Abigail Anne's pillow. In the heat of the afternoon she baked bread and cooked a pot of soup for their supper. She boiled the carcass of a chicken until the bones fell apart, then added in onions, potatoes and cabbage. Cabbage was the one thing that had grown plentiful on the Lannigan farm that summer so they ate cabbage soup, cabbage stew, cold cabbage, hot cabbage and at times, even cabbage pancakes. When the children complained, Livonia told them stories of families less fortunate, hungry families who had to leave their farms and try to eke out a living in crowded cities such as Richmond or Alexandria.

"I'd be happy if we lived in the city," Will would say but Abigail would furrow her brow and get this far away look in her eyes; it was enough to make anyone think the child could see what lay in store for those who left the Shenandoah Valley.

For hours Livonia watched and waited, then when the blistering sun crossed the mountain, she started to pray, but still there was no trace of Abigail. After the table had been set for supper, she went to the barn. "What happened between you and Abigail Anne?" she asked her husband.

"She's riled up 'cause I won't take none of her sass." William spoke with his back to Livonia, and kept to his doctoring of the sick cow.

"What did you do?"

"Told her get back to the house."

"That's all?"

"Just about." William turned, his face knotted tight with anger. "She's a girl, Livonia! A girl! But instead of accepting that, you fill her head with craziness and get her thinking she can do whatever Will does. Well, it ain't so!" he snapped.

"How can you talk this way? She's your daughter! Your own flesh and blood!"

"Women got their place in life. Nothing you say or do is gonna change that!"

"Nothing's gonna change you either!" Livonia said. "You're just a stubborn old bull frog!" With that, she whirled on her heel and marched off.

28

The Lannigan family was halfway through their soup when Livonia heard the clip-clop of a horse trotting up the dirt road. She said nothing but listened with a sharp ear until moments later she heard the familiar clunk of the pen latch. She was certain everyone else had also heard it, but William just dunked his bread in the soup and never even raised an eyebrow. A minute passed, then two, then several more, still Abigail did not come into the house. When Livonia could wait no longer, she left the supper table and walked out onto the front porch. The child was sitting on the top step with her head dropped down between her knees. Her face was hidden but with the youthful curve of her body and a tangled shank of chestnut hair hanging down her back there was no mistaking that it was Abigail Anne.

"You were gone a mighty long while," Livonia said.

"I'm sorry, Mama." Abigail did not look up.

"Your papa's pretty peeved about you taking Malvania."

"I figured he would be."

"I'll have none of your sassiness, young lady. Your papa told you not to ride Malvania for fear you'd get hurt."

Abigail jumped to her feet and faced her mother. "You blind, Mama? Don't you see it ain't just Malvania? He plain out hates me!"

Livonia saw the red welts on Abigail's cheek. "What happened to your face?" The girl just rolled her eyes and turned away but Livonia could tell it was the mark of a man's powerful hand. "Abigail, honey, you've got to get something on that. Come have some soup while I fix up a salve."

"I ain't hungry, Mama."

"Nonsense." Livonia took hold of the girl's hand and led her to the table.

With an empty stare fixed on her own feet, Abigail sat down. Livonia brought a bowl of soup and set it in front of her, then the girl dutifully picked up her spoon and brought it to her mouth. Her movements were slow and shaky, like a machine that wasn't working as it was supposed to.

William did not look up, but after he had emptied his own soup bowl, he pushed back from the table and started taking his belt off. "You hurry and finish up that dinner, girl, 'cause soon as you do you're gonna get the beating of your life for sassing me and taking that horse."

"No, Papa!" Will shouted.

"Shut up, boy. Keep to your own business."

"Abigail Anne, you take your time with that soup," Livonia said, then she turned and walked out the kitchen door. In less than a heartbeat she was back with a pitchfork in her hand. She looked straight into William's eyes. "Lay another hand on this child," she said, "and, I'll run you clean through."

"Are you crazy, woman?"

"Blind maybe, but not crazy," Livonia answered. "You've done her enough harm. Now, you let her be."

"I'll do no such thing! She needs to be taught a lesson."

"I warn you, William, harm her and I'll make certain you never sleep through another night. Even if you best me now, I'll wait till you grow so weary that you have to close your eyes then I'll cut out your stubborn old heart." Livonia's voice didn't waver, didn't show one iota of weakness, it was as flat and cold as the meadow in the dead of winter. "Believe me, William," she said, "believe me when I tell you I'll do it."

William kicked over his chair and stepped back from the table. "Woman, you have gone stark raving mad. I've half a mind to let the authorities come lock you up in the insane asylum." He took three long strides toward Livonia and grabbed hold of the pitchfork handle. She was a tall woman but narrow built and certainly no match for a man of William's size, her heart started beating faster and beads of sweat rose up on her face, but still Livonia kept a firm grip on the pitchfork. "I've been a patient man," he said, and pushed his face up into hers. "You wanted Abigail Anne to go to school and I let her, even though I *knew* a girl didn't need book learning. I give in on that, then you start in filling her head with Suffragette nonsense, telling her how women now got the same rights as men—well, it ain't so. It ain't never gonna be so! That little she-devil ought to learn about the truth of life or she ain't gonna grow up fit to be any man's wife!" With that, William yanked the pitchfork from Livonia's hand and heaved it right through the screen door. Then he turned and slammed out behind it.

The spring had barely snapped shut before Livonia straightened her back and resumed her seat at the table. Even a blind man could see how Abigail got the strong tilt of her chin, for there sat Livonia, a well of tears in her eyes but head held high and chin thrust forward in such a way that anyone would think it was she who had heaved the pitchfork through the screen door.

"Can they *really* lock you up in the insane asylum?" Will asked.

"Of course not, dummy," Abigail snapped. "He's just trying to scare us."

"Well, he sure enough scares *me*."

"You children stop talking such nonsense," Livonia said. "Your papa and I just had a family disagreement. Lots of families have disagreements and nobody ever gets locked in an insane asylum. Now, finish up that soup."

"I'm not the least bit afraid of him," Abigail said, her chin tilted exactly like Livonia's but the stony set of her eyes an indication that there was something only she knew. "Papa's got a terrible mean heart and I hate him, but I'm not afraid."

"It was just a moment of anger," Livonia reached across the table and touched her fingers to Abigail Anne's face. "Your papa didn't mean to do this; other troubles just set him off. You'll see tomorrow, there's no reason to be afraid of your papa."

"Oh yes there is!" Will said. "He's got it in for Abigail now! He'll get hold of her when she's sleeping and poke her eyeballs out so she can't see to ride Malvania no more."

"Hush talking nonsense. He'd do no such thing!"

"He just might do it," Abigail said. "He sure hates me enough. He hates me more than even I hate him and I hate him more than anybody in the whole entire world. I got enough hate for him to last long as I live!"

"Enough of this," Livonia snapped. "Will, you go get washed up for bed and Abigail, come with me so we can get some salve on your face." Livonia quickly dismissed the thought that William might harm the girl, but that night, and every other night for as long as she lived, she slept in the bed alongside Abigail Anne.

At a time of year when a cold wind blows through the Valley and the sky is thick with heavy clouds that threaten snow, William Lannigan once again unlocked his grandfather's secretary and took out the Family Bible. Beneath Abigail Anne's name he wrote Livonia Lannigan, died January 1926.

Two days later, William clumsily shifted a long wooden box onto the back of the wagon. It was a simple unadorned coffin made from wood that came from the oldest orchard on the Lannigan farm, apple trees planted two generations back. The two children sat beside their father as the plow horse carried Livonia across the north plateau and down to the far meadow where the other Lannigan wives were buried. When William stepped down from the wagon, he handed his son a shovel and nodded toward the spot that would be Livonia's final resting place, but the boy just stood there with a limp hand locked onto the shovel and a stream of icy cold tears rolling down his cheeks. Four men from the Callaghan farm were among the handful of black-clad neighbors that had gathered; it was the eldest of the boys who stepped forward and took the shovel from Will's hand. As the men tore chunks of earth from the ground, Missus Callaghan and Cora Mae walked over to stand beside Abigail.

Missus Callaghan draped a large heavy arm across Abigail Anne's shoulder. "Honey," she said, "your mama was a fine woman. I know how much you children are gonna miss her. 'Especially you, Abigail Anne. It's bound to be a lonely old time, but if you need to talk woman talk, come see me." The girl nodded but held fast to the stony set of her face, a lost look in her eyes, a look that reminded Agnes Callaghan of a new calf cordoned off from its mother. "You cry if you've a need," Agnes said and affectionately squeezed the girl's shoulder.

Abigail Anne didn't cry, nor did she speak a word; she just stood there with her line of vision set to the dark thicket of scrubby pines that marked the far boundary of the meadow. Not once did she turn to watch the men wielding shovels or the mound of dirt that kept growing larger. When they lifted the apple wood box onto the ropes and lowered it into the ground her eyes looked straight past her father and focused in on a large crow perched on the uppermost branch of a black balsam. She kept staring at that crow the whole time Pastor Broody spoke, then when he closed his Bible and said "Livonia Lannigan, may you forever rest in peace," Abigail Anne turned and walked back to the wagon.

A hard rain started up as three wagons made their way back across the plateau and followed the ridge road that led to the Lannigan farm. January was customarily a time when most Valley people stayed close to home for it was rumored that in the first month of the year a man could lose his way in a blinding snowstorm and freeze to death hours before he was found. On this particular day there was no snow but an icy cold wind roared down off the mountain and drove the rain at a slant so that it pounded against the faces of the Lannigan family and the few others who followed along.

The Terrells, who lived the next farm over, said their boy was feeling poorly and headed home even though Claudia Terrell considered herself a friend of Livonia. Beside William and the two children, there were only nine others: the Coopers, their boy, and the Callaghan family. Two of the Valley farmers had come to call yesterday; they delivered heaping dishes of meat and potatoes, biscuits and pies, said how sorry they were to hear of Livonia's death, then took their leave and headed back across the ridge before darkness could set in. Those men were somber-natured and gave little more than a nod to Abigail Anne and her brother. Clifford Callaghan was different, the sort of man who usually ate with a hearty appetite and laughed loudly. Even though Cora Mae was in the eighth grade, a full year ahead of Abigail Anne, he would still lift her into his arms and swing her around like a little kid. Last summer at the Methodist Church Annual Picnic, he did just that.

It happened shortly after the Chestnut Ridge men had beaten the fellows from Riverton Creek in a hotly contested game of horseshoes. Cora Mae was over nearby the pond when Mister Callaghan called to her. "Hey, Princess, come here and give your daddy a hug." She went running to him like he was Santa Claus offering up a bag of free toys; right then and there he lifted her clear into the air and whirled around three full turns. Princess, he'd called her. It was a sight that stuck with Abigail Anne and for a long time afterward, she kept thinking of how nice it would have been if only her mama had married Mister Callaghan instead of her papa.

"How come you married Papa?" she asked Livonia, time and time again. "How come you didn't marry Mister Callaghan?"

"Honestly, child," Livonia would say, "you get the craziest notions."

Abigail Anne didn't think it was crazy, so she kept right on daydreaming of what it would be like to be a Callaghan. It was easy enough to replace the image of Cora Mae with her own and bump Will up to being one of her older brothers, but the two oldest boys and Clifford Callaghan she had to keep exactly as they were. For the remainder of that entire summer Abigail would drift off at the most unexpected times—in the middle of feeding the chickens or setting the dishes on the supper table. Three or four times her mother could remind her to set out the milk or the butter or the salt, but Abigail forgot anyway, she wasn't paying one bit of attention because she was lost in those thoughts of the big white Callaghan house. Sometimes she'd picture Livonia standing on the Callaghan front porch calling out that supper was on the table, other times she'd see herself in Cora Mae's room with its pink flowery wallpaper and a half dozen dolls scattered across the bed.

On the day of Livonia's funeral, Mister Callaghan didn't have a hearty appetite, nor did he laugh out loud. He carried in the smoked ham they'd brought for the Lannigan family, then sat on the sofa alongside his wife until it was time to leave. It was a noticeable thing when Clifford didn't eat so William said, "Where's your manners, Abigail Anne? Go fix a plate of food for Mister Callaghan."

"She'll do no such thing," Agnes Callaghan said. "He can fix his own plate." She patted her hand against the sofa. "Abigail, honey, you come sit over here."

Abigail was weighted down by her thoughts and before she could make a move to go sit alongside Missus Callaghan, Cora Mae had already slipped into the spot. For an hour, perhaps more, the awkward little group grasped at straws of conversation, saying anything to fill the emptiness, lingering over details of the weather and precisely where the best blackberries might be found if and when spring should ever come again. Clifford Callaghan, who was generally a man to see the brighter side of things, told of the bloody way a rabid raccoon had torn apart four of his best hens. Everyone mumbled something about what a hard winter it had been, then Tom Cooper said he knew the Valley was in for a bitter cold planting season. He claimed for five nights in a row he'd dreamed of hawks swooping down on rats scurrying across an empty bean field, which was more than likely a sign. William agreed, and shaking his head in a most sorrowful way added that he'd already had more than enough bad fortune. Other than a few pleasantries offered up by Agnes Callaghan, the conversation was of a pitiful nature. When the Cooper boy fell asleep in the chair, Clifford Callaghan suggested they call an end to the visit so that everyone might get home before dark.

As the Cooper's and Callaghan's bundled themselves back into the heavy coats and wool scarves still wet from the rain, Missus Callaghan pulled William to one side. "That girl of yours is hurting way more than she shows," Agnes said. "She's got to have a loving hand. Your boy, he'll do just fine, he's open about his hurt, but Abigail Anne is froze-up inside so you take special care with her."

William nodded along as if he agreed with the statement but Abigail Anne, who had been listening with a sharp ear, knew better. She knew full well that the words would be fruitless, like seeds sown upon bedrock; still, it warmed her heart to hear Missus Callaghan speak in such a kindly way. When the woman turned and hugged Abigail to her chest, the child felt a pang of guilt about wishing her own mother was the one married to Mister Callaghan.

That night, after the coals in the kitchen stove had cooled to a crimson glow and everyone else in the Lannigan household was sound asleep, Abigail Anne slid across the sheet and moved into the spot left empty by Livonia. In this place that had been shared by mother and daughter, she could still sense the fragrance of Lavender Water and linger with memories of the gentle voice that told stories of courageous women. *Someday, Abigail Anne,* her mother had promised, *someday every girl with an adventurous heart will be able to follow her dreams.* The tears started as small droplets that slid from the corners of her eyes, and then grew to great heavy sobs. Abigail Anne buried her face in the pillow to muffle the sound.

When the cock crowed the next morning, Abigail Anne remained in bed and turned her face to the wall. She heard the footfall of William's heavy boots and the clank of iron against iron as he stoked the fire and she pushed deeper into the pillow. Long before the red of sunrise could be seen above the ridge, William came to her bedroom.

"Get up, girl," he said. "You got chores to do."

"I'm sick, Papa," Abigail answered.

"You're no such thing. Now get up!"

"No, Papa, I'm *really* sick. See." Abigail stuck her tongue out as if it might prove the point. "I been shivering and shaking all night long," she said, which happened to be the truth but not for the reason she would have him believe.

"You got a fever?"

"Uh huh."

William walked across the room and sat down on the side of her bed. He put his hand to her forehead, which was, as far back as Abigail could remember, the only time he'd touched her for something other than a paddling. "It don't feel like a fever."

"Oh, it *is*. I've likely caught my death of pneumonia."

"Nonsense." William removed his hand and let it fall limp between his knees. "What's likely is that you're feeling sorry for yourself."

"No, Papa, I'm *really and truly* sick. My throat hurts even." Abigail mustered up a pitifully weak cough, and then fell back against her pillow.

"Well, okay. You stay in bed for awhile, but come midday I want you to have a meal on the table."

"Why can't Will..."

"He's got men's work to do. We've got to fix the south meadow fence."

"Why can't I help with the fence and let Will do the cooking?"

"What's the matter with you, girl?" William looked down at his feet and shook his head. "You got the craziest notions I ever heard."

"It's not crazy. Mama said..."

William turned to face her, his eyes pitched with anger and his jawbone set hard as a wall of granite. "Your mama?" he sneered. "Well, your mama was a dreamer! A woman with a head full of silly notions and no understanding of what the world is *really* like!" He stood and walked out of the room.

Abigail remained in bed long after the sound of William's footsteps faded. She thought of things she had done with Livonia, a picture they had once painted with color sticks, a quilt they had sewn with a brilliant rose in the center to conceal the droplets of blood that had fallen when she punctured her thumb. Abigail remembered the stories of the girl in the snow globe and she also thought about something her father owned—a sailing ship sealed inside of a bottle and set atop the fireplace mantle. It was a ship that could sail nowhere.

She imagined tiny little sailors scurrying around the deck of the ship, forever trying to find a way out, a way back to the ocean. As she lay in bed, watching a light snow fall, it came to her that she was no better off than those imaginary sailors or the girl in the snow globe. She was trapped in a world of her father's making, with no seeable way of getting out.

Abigail vowed that if this was to be her life, she would remain in the bed until the day she died. Magic would be her salvation; she could dream of places beyond the high ridge, float off and become a suffragette, or a piano teacher, maybe even an actress on the stage. For a long while she watched as the snow deepened on the ground and draped a white blanket across the bare limbs of the chestnut trees but when William stomped in cold and hungry and told her to get her skinny ass out of bed, she did. She pulled on a pair of woolen stockings and covered her dress with the apron her mother had last worn; then she tromped into the kitchen and set about the task of warming foods that had been brought by the neighbors.

There was something about the wearing of Livonia's apron that helped Abigail to remember the way her mother had moved about the kitchen. It came to her where Livonia kept the iron skillet that was used to fry the meat, she remembered to wrap the biscuits in a cloth towel before placing them inside the warmer, and when dinner was finished she heated water to wash the dishes. A neighbor peering through the windowpane could have believed it was Livonia moving about the kitchen, except for the stone set of Abigail's eyes.

As the days drifted into February, Abigail developed the ability to be elsewhere as she worked. She would appear to be peeling potatoes or plucking frozen laundry from the clothesline, but inside her head she was riding horses and attending parties. She pictured a horse that was all her own, a black stallion with white markings, a horse named Thunder, so mighty that people took a deep breath and gasped as she climbed astride his back. She dreamed of taking the train to far away places such as Lynchburg and Alexandria and saw herself wearing a yellow hat with partridge feathers as she marched into President Wilson's office along with the other suffragette ladies. Yet, try as she might, Abigail couldn't imagine the fair-haired girl breaking free of the snow globe.

In early March, Abigail Anne returned to school, despite William's objections. He'd been of the opinion that seventh grade was plenty of schooling for girls, but when Miss Troy came to call with Preacher Broody, he pretty much backed off of that stance. He might not have been intimidated by Miss

Troy, even though she was said to be the prettiest teacher in Blackburn County, but he was a God-fearing Methodist and wasn't about to go against anything Preacher Broody said. Abigail hid in the pantry and listened to every word that was spoken.

It started off with William being right sociable, like this was just a friendly-come-to-call-visit. Then when Miss Troy said it was past time that *both* children returned to school, he got real huffy. "Who's to say, when my girl goes to school?" he snapped.

"Every child deserves an education." Judith Troy answered, calm and collected as if she was commenting on some mighty good weather.

Preacher Broody didn't say much but even Abigail Anne, peering through a crack in the pantry door, could see how he kept his eyes fixed on Miss Judith's pretty face.

"She already knows how to read and write," William said, his voice bristling with rancor. "And, with Livonia gone, she's got more chores to do."

"She's just a *child*!"

"She's going on fourteen. I was only eleven when I started working the farm."

"But, the world is changing. Now-a-days children need to know more than just reading and writing."

"Not for living on a farm, they don't!"

"Abigail Anne might not want to be a farmer!" At this point, Miss Troy's voice got sharper and she poked that little nose of hers out in a way that made Abigail Anne worry her papa would reach over and smack it good.

"She won't *be* a farmer, but she'll sure as hell marry up with one! You gonna educate her about caring for a family in that school of yours?"

"I'll teach *both* of the children the ways of the world so that they can choose what they want to be. The time is coming when men will travel to cities and take on jobs that their fathers never dreamed of. And women, someday they'll be able to stand shoulder-to-shoulder alongside of men. Don't you want those things for your children?"

William stood so abruptly that his chair flew backward. "I sure as hell don't!" he shouted. "I'm a Valley farmer and it's a damn good life. If it's good enough for me it's sure as hell good enough for them!" William's face was red as the noonday coals in the stove and Abigail Anne was certain if the preacher hadn't been there, her daddy would have picked Miss Troy up and bodily tossed her out the door.

Preacher Broody must have known it also, because that's when he started speaking up. "Now, William, there's no call to get riled," he said. "Miss Troy here is just trying to be helpful."

"I don't need help and neither does my kids." William picked his chair up off the floor and sat back down at the table.

"There's no way of knowing what God has in store for a body," the preacher said. "Could be there's some merit in what Miss Judith believes."

William most always addressed the preacher with respect, but this time he looked him square in the eye and said, "Henry, I ain't counting on the Lord to decide what's in store for my kids. Will is gonna work this farm and Abigail Anne damn sight better be married off by time she's sixteen."

Just when Abigail Anne thought Miss Troy didn't stand half-a-chance of changing her daddy's mind, Preacher Broody hauled out his trump card. "The Lord takes a mighty dim view of such talk," he said. "A closed mind is not the Christian way."

Whereas he had been almost nose-to-nose with the preacher, William now slumped back in his chair. "I'm as God-fearing a Methodist as any," he said, and that's when the conversation took a turn for the better. Everybody's tone of voice got a bit more easygoing and before the preacher and Miss Troy left the house, William had allowed that both children could attend school three days a week and Preacher Broody had indicated William's name was sure to be on the list when the Congregation's new Ministry Assistants were announced. In William's mind, such an appointment practically meant a reserved spot in Heaven.

Still hidden back in the pantry, Abigail Anne grabbed hold of a sack of flour and kissed it as ardently as she would have kissed Miss Troy, if she'd had the opportunity.

The second Monday in March was blustery and cold, but to Abigail it felt like the most glorious of days as she and Will rode across the ridge road and off to Bush Creek. They were riding double on the back of Whisper, who was well on in years, so by time they arrived most of the other children, including Cora Mae Callaghan, were already in their seats. Miss Troy stopped what she was doing when the twins entered the schoolhouse. "Welcome back," she said. "We've missed you, haven't we class?"

"Yes, Miss Troy," everyone echoed.

Then Judith Troy walked over and hugged both children. Abigail Anne was certain she caught a whiff of the same Lavender Water Livonia had always worn. The teacher was dressed in a brown wool skirt and a white blouse, but as Abigail watched throughout the day, she could envision Judith Troy in cloche hats, suffragette-type suits and rustling silk ball gowns. Once when Miss Troy touched the tip of her pencil to her chin, Abigail even pictured her smoking a cigarette.

That was when Abigail Anne first decided she wanted to be *exactly* like Judith Troy. She took to studying her movements, her smile, her tone of voice, the way she combed her hair and even the precise shade of lip rouge she used. Long before she turned fifteen, Abigail Anne had set her mind to becoming a teacher. Most times she could picture how she would look in wool skirts and crisp cotton blouses, hear herself speaking with Miss Troy's rounded vowel tones, even feel the rumble of the train that would carry her off to far away cities, but sometimes in the middle of those thoughts, she'd hear the echo of her father's words—*better be married off before she turns sixteen.*

Troubled Times

estiny Fairchild always reminded me of the wild roses that sprang up along the south end of Chestnut Ridge every summer. In the dead of winter, when the snow on the plateau was as high as a man's head, Mama would say "I don't expect we'll see any roses this year." But a few months later, there they'd be, millions of bright red buds twining their way along a row of split rail fences or shimmying up the sunny side of a chestnut tree. I always supposed God planted those roses so He could chuckle at the wonderment on folks' faces when they passed by. I guess He also had a hand in bringing Destiny to Middleboro, because, just like those roses she cropped up out of nowhere and made folks feel happy. What kind of a mother would name a child Destiny I'd wonder, then I'd get to chuckling and have to admit it was pretty appropriate.

I wasn't the only one who felt that way about Destiny. Every time we'd go to the market, the clerks would call out her name and wave from clear across the store, smiling like they were genuinely glad to see her. When we got home, there'd generally be an extra round of beef or package of fresh baked cookies in our bag. Once the butcher tucked in a twelve pound turkey! It was the same everywhere, the market, the gas station, the post office; people just seemed to take a liking to Destiny. That is, people other than Elliott. He only saw the girl a handful of times, but right off took a dislike to her.

"She's a *fine* neighbor," I told Elliott. "I'm lucky to have her."

"Oh, sure," he said, with that condescending look where he raises one eyebrow and lets the rest of his face fall slack. "Her kind is out for what they can get from you."

"She's not asked for a dime!" I told him. I figured it would be better to leave it at that rather than reminding him of how *he'd* borrowed money on eight different occasions and never repaid a cent of it.

Other than Elliott's snide comments, you never heard a bad word about Destiny—that is until her twenty-fifth birthday, a day when the child should have been celebrating with cake and ice cream, instead of sitting in a police station. Morgan Broadhurst, a genuinely dislikable District Attorney, perched a pair of snobby looking glasses on his big red nose and sneered at her as if she was some low-life white trash. "Miss Fairchild," he warned, "you either give this investigation your utmost cooperation, or face charges on five counts of grand larceny, forgery, failure to…"

Grand larceny? Forgery? It was no such thing! I signed that car over to her, gave it up of my own free will! It hadn't been driven since some time after Will died—four, maybe five, years ago. When her old Pinto finally gave out, I said, "Destiny, there's a perfectly fine Buick sitting in my garage, you take it so we'll have some way of getting back and forth to the market." Granted, it was Destiny who filled out the papers and renewed the registration, but you've got to remember by that time my hand was real shaky and I couldn't get around good as I once did. After she signed up for insurance, she polished and shined that car till it looked brand new. She even went out and bought a Saint Christopher medal that was going to keep us safe. I suppose Saint Christopher was looking the other way when Elliott told Detective Nichols that Destiny had stolen the car and forged my name on the papers.

Elliott, who could always make worse of a situation, contrived a slew of accusations as to what Destiny had done, then he handed the detective a typed list of family heirlooms which, according to him, had been stolen. "And," he said, "my great aunt's silver tea service is missing as well." He carried on like every one of those things were treasures of great sentimental value, but I knew what he was really after.

Detective Nichols read down the list of items. "Antique sewing cabinet, mahogany lamp tables, sterling silver ladle, cameo brooch—hmm. This is a pretty extensive list, you *sure* it's all missing?"

The way Elliott carried on, anybody would have thought me richer than the Queen of England. The truth is, that so-called tea service was nothing more than a coated over piece of tin—why, I got it with six books of the green stamps they used to hand out at the Bountiful Basket. And the sewing cabinet belonged to my mama, it had a broken hinge and any number of scratches, it meant a lot to me but other than that it wasn't worth a nickel—still, Elliott led the detective to believe it was something valuable. That was the way he was; he'd take some ordinary circumstance and blow it way out of proportion to fit his grandiose scheme of things.

"Oh, it's all missing," Elliott swore. "Every bit of it!"

It was hard to know for sure, but I thought the detective had a suspicious glint in his eye; he seemed a man well-acquainted with lying snakes.

"I've the suspicion," Elliott said, "that if you searched the Fairchild woman's house, you'd find all of it. Every last piece. Why, I've already *seen* her driving my great aunt's car!"

"Destiny Fairchild? She's the neighbor you spoke of?"

"Yes. I've only met the girl a few times, but right off I suspected she was out to swindle my poor aunt. I warned Aunt Abigail, but she was not one to listen."

"This is a serious accusation," the detective said. "Are you certain you want to file a complaint?"

"Absolutely!" Elliott answered, "Absolutely!"

"Okay." Detective Nichols eyed Elliott with a look that gave me reason think he doubted the truthfulness of the entire story. "Now," he said, "let's go through this from the start. Tell me what happened, as best you can recall."

Lord God, I thought, the world has come to a sorry state when a thieving conniver such as Elliott is a person to be listened to. If Destiny had slammed the door in his face, that man wouldn't know if I was dead or alive. Right then I started wishing Destiny had been called something else, like Lucky or Happy, some more positive name that didn't leave such an open-ended issue of her future.

I still remember the day I first met Elliott; it was back in nineteen-eighty-six, two years after Will sold the farm and moved to Culpepper. Dear sweet Becky was still alive then and she was the one who telephoned and invited me to Sunday dinner. "Will wants you to come over to meet this Elliott person," she said. "Supposedly his grandma was a descendant of the Lannigan family." I caught on to that *supposedly* and right away knew Becky had certain suspicions. Will's wife was a good woman, down-to-earth as they come, but at times she could be a bit priggish if a person didn't strike her just so.

"Okay," I answered, "but I'll want to start back early." Culpepper was a good two hours away from Middleboro and I had already reached the point where my eyes didn't adjust well to nighttime driving.

Well, if that don't beat all, I thought as I hung up the receiver. Just when I'd resigned myself to the fact that me and Will and Becky were the last of the Lannigan family, another honest-to-God relative pops up. Not being of a suspicious nature, the idea of more relatives pleased me and right off I started imagining Elliott Emerson to be a man like dear old Mister Callaghan, round-faced and happy, playfully tossing sons and daughters in the air as they laughed and laughed. It was barely September, but there I was, picturing a Thanksgiving dinner with a thirty-pound turkey on the table and a whole slew of nieces and nephews calling out for Auntie Abigail. I even considered that for Christmas I'd get a *real* tree, a big one, tall as the ceiling. Of course, I didn't dwell on how I'd get such a thing home or where I'd get the trimmings for it.

When Sunday rolled around, it was a gray morning with a thick layer of black clouds threatening to let loose a downpour. Anyone could tell this wasn't going to be a drizzle, it was going to be the kind of driving rain that makes it impossible to see the road even when the windshield wipers are set to their fastest speed. This all happened just after Ben Meyerson had moved away and the place was still empty. If I'd have known Destiny at that time, I could have gotten her to go with me. She was good that way, always willing to drop whatever she was doing to lend a hand. Why one time, she got behind the wheel of my Buick and drove all the way over to Virginia Beach just because I had a yearning to smell the ocean.

Anyway, I fretted about making the trip alone and twice I even dialed Will's number to tell him I'd come some other day, after the weather got better. Both times I hung up before he answered, probably because I was pretty eager to meet this Elliott. Finally, I started reasoning like a person with some sense—just stay in the right lane and go slow, I told myself, which is a laugh because in those days I rarely drove faster than forty miles an hour anyway. Once my mind was made up, I outfitted myself like a person visiting with the President of the United States—straw hat, silk dress, fancy bloomers, even a brand new hankie tucked into my purse.

As it turned out, the rain clouds drifted off to the east and I got to Will's house almost an hour early. When he opened the front door he had this big wide smile on his face. "Come on in," he said. "Meet Elliott Emerson!"

I had barely stepped through the door when Elliott said in his smart-alecky way, "So, *this* is Abigail Anne." A gentleman would have shown the courtesy to stand but Elliott sat there with his lanky frame stretched across the sofa and waited for me to walk over to him. "Ah yes," he said, eying me top to toe, "Abigail Anne, the twelfth child of William Lannigan. As Will here knows, my grandmother was the *first*."

Everyone knew Papa had other wives before Mama, but I wasn't about to give this Johnny-come-lately the upper edge, so letting on that such news was of small consequence, I answered, "Do tell." Right away, any hope for chubby-cheeked nieces and nephews was gone. It's funny how you can take measure of some people from the very start, not just by their looks, but things you can't even put a finger on—a lack of expression, eyes that look right past you, a hollowed out laugh. Elliott had all those, plus a bushy mustache that hung like an awning over his lip and hid the sneakiness of his mouth. When he spoke my name, he gave one of those hollowed out laughs, I suppose it was meant to sound friendly-like, but I could tell behind that bushy awning he had gritted-together teeth.

"Emerson?" I said, "I've no knowledge of any Emersons in our family."

"Emerson is my father's family name, but my mother was most certainly a Lannigan," Elliott stated emphatically. "William Lannigan was my great grandfather. Bertha Abernathy, his first wife was my great grandmother."

To my way of thinking, having a blood line that could be traced back to Papa didn't say much for anyone. I was of a mind to say so but Will seemed to be taken by the man so I kept my opinion to myself. Of course, Will was the kind of person who could never see bad in anyone. Once we were watching the television news and there was this story about a man who'd murdered his own mother—I said they ought to string him up but my brother felt sorry for the guy. "Just think how troubled that poor soul must have been," was all Will had to say. I'll grant you Elliott and me might not have gotten off to such a poor start if I'd have been a bit more pleasant natured, but from the minute that man opened his mouth there was something about him that rankled me.

"Elliott telephoned, just after I sold the farm," Will said. "Imagine, him having the where-with-all to track down a Lannigan after all this time."

"Imagine," I echoed apprehensively. "How exactly did that come about?"

"With my Lannigan heritage and given the fact that Margaret Louise, my grandmother was the *first* child of William Lannigan, I always considered the possibility that I'd one day be called upon to take over the farm. When I heard that Will here had sold the place, I knew I should get in touch."

Will nodded. "He's right about his grandma. Margaret Louise was Papa's first born. Eighteen-seventy-seven. Her name is in the Family Bible."

I didn't much care if the woman's history was carved into the side of Thunderhill Mountain; Elliott Emerson's pretentious mannerisms had already convinced me that I had no desire to be related. "Margaret Louise Lannigan?" I repeated, "That name still doesn't ring a bell." Even then it struck me how Elliott was going to great lengths to establish the fact that he was blood kin to Papa and the Lannigan family.

"My grandmother, Margaret Louise, married Fred Potter," Elliott said. "He was the youngest son of the Piney Creek Potters. My mother, Madeline, she was their only daughter, married Walter Emerson. Madeline and Walter Emerson were my parents."

"Well you certainly have a sizeable amount of history," I said with a bit of sarcasm. "Must be hard to keep track of all those Lannigans, Potters and Emersons."

"Not at all," he answered. "We Lannigan men take considerable pride in our heritage, don't we, Will?" He looked over at my brother and winked like there was some secret to which only they were privy.

At that point I'd had about enough of the pompous Elliott Emerson, so I excused myself and trotted off on the pretext of lending a hand with dinner. Becky was hiding out in the kitchen and from the look on her face I knew she'd already had quite a few tipples of sherry. "Isn't that man awful?" she said, then poured herself another sherry and set out a glass for me.

"Arrogant, for certain," I answered.

"A month now, he's been hanging around here; keeps following Will room to room, talking about how he's always loved farming. Claims it broke his heart when we sold the farm." Becky took another gulp of sherry which, no doubt, was how she'd found courage to speak up as she was. "Just look at that man's hands, why he's never done a lick of work in his life. Certainly not *farm* work."

"Could be he's lonely for some kinfolk," I said. True, I'd already developed a dislike for Elliott Emerson, but I felt I ought to make an effort for Will's sake.

"Lonely?" Becky sneered, "Hah! More likely he's looking to get something out of that farm. Mark my words, he's a man who'd chew a person's skin off then start on the bones. A scavenger, worse than a river rat!" She took a real big swig of the sherry, then said, "I worry about your brother, Abigail. He's too trusting." She heaved a deep down sigh, like the weight of the world was square on her shoulders, then switched over to her secret-telling voice. "If something happens to me," she whispered, "you keep an eye out for him." Becky wasn't one for crepe-hanging conversation, so I probably should have realized something was wrong, but I didn't. Many a time I've thought back to that day and wished I'd asked what she meant by such a thing.

All through dinner Elliott went on about how he was so successful and had all these bigwig contacts. When I'd had my fill of it, I asked, "And, just exactly *who* do you work for?" You'd guess a chicken bone was stuck in his throat the way his face turned bright red, but I knew the question had flustered him.

Maybe I should have left it at that, but I didn't—I stared him right in the eye, and waited for an answer.

"Well actually, I'm self-employed. I do *consulting*," Elliott finally said.

That answer didn't surprise me one bit. Consulting is what most people claim to do when they don't really have a job. Elliott struck me as the type of person who was looking to avoid work rather than find it. He was a sly one all right. Thing is, you don't get to be my age without having a few tricks up your own sleeve. While we were having the butterscotch pudding I brought up the subject of Margaret Louise. "I trust your grandma taught you to be a good and faithful Baptist, like Papa taught us."

"Yes, indeed." Elliott answered. "And I am a devout Baptist to this day."

Will's eyes opened real wide and Becky sniggered quietly.

"That's nice to know," I said and took another spoonful of pudding. The rat was in the trap as far as I was concerned. Everybody knew Papa was a staunch Methodist and the only thing he hated more than vagrant Negroes was Baptists. Papa always claimed that the Baptists were a bunch of rabble-rousing hillbillies using the house of God to cover up their sins. Papa had more than a few sins of his own, but in his mind being a God-fearing Methodist equalized any transgressions.

After dinner, I helped Becky do the dishes then took my leave. On the drive home I turned the car radio to the Revival station and added my voice to those of the Gospel Singers. Each time they'd bellow about the Lord God lifting them across the river of sin, I jumped in with a chorus of *Amens*. I felt right good about what I'd done.

Dear sweet Becky died three months later. Looking back, I'm certain she knew about the cancer that day in her kitchen. I suppose it was pretty far gone by then and she probably thought telling me wouldn't have made any difference. If I'd known, I'm sure I could have done something. But, maybe not.

Will just fell apart after that. He'd sit in the chair and stare at the television, not even taking notice of whether it was turned on or not. When I came over that Saturday, two weeks after the funeral, he was sitting there watching a Bugs Bunny cartoon. I snapped the TV off and said, "When's the last time you took a bath?" You could actually *smell* him as soon as you came through the front door.

"I forget," Will answered.

"Did you also forget to change your underwear? Eat dinner?" I knew I was being a bit harsh, but when someone's grieving that much you'll do just about anything to snap them out of it. When none of this worked, I told him, "Will, you're gonna have to come to Middleboro and stay with me."

He looked up and his eyes were so sad they about broke my heart. "Okay," he said. And that was how it happened. We loaded his clothes into my car and drove back to Middleboro. He never stepped foot into that house again.

A girl named Rosalina once told me that her grandmother had the ability to put a hex on people—supposedly the woman caused a wart the size of an egg to swell up on her sister-in-law's nose and Rosalina could recount plenty of other instances as well. A man who cheated the grandmother got hit by a garbage truck, a neighbor kicked a dog and got his cellar flooded, a heavy-handed butcher had thirty-six pounds of pork sausage spoil overnight, no explanation whatsoever. I've often thought if I had such an ability Elliott Emerson would have started looking like Pinocchio as he sat there telling all those lies to Detective Nichols.

After he had blurted out the worst of his accusations, Elliott told the detective, "This girl's unscrupulous; she has no job. Swindles old people out of their life's savings, that's what she does for a living!"

"Destiny Fairchild?"

"Yes! Destiny Fairchild!"

"On what is this allegation based?"

"She's stolen my aunt's money!"

"Allegedly," the detective said. "Allegedly stolen. Do you know exactly how much money is missing?"

"Not just money!"

"Well what? Stocks? Jewelry? Bank Accounts?"

"It's difficult to pinpoint all the things, but this list…"

Hearing such talk made me wonder what the world had come to. Is money the measure of things? What about a good heart? Destiny Fairchild was the sweetest soul I'd ever known. She didn't ask for anything and she didn't need much to be happy. One of those clear blue sky days would come along—the kind with puffy white clouds billowed out like sheets on a clothesline—and that was enough to make Destiny start singing like her heart was full up with gladness. The only thing that girl wanted was for folks to love her. But Elliott, now he was a person itching to grab up every dollar he could lay his hands on.

They say people can die of a broken heart and I for one believe it. Oh, the doctors give you a thousand other reasons, heart failure, kidney failure, liver failure—but the truth of the matter is sometimes people reach a point where they just quit living. That's what happened to Will. Once Becky was gone, he pretty much lost his heart for living. I'd worry and fuss over him, fold an extra blanket over his feet on cool evenings, check that he was taking his medication, cook up special foods—things he'd craved all his life such as cornbread or stewed butter beans. When I set that hot cornbread on the table, he'd smile the way he used to, but before I could fetch us a cup of coffee he'd be poking at the edges and pushing a bunch of crumbs off to the side of his plate. "I thought cornbread was something you liked," I'd comment, but he'd look at me and shrug as if what he liked or disliked was something he was too tired to remember.

"I suppose I'm not all that hungry," he'd finally say, and then an hour or so later he'd start telling me about how Becky always made her cornbread with molasses. "Yes indeed," he'd lick his lips, "cornbread with molasses, that's *really* good."

I'd make up another batch and add molasses even though it wasn't part of the recipe. Soon as the cornbread was out of the oven he'd break off a piece but before he'd swallowed that first bite, I'd see him shaking his head like a man who'd run out of hope. "I recon that wasn't it," he'd say and turn back inside himself.

The problem was that he'd been married to Becky for over fifty years and couldn't remember how to live without her. It might have been different if they'd had children—but then everything would have been different if they'd had children.

Elliott Emerson came to visit Will every few weeks. "How you feeling?" Elliott would ask. "Anything you want me to take care of for you? Insurance, maybe? Banking? Investment business?" Will would just shake his head from side to side without turning away from whatever television show rerun he was watching.

It was enough to make you cry because my brother had always been a smart man. The year we turned seventeen he went off to William and Mary College. *I wish you could be here, Abigail,* he'd written in his first letter. *This school has a million books and a library bigger than the Lynchburg City Hall;* he enclosed a picture of himself standing in front of the big stone building. For two years he studied at William and Mary but the third year Papa had his stroke and Will had to go back home to take over the farm, which wasn't easy because by then Papa was more cantankerous than ever. Even though he was flat on his back, things still had to be done *Papa's* way. After Papa died, Will ran the farm the way it should have been run in the first place; he put in fields of winter wheat and rotated the crops till he got four, maybe five harvest seasons. Believe me; my brother deserved every nickel that came his way when that farm was finally sold. I still remember the day Will signed those papers; it was five o'clock in the afternoon when he telephoned and he sounded like he'd been nipping at the whiskey.

"Abigail Anne, you're not gonna believe what I got for the farm," he said.

I told him that if it was me, I wouldn't give fifty cents for the entire place.

"Times have changed," he said. "These folks are investing in the *land* and it's not because of farming. They're gonna build houses—hundreds of nice little three-bedroom houses right here on the Lannigan farm."

"Hundreds?" The way I remembered it, there wasn't more than one-hundred and twenty houses in the entire valley.

"Yes, indeed. Two hundred and forty to be exact. They'll divide the bottomland into individual lots and put in cement streets that run clear out to Ridge Road." Will hesitated for a second, then said, "Becky and I have already discussed this and, Abigail Anne, we both feel you're entitled to half of that money; you're as much a Lannigan as I am and that land was Lannigan land."

"Hogwash!" was what I answered. "You worked that farm, Will. Papa left it to you and justifiably so. A person doesn't get *born* into owning something. You work for it, long hard hours of work, *that's* how you get to own it."

Well, our conversation went back and forth for heaven-knows-how-long, but in the end I flat out told Will that I didn't need the money and I wasn't taking any. At any rate, it was the end of the discussion. I never did ask how much Will got for the farm or what he did with the money.

Will died fourteen months after he came to live with me. As much as I tried, I just couldn't help him get past loosing Becky. The doctors claimed it was the emphysema, but I still believe it was a broken heart.

Elliott was, of course, first in line at the funeral parlor. That big phony had a black band around his arm and a hang-dog look on his face—why, he didn't care about Will anymore than I did Adolph Hitler. The preacher had barely finished the '*from ashes we came and to ashes we shall return*' part of his sermon when Elliott whispered to me, "Do you have a date set for the reading of the will?"

If I was a few years younger I might have lambasted him square in the nose, but in deference to my brother, I held my temper and in a very ladylike manner whispered back, "Go to hell!"

Detective Nichols opened his desk drawer and removed a yellow pad. "Okay," he said, "I'll need your name, address and phone number."

"Elliott Emerson. Fourteen-twelve Pine Street. Hazleton, Virginia."

"Hazleton? Way down in Hazleton? What are you doing in Middleboro?"

Elliott fidgeted a bit, like people are prone to do when they're telling a big fat whopper, "Well," he said, "this is where the crime was committed."

"Hmm." Detective Nichols looked eyeball to eyeball at Elliott and leaned forward; I could tell he'd started to catch the stink of a skunk. "Interesting," he said. "Most folks would just go to their local police station—how'd you know a complaint had to be filed in the township where the crime occurred?"

Elliott coughed several times and cleared his throat as if a pork chop was stuck in his windpipe. "I suppose," he finally mumbled, "I read up on this sort of stuff."

"Hmm." The detective made a check mark in the margin of his notepad. "Now, let's go through this again. Is it your allegation that this neighbor— Destiny Fairchild, right?—has stolen your aunt's money along with other personal property?"

"It's not an allegation, it's a fact!"

"That's yet to be determined. I'll need more information. What's her address?"

"My aunt?"

"The neighbor, Destiny Fairchild."

"I'm pretty sure she's moved herself into my aunt's house, even though she has her own place right across the street. My aunt's house is number fourteen, hers is seventeen. Seventeen Oakwood Drive, that's it."

"Do you know her social security number?"

"Of course not," Elliott replied. "I hardly know the woman. She's certainly not the type person I would associate with!"

"Why?" the detective asked, "Has she been in trouble before?"

Elliott shrugged. "That's something I can't say with absolute certainty, but given her larcenous nature, I wouldn't be one bit surprised."

"I take it she's still at this address. Do you know how long she's resided there?"

"Not long."

"Less than a year?"

"Longer."

"Two years? Three?"

"Four or five, maybe six. But, soon as she moved in, she started grubbing money from dear sweet Aunt Abigail."

"How exactly did she do that?"

Elliott started telling how Destiny would pop in most every day, but he made it sound as if she was up to no good; not once did he mention how she came there to help with my housework or take me to the grocery store or the doctor. "She started helping herself to my aunt's assets little by little," he said, "then, before anybody realizes what's happened, she's got *her* name on the checking account and she's driving around town in Aunt Abigail's car. Now, virtually all the valuables are missing from the house!"

Detective Nichols listened to the story Elliott was concocting. Every so often he'd jot another note on that yellow pad, as if he had heard some significant fact, but I could tell by the way his eyes were narrowed, the detective had his doubts about the truth of it all. I suppose that's when I took such a liking to Tom Nichols. He had a way about him that made me think; *now, here's a man who can sort out truth from falsehood.*

"Do you know where Destiny Fairchild came from? The state? City?"

"I couldn't even venture a guess," Elliott answered. "For all anybody knows, she's an escaped convict on the run!"

I noticed how Detective Nichols had started penciling in a bunch of interlocked boxes along the margin of the yellow pad. It seemed the more Elliott talked, the less the detective was inclined to write down.

"Can you give me a physical description of the woman? Height? Weight? The color of her hair? Eyes?"

One week after Will's funeral, Elliott telephoned me. "Being the only other Lannigan heir," he said, "I was wondering when there is going to be a reading of my great uncle's will."

Of course, I was missing Will something fierce and feeling pretty blue to begin with, but the sound of that man's voice edged me into a downright foul mood. "Stop pestering me," I told him.

"Well, Aunt Abigail, there's a sizeable estate involved here, and my grandmother told me that Lannigan property is always passed along to the eldest male. As you know, I'm the *one and only* remaining male in the Lannigan family."

"You're no Lannigan! Shit, you're a Baptist! Papa would roll over in his grave if Will ever left one nickel of his money to a *Baptist!*"

"But," Elliott stammered, "you said…"

"I lied!" I slammed the received down so hard it probably made his ears ring.

At that point I thought I might be rid of that nuisance, but no, two weeks later I get a call from this lawyer who claims to be representing Mister Elliott Emerson.

"Oh, really?" I said. "And just what does that have to do with me?"

"My client has grave concerns," Mister Binkerman said, that was the lawyer's name, August J. Binkerman. "Grave concerns, regarding the distribution of assets belonging to your late brother, one William Matthew Lannigan."

"Anything that belonged to my brother is none of Mister Emerson's concern."

"Mister Emerson feels differently. He believes that William Lannigan left a will which has not yet been submitted to the court for probate."

"Listen here, Mister Binkerman," I told him, "you've no cause to say such a thing. First off, I don't even know if my brother had a will. Second off, Elliott is *not* real family and my brother knew it."

"Oh, don't misunderstand, Miss Lannigan, Mister Emerson is not *accusing* you of anything. He's just questioning whether you might need help in bringing such a document to probate."

"Elliott, helpful?"

"Yes, indeed. He's quite prideful of his Lannigan heritage."

"Lannigan heritage, my foot! My brother came into some money, *that's* what brought Elliott Emerson knocking at his door!"

"Mister Emerson can establish the authenticity of his bloodline, so I hardly think the fact that your brother realized a profit from the family farm means…"

"Related or not, my brother wouldn't have left a dime to a conniver like Elliott."

"Well, we can't know that for certain unless there is a will."

By the time I hung up the receiver, my blood was boiling and off I went, hell-bent on sorting through every sheet of paper packed away in my garage. After Becky died, Will didn't much care what happened to anything, "Do as you want," he told me. So, I hired a bunch of movers to come in and pack up their personal effects, then I shipped most of the furniture off to The Salvation Army. I didn't get rid of Mama's sewing cabinet and some other things that brought to mind pretty good memories.

I certainly could have used Destiny's help in going through those boxes, but she didn't move into the Meyerson place until the following summer so I was on my own. It took me almost four weeks, probably because when I'd happen upon one thing or another, I'd get to thinking about the farm and the happy times we'd had before Mama died. I'd stop my sorting, fix myself a cup of tea and visit with those memories for a while. I'd never realized Becky was such a saver but she'd held on to most everything, even the storybooks Mama would read from. The day I came upon that old copy of *Grimm's Fairytales* I sat there all afternoon leafing through those crinkled pages and hearing the stories in Mama's voice.

It was the first day of April—April Fools Day—when I found the flowered box tied with a pink ribbon. It was sort of frilly-looking, the kind of box where you'd expect to find things like gloves and lace hankies, but instead it was filled with papers and sealed up envelopes. Right on the top was a blue envelope marked *Abigail Anne*. I could have sworn it was Papa's handwriting, but of course there was no way of knowing for sure. I opened that envelope first and found a gold wedding ring, a tiny narrow band, plain as could be and probably just like a million others, but I knew it was Mama's. I could picture the way she'd fidget with that ring when she was fretting about something, one hand folded over the other, twisting the ring round and round on her finger. Holding her ring in my hand I realized how slender my mama's fingers must have been. Mama had always seemed bigger than life to me, strong and powerful, like she could move a mountain if she had to, but here was her ring, too small to fit my pinky. Even though she'd been gone for over sixty years, seeing that ring made me miss Mama so much I sat there and bawled like a baby. I'll admit it's pretty strange, an old woman crying over something like that, but it don't matter how old you get, your mama's always gonna be your mama, and that day I'd have given everything I owned just to have my mama hug me one more time.

I brought the flowered box inside the house and set it on the kitchen table, but by then my heart was so heavy, I couldn't look at another thing for two days. When I finally did get around to going through the rest of the box, I found a receipt for a tractor Papa had bought, letters Will had written in college and Mama's recipe for chocolate cake. Way down near the bottom of the box was a bulky white envelope from Scott C. Bartell, Attorney at Law. I was pretty sure this was the will, but I was almost afraid to open it, mostly because I didn't want to see that my brother had left something of Mama's to Elliott Emerson. The will had been written three years ago, before Becky died, it told how if Will died first everything he owned should go to Becky and if she died first, everything should go to Will. On the second page it went on, *In the event both parties are deceased, all tangible personal property and estate assets are bequeathed to Miss Abigail Anne Lannigan, twin sister of William Matthew, and daughter of William John and Livonia Lannigan.* There was no mention whatsoever of Elliott Emerson.

Scott Bartell turned out to be a right nice person. I telephoned him and he said he was real sorry to hear about Will's passing but for me not to worry because he'd take care of everything, even August J. Binkerman. "Will only had three bank accounts," I told him, "and a handful of personal stuff that came from the farm." I wasn't lying, because back then I didn't know diddley-squat about the bonds. I knew Will had gotten a sizeable sum when he sold the farm but I figured he used that money to buy his house in Culpepper.

"You get me the numbers for those bank accounts," Mister Bartell said, "I'll make sure that everything is transferred over to your name."

Scott Bartell did just that, and in no time at all I had one-hundred and sixty-seven thousand dollars in the Middleboro Savings Bank. God knows that was the most money I'd ever had and I suppose it went to my head 'cause I got to feeling a bit guilty about the way I'd turned my back on Elliott. In the middle of dusting a table or washing dishes, I'd get to thinking back on how my brother was so pleased when he found out there was another Lannigan. Unlike Becky, Will believed Elliott to be a direct descendant of Papa, "Distantly related," he'd say, "but still a Lannigan." Maybe if Will hadn't fallen apart the way he did, he'd have provided some sort of remembrance for Elliott.

In August I called Elliott. "My brother felt fondly toward you," I told him, "and I think he would have wanted you to have his watch."

"Is this really Aunt Abigail?" Elliott asked, like he thought it might have been somebody else playing a trick on him.

"Of course it is, you fool," I said. That boy had a way of agitating a person the minute he opened his mouth and I had to practically grit my teeth to keep on talking. "I know we've had our differences, Elliott, but Will believed you're Lannigan kin, and I want to do right by my brother."

"You want *me* to have his watch?"

"Yes, and a bit of cash."

Two days later, there was Elliott, standing on my doorstep with his hand open. "I came to visit," he said and plopped himself down on my sofa. "Got anything cold to drink, lemonade maybe?"

I went into the kitchen, fixed some iced tea with a slice of lemon and served it to him in one of my very best glasses. The gracious thing would have been to take polite sips, but Elliott gulped it down like a man dying of thirst then set the glass down on the wooden end table—not on the coaster I'd put out for him, but smack on the wood. "Thanks Aunt Abby," he said in this smart-alecky but supposed-to-be-funny way.

"You're quite welcome," I told him then I ceremoniously picked up that glass and moved it over onto the coaster. Elliott and I never had much to say to each other and being together was awkward—we were like two foreigners who spoke different languages. So, once he'd collected Will's watch and a check for two-thousand dollars he took his leave. I suppose I'd been hoping a different Elliott would show up, one who was thoughtful and pleasant, one who could sit and visit with an old lady without fidgeting like his pants was on fire. As it turned out, I can't say I was sorry to see him drive off, nor did I feel bad about giving him that money. I'd planned to write out a check for ten thousand dollars, but when he set that wet glass down on my fresh-polished table, I decided to make it two. Knowing what a good heart Will had, I imagine he would have given Elliott the ten thousand, but I felt two was more than he deserved.

Mama always used to say that God watches everything you do, and if you do right by other people, He'll do right by you. I expect it's true, because a month after I gave Elliott the money, Destiny came along.

Beyond the Valley

1927

The summer following Livonia's death the Valley experienced a growing season such as the farmers could never before remember. Tomatoes grew to the size of melons and the corn became so tall that a man walking between the rows was hidden from view. William spent hard-earned money to buy a new gasoline powered tractor and Will started riding Malvania back and forth to Cobbs Corner so he could visit with Rebecca Withers. Most everything in the valley changed that year, everything except Abigail Anne; she remained firm in the conviction that she would be a teacher like Miss Troy. From morning until night, she had her nose in a book. She'd be cooking potatoes or frying up a piece of pork and on the table alongside the stove would be an open book. She'd stir the pot absentmindedly and marvel at things she'd never thought possible. "Imagine," she told Will, "talking movies!"

Emma Hopkins, the librarian, allowed Abigail Anne to take home six and seven books at a time even though the rule was no more than three. "Abigail dear, have you read this one about our United States Presidents?" Emma would ask, then she'd stack another book on top of the pile of those already selected.

On the first Sunday in August, William told Abigail to fix an especially nice dinner. "The Kellers are coming to visit," he said, "and they're bringing that nice young boy of theirs with them. Name's Henry, I believe."

Abigail, who now wore Livonia's apron day in and day out even though it had been washed a hundred times and long ago lost the scent of her mother, fried up a platter of chicken and boiled a pot of potatoes. It was the hottest day of the season, so hot that even the livestock left the grass of the field and clustered together under shady maples, but Abigail baked biscuits and a peach pie. When William saw the sideboard laden with food, he smiled. "Ah yes," he said, "that boy's gonna like this."

Abigail didn't answer because she was engrossed in a news story telling how a woman from Montana had been elected to Congress. "See, Papa," she said. "Mama was right; women can do anything they set their mind to!"

"What are you talking about, girl?" William looked over Abigail's shoulder and saw the headline that read *Jeanette Rankin—the U.S.'s First Congresswoman.* He turned down his mouth and shook his head from side to side. "Lord God," he mumbled, "what next?" Then he told Abigail she ought to clean herself up, maybe rouge her cheeks a bit.

The Kellers arrived just after two o'clock with their son Henry, who was already taller than his father and skinny as a fence post. With a real friendly looking smile on his face, William led them into the parlor, the room usually reserved for very special company. "Sit here," he told Mister Keller and motioned to the biggest chair. He told Abigail to fetch some cold tea, then turned back to Mister Keller. "Well, John," he said, "how's that spread of yours doing this year?"

John Keller was a somber faced man who had the habit of rubbing his chin whenever he had to think about something. "Better than ever," he answered and cupped his palm to his chin. "We got twenty-two calves. Herd's so thick I had to open up the far meadow. You?"

"The same," William answered. "Looks like we'll need two, maybe three, pickers, come harvest." He looked over at Henry, who was all arms and legs. "I'll bet a stropping lad like you is a mighty big help to your pa. Is that so, boy?"

Henry shuffled around in his seat, as if being the topic of conversation made him uncomfortable. "I suppose," he answered.

"My Abigail, she's a born housekeeper. Since I lost Livonia, she's taken over all the cooking and cleaning. Why, just wait till you taste the dinner she's cooked up today. Even Livonia couldn't make a better peach pie than this girl!"

"Papa!" Abigail blushed.

After dinner, William suggested that the young folks ought to visit on the front porch for a spell, but then he turned to Will and told him to take care of the evening chores. Henry led Abigail outside and they sat on the swing.

"Your papa's a right nice man," Henry said as he reached his arm around Abigail's shoulder.

"He means well," she answered.

"He was right about that pie. Best I've ever tasted."

Abigail smiled. "Pie-making's nothing, I'm gonna be a teacher."

As soon as the Kellers had taken their leave, William turned to Abigail, "Well?" he said, "Did you like him?"

"He's nice enough," she answered then stuck her nose in a book about India.

"His family's got the biggest spread in Blackburn County, and Henry, he's their only boy. A fine looking lad. Of marrying age, I'd say. A boy like that is bound to be a good provider." Abigail didn't answer, so William walked away grinning to himself.

From that point on, Henry Keller became a regular visitor at the Lannigan farm and William went out of his way to make the boy feel welcome. "Have another piece of pie, son," he'd say and clap the boy on the back so vigorously that the skinny lad wobbled. The minute Henry walked in the door, William settled a grin on his face. "You remind me of myself," he'd say, "salt of the earth, hard working. Yes sir, not a whisker of foolishness about you."

When school started again, Abigail was overjoyed. She'd practice the multiplication tables in her head as she washed William's workpants, or she'd think about the rules of sentence structure as she swept the kitchen. "School is so exciting," she told Henry, but he pretty much shrugged the thought off. "Miss Troy said there are airplanes that can fly from one end of the country to the other," she told him but Henry preferred to grapple her into a position where he could steal a kiss. "Don't you care about what goes on in the world?" she'd ask, and he'd shake his head no.

By the time fall turned into winter and the air became so cold and brittle it hurt a person's lungs to breathe, Abigail's worlds began to collide. It seemed that dinner was never ready on time, the biscuits were usually burned, she'd forget to feed the chickens then have to get out of bed in the dead of night to do it and she hadn't read a book in months. One Sunday she told Henry he shouldn't come over so often. "Once or twice a month," she said, "that's enough till I catch up on my schoolwork."

William bolted out of his chair, "Abigail Lannigan!" he shouted. "Have you lost your mind?" He glared across the table like she'd committed the worst crime ever. "The girl's just had a bad day," he told Henry, "pay her no mind."

"Papa, that's not it," Abigail said. "I've got studying to do."

"Young lady, you can just march yourself right into the bedroom and don't come out till you get some manners!"

"But, Papa…"

"March!"

Abigail went to her room but left the door slightly open, enough so that she could listen to the voices that came from the kitchen.

"I'd best be going, Mister Lannigan."

"Nonsense, boy. You wait a few minutes; she'll be out here full of apologies. Abigail's a good girl, high strung at times, but well worth a body's trouble."

"I don't know, Mister Lannigan, Abigail sure don't seem to care about me the way I care about her."

"Of course she does. I know that for a fact. This playing hard to get, it's a woman thing—they do it so you'll cozy up to them a bit more, you know, bring flowers, tell them their hair smells nice, stuff like that."

"You don't mean…" Henry started rubbing his chin just the way his papa always did. "It might be that Abigail *loves* me?"

"I wouldn't be a bit surprised. A man can't judge what's on a woman's mind by what she *says*. Why her mama, turned me down three times and I practically had to get down on my knees and beg before she agreed to marry me."

"Honest?"

"Yes indeed. And Abigail Anne, she's got ways just like her mama. Fire and brimstone on the outside, but inside," William shook his head as if some special instance had suddenly come to mind. "Well inside, she's cuddly as a newborn kitten."

"I'd sure marry up with Abigail Anne, if she'd have me."

"Have you? Why, there's not a doubt in my mind that she'd have you!"

Henry had a tendency to slump like a person trying to hide their tallness, but when he heard what William said, the boy straightened his shoulders to their full height and put on a grin so wide it appeared that his mouth had somehow gotten hooked onto his ears. "You mean…" he cleared his throat, "Abigail Anne, would say *yes*, if I asked?"

"Well, she's a mite young right now and hell-bent on finishing up eighth grade—but you wait till she turns sixteen in August, that's when she'll be ready for marrying."

"But—Abigail Anne said next year she's going to the high school over in Buena Vista. Told me she's gonna study to be a teacher."

"That's just young girl talk. Foolishness. You wait till she's sixteen."

The voices continued for a while longer, then Henry asked William if he thought Abigail Anne was gonna come back out anytime soon.

"Might be she's too embarrassed," William said. "You come for supper Tuesday evening. She'll be all prettied up and smiling like nothing ever happened."

"You suppose she'd make that apple cobbler of hers?"

"I'd bet on it, boy!"

Abigail Anne eased her door shut, then crawled into bed and pulled the quilt up around her ears. She turned on her side and let the tears fall into her pillow. "Oh, Mama," she sobbed, "I miss you so much." That night a flock of black crows gathered in the maple tree, screeching and cawing like they were angry enough to tear the skin from a grown man. As Abigail lay listening in the darkness, she came to believe the sound she heard was the protest of her mother.

The following morning Abigail dutifully set breakfast on the table, but before her father had his first sip of coffee, she said, "You're wrong, Papa."

"Wrong?" he replied, like he hadn't the faintest notion what she might be talking about. "Wrong about what?"

"You as much as told Henry I'd marry him."

"Well?"

"I'm not gonna. I already said, I'm going to school in Buena Vista."

"Abigail Anne, I've had enough of that nonsense about you being a teacher. Henry Keller is a fine young man and he's gonna come into his family's farm one of these days. You ought to be thankful he's so taken with you!"

"But, I don't *love* him, Papa. I can't marry a boy I don't love!"

"Love!" William shouted. "What in God's name does a fifteen-year-old girl know about love? Is love gonna put food on the table? Build you a fine house? Take care of your babies?" William reached across the table and took hold of his daughter's hand. "Abigail Anne, love happens after a woman goes to a man's bed, after they have babies together and come to know each other. The important thing is for you to marry a good man, someone who's got his own land and a means to provide for you, a man like Henry can take care of you, make it a bit easier in hard times."

"But Papa, if I learn to be a teacher I can take care of myself."

"Take care of yourself? Now wouldn't *that* be a fine life!"

"For me it would."

"For the love of God, Abigail Anne! It's high time you start realizing that this ain't some storybook tale! You might not fancy you're in love with Henry

Keller right now, but that boy cares about you! He's one who'll take good care of you and your babies, the way I did your mama."

"Mama's life wasn't so good."

"That's enough!" William slammed his fist against the table so hard that a plate of eggs flew off and splattered on the floor. "You'll do as I say!"

Abigail heard the cawing of a whole flock of black crows ringing in her ears and she snapped back, "I'll not marry Henry Keller!"

William smacked her face so hard she fell to the floor. "You'll do as I say!" he repeated, then stomped out the kitchen door.

When Abigail arrived at school that morning she still had a large red welt on her cheek. "Why honey," Miss Troy said, "what has happened to your face?" When the other students turned to look, Abigail Anne burst into tears. Miss Troy, being the kind of woman who could make her intent known with a single glance, gave out a reading assignment then went over and put her arm around Abigail's shoulder. "Now, now," she said, "nothing's that bad." She pulled a lace handkerchief from the pocket of her skirt and dabbed at Abigail's face. "Come with me, honey," she whispered, and guided the teary-eyed girl to a side room that was used mostly for storage. "Now tell me what's troubling you," Judith Troy said in the same comforting way as Livonia might have.

After she'd heard the complete story of how William expected Abigail to marry Henry Keller, Miss Troy called Will into the side room with them. "Is such a thing true?" she asked the boy and when he answered that it was, she huffed and puffed like an angry bull. "William Lannigan must be living in the Middle Ages!" she said. "Now-a-days young ladies are free to marry whomever they choose!"

"Papa's mighty difficult to reason with," Will said, "even when he's dead wrong."

"Oh, is he? Well, we'll see about that!" Miss Troy waggled her finger and stuck out that pointy little chin of hers, "You just tell your papa that I'll be out to see him this Saturday! Times have changed and it's high time he changed with them!"

"If I was you, I'd bring along Preacher Broody," Will told her.

"I'm not one bit afraid of your papa!" Miss Troy snapped.

"Maybe not," Will said, "but Papa's more inclined to listen to the preacher."

Abigail's black crows were cawing louder than ever.

The following Saturday morning Abigail was so nervous that she burnt the biscuits and brewed coffee so bitter William left a full cup sitting on the kitchen table. Given the irritating nature of these things added to the fact that she'd forgotten to feed the chickens again yesterday, Abigail was earnestly praying Miss Troy would have Preacher Broody in tow. When the surrey pulled up at the house and Judith Troy was alone, Abigail's heart fell.

"Morning, Mister Lannigan," the teacher said.

"Morning." William was stacking wood and didn't bother to stop.

"I've come to talk about Abigail," Judith Troy said. "Abigail Anne wants to continue her education instead of getting married; and I believe you should respect her wishes…" Miss Troy didn't get the chance to finish what she had in mind for William turned his back and walked into the barn. "Mister Lannigan," she called after him but there was no answer.

Abigail, who had been standing there wanting to take it all in, shrugged as if to indicate she had no idea what her father's actions meant.

Judith Troy stepped down from the surrey and started toward the barn.

"Get back in the buggy and get off my farm!" William said as he came out of the barn with his shotgun leveled at her head.

"Now, Mister Lannigan, there's no need…"

"Get off my farm," he repeated.

"Mister Lannigan, the girl needs…"

"Needs? *I'm* the one who decides what she needs and don't need."

"But…"

William fired a shot into the air. "I'm warning you!"

Abigail went running over to her father, "Stop, Papa! Please stop! Miss Troy don't mean no harm. She's just trying to help."

"I ain't in need of any *schoolteacher's* help raising my family!" William lowered the barrel of his shotgun just enough to indicate that he was willing to allow Miss Troy to walk safely back to the surrey.

"Please, Miss Troy," Abigail pleaded, "It's best you go."

Now, Judith Troy was willful and stubborn but she wasn't foolish enough to take on a twenty-two gauge shotgun, so she climbed back into the buggy and left. But after she'd turned the surrey around and had gotten no more than a few feet along the road she looked back and shouted, "You think about it, Mister Lannigan. Think about it!"

William fired another shot into the air.

After the confrontation with Judith Troy, William flew into a rage the likes of which Abigail had not seen for three years. He grabbed the girl by the arm, yanked her into the house and pushed her down into a straight-backed kitchen chair. "You sit there," he shouted, "sit there till I say you can get up!" Then he stomped back and forth across the room ranting on and on about how he would not have some meddlesome busybody telling him what to do with his children. "You'll not go to that schoolhouse another day!" he told Abigail and that's when she started to cry. Of course, she could have shed enough tears to fill the Rappahannock River and it wouldn't have made a difference to William, for at this point his mind was made up.

"Papa, please..." Abigail sobbed, but she was told to shut up.

"I'm not interested in anything you've got to say," he stormed, then kicked at the stove with a vengeance. "Blabbing our family business to that know-it-all teacher! What in the name of God possessed you?" he asked, but when Abigail started to stammer out an answer, he said, "I told you to shut up!"

After this had gone on for well over an hour, Abigail whispered, "I'm sorry, Papa. I know I had no right."

"You ought to be sorry," William replied, but this time he wasn't shouting the way he had been. "I'm your papa, girl. I'm looking out for *your* welfare. Your mama would have wanted me to do that—and I'm doing it as best I can."

"I know, Papa. I know."

"Then why do you fight me, every step of the way?" William stopped pacing and sat down at the table. He took hold of Abigail's hand. "Why?"

"I'm sorry, Papa. I won't fight you anymore. If you let me finish the school year, I'll marry Henry Keller like you want."

"It goes against my grain to let you go back to that schoolhouse," he said. "That teacher is a bad influence on you."

"I won't tell her another thing about our family business, Papa. I swear I won't. For certain she'll never bother you again."

"Well, if you're dead set on finishing, I suppose I can tolerate five more months."

"Oh, thank you, Papa. Thank you so much!"

"Just you make sure that your schoolwork don't get in the way of your chores!"

"No sir! I'll make sure of that!"

That was how William's tirade finally ended. It wasn't so much an end, but more or less a peace agreement, based on the premise Abigail would marry Henry Keller.

Abigail knew she'd made a mistake in promising to marry Henry, but without that promise she'd never again lay eyes on Miss Troy which was something she couldn't live with. That night, as she lay in bed and listened to the black crows beating their wings against the icy cold air and cawing out a message she was certain came from Livonia, Abigail came up with a plan.

For three weeks she kept this plan to herself, letting it roll around her head and settle. Twice she made potato pancakes and pork with gravy, a dish that took considerable effort, and Henry, who came for supper more often than not, licked his plate clean. He'd smile across the table at Abigail and she would smile back. William seemed satisfied that the girl had come to her senses, so he also was in exceptionally good humor. With Henry being there evening after evening, Will was free to spend time at the Withers place, which was exactly what he wanted to do now that he'd gotten moony-eyed over Rebecca. To most outsiders it seemed the Lannigan household was downright happy, but there was one person who took notice of the far away look in Abigail Anne's eyes.

Miss Troy would ask, "Can you tell me the capitol of Pennsylvania?" But Abigail Anne would look up as if she'd never even heard of Pennsylvania. This alarmed Judith Troy because she knew the girl could recite the capitol city of each and every state, so she'd try again. "How about Maryland?" she'd say but Abigail's face still didn't register a thing other than an absent-eyed look of confusion.

One morning when the rest of the class was working on a study assignment, Miss Troy whispered in Abigail's ear, "Please, come with me," and she led her back to the storage room. "Abigail Anne," she said, "you're a bright girl, a girl with a lot of ability. I know you know the answer to these questions so what's causing you to act this way?"

"Nothing," Abigail answered looking down at her feet.

"It's something, or else you wouldn't be acting this way. Has there been more trouble with your father?"

"Don't ask me that," Abigail Anne answered and her eyes filled with tears. "I can't tell you things about our family cause if I do, I'll have to stop coming to school."

"Nonsense! If your father tries a thing like that I'll notify the state authorities!"

"Papa don't care about the state authorities."

"Well, he will care if I go out there with—"

"Oh, please, Miss Troy, please don't come! Papa will claim you're a trespasser and shoot you dead in the heart!"

"There is a law against such behavior."

"When Papa gets mad enough, he don't care about the law."

Judith Troy took hold of Abigail's hand and clasped it tightly as she looked into the girl's eyes. "Child," she said, "you've got to talk to someone. You can't keep troubles bottled up inside you. You've got to pour them out so that somebody can help."

Maybe it was the fact that Judith Troy's voice sounded so much like her mother's, or maybe it was because the crows had stopped cawing in her ears, but whatever the reason, Abigail opened up and told Miss Troy how she'd agreed to marry Henry Keller after she turned sixteen.

"Marriage is a serious thing," Miss Troy said. "Do you love the boy?"

"No. I like him real well, but…"

"If you're not sure you love him, Abigail Anne, you shouldn't be marrying him."

"I'm not going to."

"But, you said…"

"I'm gonna leave the farm before my birthday."

"Leave? For where?"

"The city. I'm going to Roanoke and get a job in one of those factories."

"Oh, Abigail Anne," Miss Troy said and hugged the girl to her chest. "You don't want to do such a thing, honey. That's a hard life. A real hard life."

"The places in Roanoke have electricity and water spigots inside the house."

"Maybe so, but you work long days and come home exhausted. You're a smart girl; you can do better than that."

"Better? Marrying Henry Keller and getting stuck on his papa's farm for the rest of my life, that's better? I'd sooner jump off the top of Thunderhill Mountain."

"There are things besides marrying Henry."

"Not for me."

"Yes, there is, Abigail Anne. I don't know what, just yet, but you give me a bit of time and I'll think up another way to handle this situation."

"Don't come out to our place, Miss Troy! I swear, Papa will shoot you dead!"

Judith Troy assured the girl that she wouldn't come near the Lannigan farm, but when they left the storage room the teacher was wearing that same far away look as Abigail Anne. She told the class it was time for a recess and then she took a piece of paper from her desk and started to write. After she'd penned three pages, she signed her name, folded the letter and placed it inside an envelope. The envelope was addressed to Miss Ida Jean Meredith, 10 Jefferson Square, Richmond, Virginia.

After that, things went along pretty much the way they had been—Henry came to supper most every night and ate so much that the gauntness of him started to disappear. His face got so rosy and round that even his mother noticed. "That girl's having a mighty fine effect on you," she told her son.

But Abigail grew hollow-cheeked and developed dark circles beneath her eyes. Most nights she'd stay awake counting up how many days she had before her sixteenth birthday, or listening to the cawing of the crows that had taken up residence in the maple tree right outside her window. It seemed the more intense her troubles became, the louder the crows squawked, and finally she came to believe the birds were trying to warn her of something. Crows were troublesome birds that most people would have shooed away, but Abigail took to leaving seed at the base of the tree. Every time she'd pass that maple she'd look up and on the bare limbs there would be seven or eight black crows with beady eyes staring down at her. "What are you trying to tell me?" she'd ask. The crows just sat there like a line of black-robed hangmen.

"Abigail Anne," William would say, "you're looking mighty peaked. Could be you need a dose of tonic to fix what ails you." Then he'd start in talking to Henry and wander off onto some subject that had to do with breeding cows or planting crops.

There wasn't much said about the upcoming marriage, but it seemed that everyone pretty well assumed such a thing would happen. "We've got a pump inside the house," Henry would say, "Abigail Anne's gonna love that!"

William would nod his approval and make it obvious how he felt about the whole thing. Long before there was even a trace of spring in the air, William came home from Buena Vista with a bolt of white organdy tucked beneath his arm. He handed it to Abigail Anne and said, "This here is for your wedding dress."

"But, Papa..." she gasped.

"No buts about it. Will can take care of your chores for a few days. Now, you get inside and start sewing. Make something real pretty," he said and smiled like he was proud of himself.

For almost three days Will fixed the supper, fed the chickens, and slopped the dirty clothes up and down the washboard while Abigail hunched over the sewing machine. She pumped the foot pedal back and forth, just as Livonia had, and carefully eased yards of organdy along the guide line. She fashioned the dress with balloon puff sleeves and a wide ruffle along the hem, both things she'd never before done. She stitched buttons down the back of the dress as carefully as any prospective bride might do, then when she was finished she hung the dress in her closet.

"Let's see what you've done," William said, and when he saw the dress he smiled. "That's a real nice piece of work," he told her. "Real nice. Henry Keller's gonna get himself one fine, beautiful wife."

"Thank you, Papa," Abigail answered then she went right back to doing her daily chores. Night after night she'd set supper on the table, food that she'd prepared as carefully as she'd sewn the organdy dress, but she herself hardly ate a thing. She'd nibble on a biscuit or little wedge of potato, then push back her plate as if she couldn't stand to swallow another mouthful. By time there were only eighty-seven days left until the Sunday of the wedding, Abigail had grown so thin her collarbone circled her neck like the yoke of a harness.

The Monday morning before school was to close for the summer, Miss Troy tapped Abigail on the shoulder and motioned her into the storage room. "I've good news," the teacher said.

"Good news?" Abigail asked.

"Yes. I've written to someone about your situation—a woman who was once my teacher, a fine woman, intelligent and kind, Miss Ida Jean Meredith, that's her name. She's no longer teaching, she's retired now and writes poetry. Anyway, I told her of your abilities and explained the problem. I then inquired if perhaps she could employ the services of such a remarkable young lady."

"Employ?" Abigail repeated her eyes big as squirrel holes in a hollow oak.

"Yes. I suggested you would make a most suitable companion and assistant. I was direct about the fact that you had not yet learned to use a typewriting machine but assured her that you were a quick learner and would certainly be able to master such a task in no time."

Abigail's heart was pounding so vigorously you could see the movement beneath the bosom of her dress. She let out a whoosh of air and left her mouth hanging open.

"For a while I was concerned that I had received no answer, but yesterday this letter came." Judith Troy reached into her pocket and took out a pale pink envelope. She handed the letter to Abigail, "Read it yourself," she said.

Abigail took the letter in her trembling hands and with her first look at the looping slant of Ida Jean Meredith's handwriting, she knew that this woman must be the finest on the face of the earth. She read the words, Miss Meredith had written:

> *Dear Judith,*
> *I would be most delighted to take on your young student. This offer comes at a most opportune time for I am currently compiling my fourth volume of work and am in serious need of an assistant.*
> *These days, my step has slowed a bit, so I would also welcome a youthful companion to accompany me around town. Rest assured, the girl will be well cared for and most comfortable as I have readied the small bedroom overlooking the rose garden. Hopefully your young protégé will enjoy theatre and the ballet as you once did. I am enclosing a train ticket for the girl's travel from Lynchburg to Richmond. Please advise when she will be arriving and I will have Frederick meet her at the station.*
> *As always, I remain your devoted friend.*
> *Ida Jean Meredith*

There were tears in Abigail's eyes but she was smiling. "Does this mean—?"

"Yes," Judith Troy answered before the girl had completed the question. "This means that you have been invited to Richmond to work with Miss Meredith."

"You won't tell Papa?"

"It's not my business to tell. If you have anyone you want to tell, then you're free to do so." Miss Troy smiled, almost exactly the same way Livonia did when she was up to some sort of mischief. "But, if I were you, I wouldn't say a word to your father."

That night Abigail slept as she had not slept in years. There was no sound of crows, just songbirds chirping away like it was the middle of summer.

On the final day of the school year, when almost anyone in Blackburn Country would have sworn that Abigail Anne and her brother would be sitting at their desks, Will hitched the wagon to Whisper and rode off in the direction of Lynchburg. Abigail Anne was sitting beside him and two suitcases rattled around in the back of the wagon.

"You sure you want to do this?" the boy asked his sister.

She nodded.

"You're gonna keep in touch with *me*, right?"

"Of course, I am," she said. "Just don't tell Pa, where I've gone. He's so crazy to have me marry Henry Keller, he might decide to come down to Richmond and shoot poor Miss Meredith in the heart."

"I'm not gonna say a thing," Will answered. "Now, when you write, send the letter to Rebecca, she'll make sure I get hold of it."

"I'll do that."

"You got your train ticket and the money?"

Abigail tugged open the drawstring and took another look inside her purse. "It's right here," she said and held up a pink envelope. The smile on her face faded as she took out a second envelope, a plain white one. "This here's a letter for Henry," she handed the envelope to Will. "Please make sure he gets it."

"Okay," he said and slipped the envelope into his pocket.

When they arrived at the Lynchburg Station, Will took both suitcases from the wagon and carried them to the platform, his face pinched up as a prune. "I wish you wouldn't do this," he said. "A woman alone in Richmond..."

"I won't be alone; I'll be living with Miss Meredith." Abigail had the look of a woman in love. "Judging by the letter, I know, she's a *wonderful* person. She's planning to take me to the theatre and the ballet. Imagine, me at the ballet!" Abigail twirled around and her cotton skirt billowed in the breeze.

"There's plenty to worry about in the city," Will said, shaking his head. "Troubles such as you never even heard of."

"Sure, like turning on all those electric lights or making your way to a toilet that's *inside* the house," she teased.

Will was about ready to tell her of how folks who got out of work sometimes had to sleep in the streets and of how evil intentioned men could lead innocent girls astray, but just then the train pulled into the station so all he said was, "Goodbye, Abigail Anne. Remember, I love you." A moment later she was gone and he was left standing there with a single tear rolling down his cheek. "Be careful," he whispered, then he turned and walked away.

That evening when William came in from the field and found Will putting supper on the table, he asked, "Where's your sister?"

Will shrugged.

"Didn't she come home from school with you?"

"She didn't go to school today," Will said.

"Hell's fire!" William growled. "She's probably got herself in a twit because of that blasted teacher. Soon as school lets out, Abigail Anne thinks she can start acting up again. Well, this time she ain't gonna get away with it!"

Will tried to avoid looking his father in the face and when William said, "It's mighty strange that *you* don't know where she's gone to!" the boy fixed his eyes on the pot of stew as if he expected to find his sister in among the carrots. After supper Will didn't complain about doing Abigail's chores, but it made no difference—William went right on ranting and raving about how such a rebellious girl ought to be locked up in the state reformatory. When William got tired of stomping around the house, he took a hickory switch in his hand and sat on the front porch to wait for Abigail Anne.

He sat there all night.

When dawn rolled across Thunderhill Mountain, William saddled Malvania and rode into town looking for Miss Judith Troy.

Her tiny white house was at the far end of Belmont Street. William walked up to the door and began to pound on it with both fists. "Open this door, you troublemaker!" he shouted. "I want to talk to Abigail Anne!" By the time Judith Troy opened the door, the neighbors on both sides of her house and the deputy who lived directly across the street were all looking out their windows to see what the ruckus was about.

"Mister Lannigan, lower your voice!" Judith Troy said.

"You tell me where my girl's gone, then I'll lower my voice!" he screamed louder than ever. "You tell me right now!" He grabbed hold of Judith Troy's shoulders and started shaking her like a rag doll, that's when Deputy Greer came flying across the street and walloped William to the ground.

"We don't allow folks to beat up on women!" the deputy said and twisted William's arm back so far you could almost hear it crack. "If you want to ask Miss Judith something, you ask her nice and polite—understand?"

"She's got my girl to run off," William told the deputy.

"Is that so?" Deputy Greer asked Judith Troy, but she shook her head like she had no idea what the man was talking about.

"She run off yesterday," William said, still addressing his words to the deputy.

"Abigail wasn't even in school yesterday," the teacher said, "so, how could I possibly know where she might be?"

William looked right at Judith Troy, "You know!" he said. "You know, 'cause you're the one who put those crazy notions in her head."

"Miss Judith says she doesn't know where your girl is," the deputy told William. "If she says she doesn't know, then that's all there is to it—she doesn't know!"

When it began to look like William wasn't going to accept such an answer, Deputy Greer pressured his hold on the twisted back arm and shoved William Lannigan down the walkway. After Judith Troy closed her door and the deputy was able to let loose of William, he warned, "You don't want this kind of trouble, so stay real far away from Miss Troy. You understand? Real far!"

Malvania had been ridden at a gallop all the way into town, but on the way back to the farm, William walked the horse at a slow trot.

When he arrived back at the farm, William sat on the front porch and buried his face in his hands. Later that evening he noticed that Livonia's apron was not hanging on the peg in the kitchen, he then walked into Abigail Anne's room and found the closet door standing open. Her clothes were gone—only the white wedding dress was left hanging in the closet.

Just as Abigail had climbed aboard the train, she'd paused for a moment and glanced back at Will, half expecting him to be waving and smiling, but instead he'd already started walking back down the platform. She couldn't see the way his eyes had filled with tears or the sorrowful droop that had settled on his mouth, all Abigail saw was her brother's back, turned away—as if she'd already been forgotten. "Bye, Will," she whispered softly, then lifted herself onto the last step and left the Shenandoah Valley behind.

For as long as she could remember, Abigail had harbored a wonderful image of what it would be like to travel on the train—dressed up folks chattering about places they were off to, Pullman porters serving champagne, everybody happy just to be aboard—not once had she imagined it would be so hot and stuffy. For a moment she tried to see things as she had pictured they would be, but with the cramped together seats and peeling paint it was impossible. On the platform there had been a cool breeze and the smell of summer apples but inside the railroad car the air was thick with other smells— gasoline, whiskey, cheese that had gone bad. Most folks were waving a cardboard fan back-and-forth in front of their faces, but Abigail had not thought to bring such a thing.

In the back of the car a group of men were having a heated discussion about a game of cards they'd been playing. "I ain't never cheated in my life," the skinny one argued but the others seemed pretty adamant about the fact that he had.

"Pipe down back there!" the woman sitting in front of them called over her shoulder, then she went back to clacking a pair of knitting needles and counting aloud, "Knit one, pearl two, knit one…"

Abigail looked down the row of seats. She had hoped to sit beside a window and watch as the Shenandoah Valley gave way to new places, but the passengers had scattered themselves about like isolated towns, solemn-faced people each one taking up a space alongside of a window. No one looked as if they might welcome the thought of someone sitting down beside them. These weren't anything like the folks Abigail had imagined—a narrow nosed man reading a newspaper, several more sleeping and one of those snoring loudly, a red-faced woman banging on the window and trying to cuss it open—all people who seemed exasperated to be in such a hot place. Halfway down the aisle, there was an empty seat alongside a pleasant looking woman with a fast-asleep baby in her arms. Abigail made her way through the aisle, stopped alongside of the woman and hoisted the largest of her suitcases onto the overhead rack, the satchel she placed on the floor beneath the seat.

"I'd clean that seat 'fore I sat down," the woman said. "Isaac here, spit up a bit."

"Oh my," Abigail said and pulled Livonia's good lace hanky from her purse.

"It wasn't much," the woman said. "Hardly worth mentioning."

Abigail swished her hanky over the velour seat then sat down.

"The soot, now that's way worse than any mouthful of milk. The soot settles into things, turns them black as coal. These seats is covered with soot."

Abigail checked her hanky and saw a residue of black dust. "My goodness!"

"Crying shame folks has to sit in a dirty seat! They ought to do something!"

Just as she was about to ask *who* would be the one to do something, the conductor came through the car hollering "Tickets, please!" so Abigail fished in her purse and pulled the one-way ticket from Miss Ida Jean Meredith's pink envelope.

When the conductor stopped alongside Abigail, the woman leaned forward and said, "These seats have soot on them! A body ought not pay *full fare* for seats with soot."

The conductor looked at Abigail and said, "Ticket?"

Abigail handed it to him and asked, "How long till Richmond?"

"Richmond? Well, that's quite a ways." The conductor swiped at his face, which was shiny with perspiration, then punched three holes in Abigail's ticket. "Eight hours, give or take." He smiled and moved on to the next passenger.

A few seconds later the whistle blew and the train started to rumble along the tracks. Isaac stirred a bit and twisted deeper into his mama's arms, but when the whistle blew a second and third time he started screaming like he was being killed. "Oh, mercy," the woman moaned, then she shifted the baby onto her chest and started rocking back and forth. "That noise woke him."

"Maybe he'll go back to sleep," Abigail suggested.

"Isaac? Go back to sleep? Uh-uh. He's got the colic!" The woman moved the baby to her lap and jiggled him up and down. "Now, now, darlin'," she said in the most soothing voice, but Isaac just screamed all the louder.

After about an hour, the conductor, who'd already taken a dislike to Isaac's mama because of what she'd said about soot on the seats, came through calling out, "Next stop, Hampton Crossing," but he had to shout it three times before folks could catch the name of the station above Isaac's wailing.

The baby carried on that way through Millerton County and halfway through Somerset. At times, Isaac would wail so hard you'd swear his mama was pinching him, but of course she wasn't. Abigail knew if that baby belonged to her papa, he'd have gotten a royal slap on the rear end, but Isaac's mama kept rocking him back and forth, no matter how hard he screamed. Twice Isaac fell asleep, but the minute the train whistle blasted, he woke up screaming louder than ever. At Bogbottom, which is at the far end of Somerset County, a peddler climbed aboard and shuffled through the aisle selling sandwiches and little bitty containers of milk at twice what the price should have been. Abigail, who by now had grown weary of listening to Isaac, suggested, "Maybe he's hungry." The woman paused for a moment like she might consider feeding the baby an overpriced cheese sandwich, but then she shook her head and went back to rocking.

Halfway through Buckingham County, Abigail was certain she should have sat next to the snoring man. She closed her eyes and tipped her head back, hoping to close out the sound, but then she started picturing Will's back as he walked away from the Lynchburg station. The louder Isaac screamed, the more she missed her brother. Abigail tried to call to mind Will's face, the crooked way he'd grin, or how he'd pinch the tip of his nose when he was studying a problem, she even tried remembering the pleased look that settled on his face when papa bragged about how *his boy* was becoming a fine farmer—but all she could picture was her brother's back.

Abigail bent down, reached into her satchel and pulled out the snow globe. It was heavy in her hand, not at all a practical thing to pack, especially since she'd had to decide between carrying the snow globe or a history book Miss Troy had given her. She shook the globe and watched the snow fall around the fair-haired girl.

"Oh, look-y here," Isaac's mama said and turned the baby toward the snow globe. "Ain't that pretty?" she oohed and aahed for a bit and finally, the baby quit screaming. "He's all wrapped up in watching the snow," she told Abigail. "Keep shaking that thing, will you, honey?"

Abigail shook the globe again and as Isaac watched the swirl of snow his little arms and legs pin wheeled with delight. "Ain't that something? Just look how he's taken to that thing." The woman moved Isaac closer to Abigail and he reached out for the snow globe. "No, no, sweetie'," she said, "you can't *have* it." Isaac obviously didn't like hearing the word *no* because he stiffened his legs out and bucked so hard that he knocked Abigail's most prized possession from her hand. It happened in a split second, so quickly there was no time to grab hold of the globe, yet in that brief moment Abigail thought she heard the fair-haired girl scream as her tiny world splintered against the metal floor.

The woman's eyes about popped out of her head. "Oh, good Lord," she exclaimed, "Isaac has *never* done a thing like that! He didn't mean it. He's real sorry! Isaac!" she snapped, yanking the baby back onto her lap, "You better be sorry!"

Isaac started wailing all over again.

Alongside Abigail's feet there was a rivulet of water draining out into the aisle. She bent over and rescued the little girl who had lived inside the globe for more years than anyone knew. The glass was shattered and bits of make believe snow scattered about; although there was a sizable chip in the Christmas tree, the fair-haired girl was in one piece. Abigail lovingly brushed bits of glass from the girl's golden hair, then folded the figurine into Livonia's lace hanky; as she carefully tucked it inside of her purse, Abigail noticed the figurine's smile seemed to be brighter than ever.

Isaac was still screaming when Abigail got up and moved to the seat across the aisle. She took out the Harper's Bazaar Magazine that Will had gotten her in Lynchburg and started leafing through the pages. The man sitting alongside her had an oversized sack of sandwiches in his lap.

"Want one?" he asked and offered out the sack.

"No thank you," Abigail replied, remembering the politeness Livonia had drummed into her head.

"I've got plenty. Cheese. Baloney. Apple butter."

"No thank you," she repeated and turned back to focusing her attention on the flapper dress in Harper's. She narrowed her eyes and squinted at the picture until she could see her own face on the flat-chested model.

"How about an apple? Or homemade cookies?"

Homemade cookies—now that was a thing Abigail couldn't resist. "Well," she said, "perhaps a cookie."

The man reached beneath his seat and hauled up an even bigger bag. "Go ahead," he said, "help yourself to a handful."

Abigail stuck her hand into the sack and pulled out two big round oatmeal cookies. "Umm," she said, "my favorite."

"Me, I like cheese sandwiches. Could eat twenty of them, I suppose." As the man chomped down on the sandwich he was holding, a sizable chunk of cheddar spit off and dropped into his beard. The man seemed not to notice. "Where you headed?" he asked Abigail.

"Richmond." She smiled broadly. "I'm going to work with an almost famous-woman who writes poetry!"

"Well, now. Ain't that something! You want more cookies?"

"Uh-uh." Abigail shook her head but her eyes got fixed on the piece of cheese in the man's beard. No matter how vigorously he chewed or talked, the cheese didn't let go. If it had been her papa, she would have reached up and brushed it away—but this man was a total stranger. She tried to focus on something else, so as not to be rude. "Where you going?" she asked.

"Parkerton. I got family in Parkerton."

Abigail had never heard of Parkerton, but imagined it to be quite a distance away, judging by the amount of food in the man's sack. Before she had a chance to inquire about the actual whereabouts, the conductor came through the car yelling, "Parkerton, next stop." He called it out twice because of Isaac's wailing.

"Time for me to go," the man said. He clambered over Abigail's satchel and squeezed into the aisle. As the train rolled to a stop, he reached into his bag and pulled out two more oatmeal cookies. "Hang onto these," he said, "you'll be hungry later."

After he left, Abigail quickly slid over into his seat, which was alongside a window. As soon as she'd settled in, she took the hem of her dress and began polishing up the glass so she'd be certain to see all there was to see.

As the train rumbled through Brownell County, she kept her nose pressed to the glass, watching bean fields and apple orchards whiz by. Here and there she'd spot a farmhouse or a town smaller than Chestnut Ridge but mostly it was endless acres of farmland. After two hours of watching long stretches of green, Abigail leaned back in her seat and took out Miss Ida Jean Meredith's pink envelope.

She reread the letter over and over again, each time trying to imagine what it would be like to live in Richmond. She pictured dwellings of every shape and size, from a townhouse so tall a person would have to stretch their neck to see the roof, right down to a tiny cottage ringed with roses. Abigail Anne had the ability to do that, draw pictures inside of her head instead of taking a pencil to paper. Once she'd settled on a wide-spread house with the veranda painted the yellow of a sunflower, she started in on what Miss Ida Jean Meredith would look like. First she envisioned a tall woman with a crown of silver hair, but that was too severe, so she changed the image to a more rounded woman with ample breasts and cheeks rosy as a ripe peach. When those pictures didn't sit right according to her way of thinking, she fashioned Miss Meredith to look like Livonia and that worked surprisingly well. By then Isaac had quieted down, so Abigail went on to wondering what her papa would say when he discovered she was gone. Then, it was Henry, poor Henry. Abigail couldn't help but worry that he might go back to being skinny now that he wouldn't be eating her pies.

Abigail eventually drifted back to studying the pages of Harper's Bazaar. As she sat there picturing herself in cloche hats and silk stockings, the afternoon sun faded, day became dusk, then dusk turned to dark and Abigail fell asleep. In her dream she'd stepped from the pages of Harper's Bazaar wearing a lace dress with a wide blue sash and she was dancing the waltz with a courtly slender-built man. It seemed her heart was running wild with excitement as they whirled round and round, but when she looked into her partner's face and saw it was Henry, she woke with a start. Just then the conductor came through bellowing "Richmond, next stop, Richmond!"

The train rumbled into Richmond, a place so lit up with electric lights it looked like the middle of the day. Abigail had always been favorably impressed with the wooden station house at Lynchburg, but this station was four times the size, and it was bustling with porters hauling suitcases and steamer trunks.

Abigail took a look out the window and felt her heart jump. *These* were the people from Harper's Bazaar Magazine! She tugged her suitcase from the overhead rack and moved toward the door. Out on the platform, a man in a brass-buttoned suit was doing nothing but holding the hand of ladies as they stepped down from the train and saying, "Welcome to Richmond." Abigail set her satchel down and extended her hand as the other ladies had, but when she stepped from the train she stumbled over her own feet. "Careful," the platform man said and smiled.

Abigail had never seen so many people in one place. She twisted her head one way and then the other, eyeing fancy ladies and men dressed as though they worked in bank. She didn't notice the man standing at the far back of the platform although he stood a good head taller than most of the others and had skin blacker than the richest soil of the Shenandoah Valley. He was the one who came up to her and asked, "You Miss Abigail Anne?"

She nodded.

"I'm Frederick," the big man said, "Miss Meredith sent me to fetch you." He bent, picked up both suitcases and told her to follow him. "Now, stay close," he warned, "else you could get lost."

Ida Jean Meredith's house was not like any of those Abigail had imagined. It was a modest two-story, painted the pink of an evening sky and set far back from the street. In the front yard were dozens of rhododendron bushes in full bloom and a weeping willow that had grown taller than any other tree on the block. Abigail believed it to be the grandest house she had ever laid eyes on.

Miss Meredith, a bent over woman who supported herself with the aid of a cane, was waiting in the doorway. "Welcome to my home, Abigail Anne," she said, and then told Frederick he should take the bags upstairs and place them in the rose bedroom. "We've a late supper waiting," she said and led Abigail into a dining room where the table was set with fine china and crystal.

"Oh, my!" Abigail exclaimed and let out a whoosh of air.

Miss Meredith smiled. "You're going to enjoy living here, Abigail. Richmond is a lovely city with many things to do."

After they had eaten a supper of cold chicken and thick slices of fresh tomatoes, Abigail retired to what Miss Meredith called the rose room, for what reason she couldn't imagine, since it was decorated in varying shades of yellow. She took her dresses from the suitcase and hung them in the closet, but they now seemed frumpy and drab in comparison to the outfits worn by the ladies at the train station. "Oh dear," Abigail sighed, then she washed her face, pushed open the window and climbed into bed. As she lay there in the darkness thinking of how she would spend her very first pay on a new frock, one with a wide sash that circled her hips, the scent of roses drifted in on the cool night air.

Abigail quickly settled into Miss Meredith's schedule which was to rise early and rest in the heat of the afternoon. By seven each morning they were at work, Abigail pecking away at the typewriter keys as Miss Meredith expounded on an abstract collection of thoughts. After lunch, Miss Meredith napped but Abigail usually returned to the typewriter and practiced; some days she remained there so long that her hands felt locked into position. At night, she dreamt of her fingers stretching out to reach letters like Y or Z and her hand gracefully sliding the carriage back to its starting position. Less than a month after her arrival, Abigail sat down at the typewriter and clacked out a letter to her brother.

> *Dear Will,*
> *I have arrived in Richmond and am doing fine. As you can see, I have already learned to use Miss Meredith's typewriting machine. She is a fine lady and is teaching me many new things. Every night we have supper in the dining room and when I use the wrong fork, Miss Meredith is pleasant enough about pointing out my mistake.*
> *Last week we went to the talking picture show which, even here in Richmond, is considered most modern. Tomorrow*

*evening we are going to the Symphony and Miss
Meredith bought me a new dress to wear. It is the latest
fashion. Papa would fall over dead if he saw me in it.
Mister Frederick, who is also in Miss Meredith's employ,
drives us around town in a Pierce Arrow automobile that
is so shiny you can see your face in it.*

*I am very happy and know for certain that I have done the
right thing in coming here. I am hoping to become a writer
like Miss Meredith, but instead of poems I shall write
stories of courageous women, which is something Mama
would be proud of. I pray that you and Papa are doing
well. I hope he has forgiven me for running off the way
I did, but knowing Papa, he likely never will.*

Abigail typed her name then removed the sheet of paper and folded it into an envelope addressed to Rebecca Withers.

Throughout the entire first year she continued to write such glowing letters. Week after week, she told how Miss Ida, as she came to address her benefactor, had taken her to Carter's Department Store, the largest in all of Richmond, and how they lunched in a tea room with fresh flowers on every table and brocade draperies at the windows. She told of the concerts and ballets they attended and how she had gotten her hair cut into a bob. It's the very latest, she wrote, the most fashionable ladies are all wearing it. In most every letter she inquired about her father and whether or not it appeared that he had forgiven her behavior. Although Will answered every letter, he never answered that question.

Abigail slipped into her new life as if it were a satin dress. She'd start out walking across the street and suddenly she'd be floating, stepping along on a feathery cloud with her toes barely touching the ground. Every evening the housekeeper drew a warm bath laced with fragrant crystals of jasmine, then Abigail would soak herself in the claw-footed tub and smooth her skin with rosewater and glycerin. After a while, the calluses on her hands disappeared and along with them went the memory of her life on the farm. Livonia's apron was folded and tucked into the bottom drawer of her dressing table for Abigail no longer had need of such a thing, she'd become a fine lady.

Everything changed after her second summer in Richmond. It happened on a Monday in October, when the crackle of fall was in the air and pots of yellow chrysanthemums were lined up along the walkway. Miss Ida, who usually insisted they dine at six so that at seven she could listen to Amos and Andy, wrinkled her brow and said, "There's been stories of terrible happenings in New York. Tonight we must listen to Mister Winchell and learn the truth of the matter." After supper, she called for Abigail, Frederick and Anna Mae, to join her in the parlor; then she turned the radio dial to the somber-voiced newscaster telling how people in New York City were jumping out windows because they had lost everything they owned in the stock market. "Oh, my Lord," Miss Ida repeated over and over, twisting her lace hankie into a knot.

Anna Mae, who had spent the last thirty years cooking for Miss Ida and never been outside of Richmond, had no knowledge whatsoever of the New York Stock Exchange, but she knew by the tears in Miss Ida's eyes that the situation was serious. "Now, don't you go fretting, Miss Ida," she said, "Them New York folks is plain out crazy, ain't no such thing gonna happen here." After that Anna Mae scurried out of the room saying that she'd fix up some hot chocolate to make everyone feel a bit better. But before she could return with the tray of cocoa and shortbread cookies, Miss Ida had poured herself a full snifter of brandy.

Abigail thought Anna Mae spoke good sense, and reasoned that poets *did* have a tendency to portray things in a far too dramatic fashion. She remembered the day Miss Ida had gotten herself into a tizzy over an article she'd read in *Ballyhoo* Magazine—she steamed and snorted for days, even wrote letters to three congressmen, a senator and President Hoover, but eventually it was all forgotten. Abigail decided that this stock market thing was just such another instance and would soon enough blow over. Before the sound of Walter Winchell's voice died away she had drifted off to thoughts of attending the ballet in the green satin dress she'd seen displayed in the front window of Carter's Department Store.

One week later Ida Jean Meredith received a telephone call from Walter Crimmins at the bank. He did most of the talking; she just stood there with the receiver pressed to her ear and a stream of tears rolling down her face. Once she'd replaced the receiver, she didn't repeat a word of the conversation to anyone; she simply lowered herself into the rocking chair and started humming—no specific song, just a monotonous drone that had the sound of a hurt dog. When Anna Mae announced lunch was served, Miss Meredith didn't even turn an eye, she just kept creaking her chair back and forth, back and forth. The very next day she told both Anna Mae and Miranda, the cleaning woman, that she would no longer be needing their services. "We'll have to make do" she tearfully sobbed to Abigail. "There's no other choice."

"Make do?" Abigail replied soulfully, never imagining that it would fall upon her to do the cleaning and cooking. "Does that mean we won't…"

"It means I've barely enough money to feed us!" Miss Ida moaned, and then she started to cry in huge shuddering sobs. After that, Miss Meredith did little more than wobble back and forth in her rocking chair from dawn until dark, no longer bothering to bathe or dress herself. "It costs too much to heat bath water," she'd say, "We've no money for such luxuries."

In November, the chrysanthemums wilted and turned brown but no one bothered to cart the pots away. A curtain of gloom settled over the once cheerful house and day after day the shutters to the study remained closed. Ida Jean Meredith had been halfway through the third verse of a poem about the simple joy of a songbird, but she ceased writing. When prompted to continue on with her verse, Miss Meredith replied, "Joy?" her eyes glazed over with a bewildered expression as if she could no longer comprehend the meaning of such an emotion.

Abigail's silk dresses hung in the closet gathering dust as she scoured the floors and laundered their clothes in cold water and lye soap. Her hands once again grew raw and callused; the skin on her right thumb split open and bled, then it crusted over and split open again. She rummaged through cupboard after cupboard searching for a bit of cream or rosewater and glycerin to soothe her skin, but there was nothing and she cursed the fact that she had used it up so wastefully. Most every night she cried herself to sleep, praying that when she woke in the morning this horror would be a nightmare that had come and gone, instead she would wake to find a lump of self pity stuck in her throat and the thought of food banging away at her brain. For breakfast she'd gulp down a bowl of oatmeal, all the while dreaming of hot chocolate thick with cream, and at dinnertime she'd imagine the watery soup of potatoes and onions to be a thick stew. Once in a great while there might be a hambone in the pot and then she would lose all pretenses and gnaw at it until every last drop of marrow was sucked clean. On nights when she crawled into bed feeling the emptiness of her stomach press against her spine, Abigail called to mind a picture of the fat bellied cook stove that warmed the old farmhouse kitchen—she could almost smell the thick slabs of bacon sizzling in an iron skillet and taste the biscuits, so buttery they drizzled down onto her chin.

When winter came, she took to wearing heavy wool stockings in the house because Miss Ida was fearful of wasting the meager supply of fuel. "We're fortunate to have a roof over our head and a bit of food for the table," the old woman would say—but Abigail did not feel fortunate, in fact she felt miserable. Despite the wool shawl pulled tight around her shoulders, a chill needled into her spine and at times caused her to long for the warmth of Henry Keller's embrace. When the wind blew and frost iced the ground, she sunk into a bottomless sense of loss and began to wonder if there was such a thing as going back.

That January was the coldest Richmond had seen in many years. On a bitter morning when the trees were bare of leaves and the sky such a dark gray it looked to be night, a noisy black crow settled on the window sill. Abigail believed it to be the very same bird that summer before last perched in the tree outside of her old bedroom. The bird had the icy stare of a black-robed clergyman and she sensed it had been following her ever since she left Chestnut Ridge. Last summer she had seen sparrows and bright red cardinals nesting in the lilac trees, now there was only one hateful crow gleefully cackling at the misfortune that had fallen upon her. Abigail rapped hard against the windowpane but the nasty bird pecked at the place her hand had touched and cawed arrogantly. She pictured Preacher Broody banging his fist against the pulpit and hammering home the message *as ye sow, so shall ye reap.*

Ida Jean Meredith, who was a frail woman to begin with, died in the spring of 1930, just one month before the bank foreclosed on the two-story pink house and by some odd circumstance, the very same year the rhododendrons never bloomed.

For the first time in her life Abigail was alone, so alone that she took to talking to inanimate objects—a chair, a table, a cooking pot. "I don't expect you'd know what time it is," she'd say to a chest of drawers, or mumble some question as to the state of the weather as she passed by the sofa. Without the responsibility of doing for Miss Ida she became lost and wandered aimlessly from room to room, forgetting to eat and falling asleep at odd times and in odd places. One afternoon she awoke draped across Miss Ida's desk—the inkwell tipped over and a blue-black stain on her left cheek. She might have continued on that way, except that six weeks after the funeral, Harold Wigbottom, who was Miss Meredith's attorney, knocked at the door and told her she had to be out of the house by the end of the month.

"Miss Meredith willed her entire estate to The Artists and Poets League," he said. "They plan to take possession of the house and it's furnishings on May first."

"But," Abigail stuttered, "I'm *living* here!"

"You can stay until April thirtieth," he said. "No longer. I regret that such is the circumstance, but…" he shrugged then doffed his hat and walked off as if the conversation had been of little significance.

"Where am I to go?" she called after him, but Mister Wigbottom rounded the walkway and kept going. As soon as the door clicked closed, Abigail threw herself onto the sofa and started to bawl. She pounded her fists against the pillows and cried for hours on end, she cried until it felt as though there could be no more tears inside of her, then sometime during the wee hours of the morning she fell asleep on the sofa.

That night she heard thundering hooves pounding against the pavement, she saw wild horses running through the streets of Richmond. At the forefront of the pack was Malvania—his mane billowing recklessly, his nostrils flared and snorting, astride his back was a straight up Abigail with her nose tilted in the air and a look of determination in her eyes. As the herd thundered closer to the center of town, people clambered back against the walls of the buildings, all but one man, that one man was her father. He planted himself in the pathway of the horses and stood ground. Abigail could sense a collision coming, a collision that would shatter one of them into tiny shards of hopelessness. She had to do something. She spurred Malvania into a hard right and the herd followed, circling around him. When Abigail looked back, her father was standing there, his arms folded square across his chest and a look of hatred frozen on his face.

Abigail awoke with a start. She suddenly understood why the question about her father's forgiveness had never been answered. It was because there was no forgiveness, there never would be. Any thoughts she'd had about going home were no more than foolish daydreams. She'd made her decision the day she stepped on a train bound for Richmond. Now, there was nothing for her in Chestnut Ridge—nothing but the collision that would reduce her to a fragment of hopelessness. There was no going back now. There never had been.

On April thirtieth Abigail closed the door to Miss Ida's house and turned back only long enough to slip the key beneath the doormat as she'd been instructed to do. She trudged across town to a small flat on the third floor of an apartment building. A flat that had one tiny window overlooking an airshaft and a narrow bed left there by a previous tenant. It was only temporary, she told herself as she handed the landlord seven dollars for the month's rent. Abigail planned to get a job and move on to a better place, a place where sunlight sprawled across the floor and the scent of night blooming jasmine drifted in on the evening breeze. *It's only temporary* she reminded herself as a stream of tears rolled from her eyes.

The following morning Abigail tugged a black wool suit that had belonged to Miss Meredith from the bottom of her valise. It was a bit dated and heavier than the season warranted but she smoothed the wrinkles from the skirt, dressed herself in it and left the building. Once out on Cleary Street, she crossed over to Hansen Drive and turned left toward the business district, choosing to walk rather than spend the money for a trolley. She tromped in and out of every building on Central Boulevard inquiring about employment, but there was no work to be had. "Sorry," they'd say and squash the door closed in her face. That night she returned to the flat exhausted and soaked through with perspiration.

The next day Abigail marched herself downtown again; this time she inquired at the newspaper office, the hospital, the bus company and every doctor's office in town, but everywhere she went it was the same mournful answer—"No jobs." After a week of searching, she began to ration the remaining bit of foodstuff she'd brought from Miss Meredith's house. She found she could make do with one meal a day and a sparse one at that. A can of sardines could be stretched out over three days and a small size muffin over two. She found a bakery that sold perfectly good two day old bread for three cents. When there was nothing but a can of black pepper left in the cupboard, she bought a jar of peanut butter and a tub of grape jelly, and lived on those sandwiches for a full month.

Abigail was down to her last dollar when she met Gloria Polanski.

It happened on a July afternoon, in the full heat of the day, when she was sitting on a bench in the park across from the Government Services Building. "Fill out an application," they'd said, "We'll let you know if something turns up." But Abigail understood that this was something people said to be polite— nothing would *turn up*, nothing ever did, which was why she was crying.

Gloria plopped down on the same bench and started eating a foot long sausage sandwich. "You hungry?" she asked, then broke off a good-sized piece of the sandwich and held it out. "Go ahead," she said, "I already ate a big breakfast." Gloria had a broad smile and the curvaceous body of a person who seldom skipped meals.

Abigail paused amid a snuffle, "You sure?" she asked.

Gloria nodded. "You'd be doing me a favor. I probably ought to lose some weight, but I got terrible will power."

Abigail took the piece of sandwich and chomped down on it. "Oh Lord, this is so delicious!" she said, licking a spot of grease from her hand. "I haven't had a piece of meat in months!"

"You out of work?" Gloria pulled a banana from her purse, broke off a section and passed it over to Abigail.

"Uh-huh." Abigail shoved a chunk of banana into her mouth and kept right on talking. "I've been everywhere and there's not a single job in this entire city. I can even type—got my own typewriter—but that doesn't make a bean of difference. 'Sorry,' they say, 'we don't have any jobs—not even for *men.'* Like it would make a difference if a man was starving to death!"

"You really know how to type?"

Abigail nodded as she was swallowing the last of her banana. "Miss Meredith taught me. She's the woman I used to work for."

"How come you quit?"

"I didn't. She died."

"Rotten luck." Gloria pulled out two chocolate cookies wrapped in wax paper and passed one to Abigail. "You got family?"

"In Chestnut Ridge. Not that I could lay claim to them since I ran off. Papa wouldn't let me back even if I had the train fare, which I don't have." Abigail wrinkled her nose and grimaced at the thought. "He's not the forgiving type," she sighed.

"What about your mama?"

"She died almost five years ago."

"Whew. You got bad luck coming and going!"

"I suppose. Some I brought on myself. I probably should of married the Keller boy, like Papa wanted. Henry, he was a fine young man with a rich Daddy, I'd have had things pretty easy if I'd of married him."

"You love him?"

Abigail paused for a moment, as if she was tallying up the good and bad points of Henry before deciding, then she answered. "Not in a do or die sort of way."

"Well then, you did the right thing. A person oughtn't marry unless they're one-hundred-percent in love." Gloria pulled out a glass jar, gulped down some of the red liquid then passed it over to Abigail. "Raspberry tea. Want some?"

"Thanks." Abigail took a drink then handed the jar back.

"Hell's fire!" Gloria moaned, swiping at a red droplet that drizzled down her bosom. "I've ruined my brand new blouse!"

"Ruined?" Abigail laughed, "Why, that's just a teeny-weenie spot. That comes out when you catch it right away." Together they walked over to the water fountain on the far side of the park and Abigail using her handkerchief washed the spot from Gloria's shirt. "Good as new," she smiled.

As they left the park, Gloria said, "Could be, I might be able to fix you up with a job. That is," she added, "if you ain't squirrelly about what you gotta do."

"Me? Squirrelly? No indeed! Why, I used to scrub out my papa's chamber pot! I'm one who believes you gotta do what you gotta do."

Gloria laughed thunderously. "This ain't no scrub lady job. It's hostessing."

"Hostessing?"

"Yeah. Smile, give guys the big eye; let them buy you a drink, stuff like that."

"A whiskey drink?"

"Whiskey, gin, whatever."

"But, that's illegal."

"Oh well, excuse me for breathing! I thought you was desperate."

"I am."

"Well, then."

"Is this a speakeasy?"

"Itchy don't call it no speakeasy, he calls it a club."

"Can't the people who work there get arrested?"

"Uh-uh," Gloria shook her head. "Itchy takes care of the cops."

Maybe if she hadn't been hungry for so long, maybe if she wasn't down to her last dollar and fearful of being evicted, maybe then Abigail would have stopped to think of what her father or Preacher Broody might say about such thing, but as it was she simply smiled and told Gloria that she'd *love* to get such a job.

"If I get you the job," Gloria said, "will you teach me how to typewrite?"

"Absolutely!" Abigail answered. "Absolutely!"

Two days later Abigail accompanied Gloria across town to Club Lucky. "This is the place?" she gasped when they rapped on the back door of a building that gave the appearance of a closed-down factory.

"Yeah," Gloria answered with a grin.

Club Lucky was a place where a pair of eyes peered through an opening in the door and then decided whether or not to allow a person inside. There were no introductions, no applications to fill out, no references needed.

It was late afternoon so other than the watchdog who opened the door and an old man stacking glasses on the bar, the club was empty. Gloria guided Abigail through a clutter of empty tables and into a brightly lit back office. "This here's the girl I told you about, Itchy," she said and shoved Abigail forward.

Itchy peered over his glasses and told Abigail to swing around so he could get a gander from behind. She'd expected that he might inquire about her previous experience or possibly even ask about her qualifications but she hadn't thought he'd want to inspect her rump so she just stood there looking bewildered. Gloria suddenly took hold of Abigail's shoulders and whirled her around. "See that," she said, "nifty, right?"

"Kinda skinny," Itchy answered, "but she'll do." He lowered his gaze back to the newspaper he'd been reading. "Thirteen bucks a week, plus tips," he grumbled, "You keep a smile on your face and order champagne when you got a big spender."

"Yes sir, Mister Itchy," Abigail answered. She was going to say that it was a true pleasure to be working for him but before she had the chance, Gloria hustled her back out the door.

What Itchy said was true. Abigail had grown thin, bone thin in fact, skinny enough that the blue silk dress hung from her shoulders like a shapeless curtain. She'd chosen that particular dress based upon Gloria's description of the job— with its pale ivory lace and seed pearls rimming the neckline, it was the most elegant frock in her closet. But she hadn't worn the dress for well over a year, not since the last time she'd accompanied Miss Meredith to the ballet, and by some odd circumstance, it had come to be weary looking during that time, droopy and tired, lackluster, almost as drab as Abigail imagined herself to be.

"You need something jazzier," Gloria said. "Something with fringe, maybe?"

Abigail sighed. She'd never pictured herself in fringe, but the sound of it was silky as rosewater and glycerin. "Fringe?" she repeated wistfully.

"Yeah, that's it!" Gloria squinted at her protégé, then walked full around her as if she were registering a measurement. "You look to be the same size as

Lucy; I'll bet one of her dresses..." Gloria tugged a rose-colored gown splattered with silver beads and rows of fringe from the rack and handed it to Abigail. "Try this."

"Without asking?" Abigail replied, but she could already see the fringe swaying to and fro as she danced the Charleston.

"Ask who? Lucy? She don't even work here no more!"

"But ..."

"These hostess clothes belong to Itchy."

"You sure ..." Abigail offered up a half-hearted protest, but as the words rolled from her mouth she untied her own sash and allowed the blue dress to drop to her ankles. The rose-colored gown cascaded across her shoulders, the silver beads clinking softly as rubbed-thin dimes jingling through the bottom of an overcoat pocket. "I sure hope Mister Itchy doesn't mind," she mumbled, but by that time she was already grinning at the reflection in the dressing room mirror.

"See!" Gloria said, nodding her approval. "Much better. 'Course you need some rouge and a bit more lipstick." That night when Club Lucky opened there was a new hostess on the floor, a girl with darkened eyelashes and rose-colored lips, a girl who didn't exist a few days ago.

As they walked out onto the floor of Club Lucky, Abigail whispered into her friend's ear, "Now, what am I supposed to do?"

"Do what I do," Gloria answered. "Look available. Flirt with the men. Be real polite to the ladies, especially the hoity-toitys."

"How will I know—"

"You'll know," Gloria answered and then she sashayed across the room before there was time to ask anything else. Abigail suddenly felt awkward—a scarlet rose in a garden of white lilies—a child dressed in grown-up clothes. Maybe, she thought, she'd been wrong about the gown—it now seemed somehow gaudy, something a woman of low morals might wear. Trampish. For a long while, she considered going back to the dressing room and resurrecting her blue silk frock, despite its prissy sash. At least that dress wasn't gilded with silver spangles. Rolling this thought over in her mind, she lingered along the far edge of the room, a spot where a person could slip off without being noticed. But instead of leaving, she stood there shifting her weight from one foot to the other, trying to make herself look inconspicuous, trying to convince herself that the hostessing business was a perfectly proper thing.

She couldn't guess how long she'd been standing there—maybe ten minutes, maybe three hours—but in whatever time had passed, the room became noisy and filled with people. Sounds of raucous laughter ping-ponged from wall to wall and the musicians honked out one brassy tune after another. Abigail tried envisioning herself as a puff of smoke, floating across the room, disappearing through the vent—avoiding the heartbreak of another mistake. She had already started ruminating on how she should never have taken the hostessing job, when a heavy arm settled across her shoulder.

"Hey, Cutie," a man older than her father said. "Can I buy you a drink?"

"Umm." Abigail nodded and tried valiantly to dredge up a smile, but it felt like the muscles in her face were paralyzed. "Actually," she confessed, "I'm a hostess." She whispered the word hostess.

The man laughed. "New, huh?" At first he had seemed almost threatening, but as he spoke, his expression eased into a rounder, softer countenance and his smile was as kindly as any Abigail had ever seen. She nodded and returned the smile. "Don't worry, kid," he said, then took hold of her arm and led her to a small table alongside the bar, "You'll do fine, you got pizzazz." He slid the chair out and motioned for her to sit.

As far as Abigail could remember, it was the first time anyone had ever suggested she had pizzazz—in fact, she wasn't all that certain what the elusive quality actually was. She knew it had nothing to do with making great pies or aspiring to someday be a writer. *Pizzazz* was a special kind of sparkle reserved for wealthy debutantes and the flapper ladies of Vanity Fair magazine. "Gosh," she murmured breathlessly, her cheeks blossoming to the same shade of scarlet as her dress.

"Pete," the man called over to the bartender, "fix us up with some gin and a bottle of champagne for the little lady." He turned back to the table and said, "I'm assuming Itchy told you to order champagne, right, cutie?"

She nodded, then shyly offered up her name.

"I'm Tommy." He said. "Tommy Anderson."

For the remainder of the evening Abigail sat alongside Tommy Anderson and listened as he told her of how he'd been smart enough to steer clear of the stock market and how he was now buying up real estate for a song. He told of how he'd hooked a big fish and then tumbled overboard into the lake. He laughed and Abigail laughed with him. He poured champagne and she sipped it, hesitating just long enough to allow the bubbles to tease the tip of her nose. As the evening wore on Abigail began to picture the years erasing themselves from Tommy's face—first the deep forehead ridges, then the fleshy valleys that traveled down toward his jaw and finally the small crease that bridged the gap between his eyebrows. They danced to a mellow rendition of *Who Stole My Heart Away* and swaying to the sound of a muffled trumpet, Tommy Anderson eased her head down onto his shoulder. She didn't pull away because it was, for the moment, a comforting feeling, something she could snuggle down into—a warm place, a safe harbor. When the song ended she noticed that the silver-haired man was wearing a much younger face.

As the evening drew to a close, he leaned across the table and took hold of her hand. "How about you and me having some fun?" he whispered. "I got a hotel room."

Abigail yanked loose her hand. "What kind of a girl do you think I am!" she stammered indignantly.

"You're a *hostess*!" Tommy snapped back, then he stuffed the handful of bills back into his pocket and lumbered away.

By the time Abigail pulled herself together and started back to the dressing room, the crowd had been reduced to a few lingering drunks. As she inched her way across the floor, Itchy grabbed hold of her arm. "How'd you do?" he asked as he stood there scratching his crotch.

"Do? I did what any girl ought to do when a man tries to get fresh!" Abigail answered indignantly. "Being a hostess is not the same as being a *trollop!*" She was trying to hold back the tears and at the same time keep her eyes fixed on Itchy's face.

"Huh? Who said any such…" Itchy grimaced a bit and switched over to digging at his crotch with the other hand.

"Mister Tommy Anderson, *that's who!*"

Itchy laughed. "Tommy? He's harmless. A sweet old guy—but gets a load on and right away thinks he's a jazzbo."

"He asked me…"

"Guys do that. Just tell 'em to go fly a kite!" Itchy shrugged and walked off, still scratching like he'd zeroed in on a nest of fleas.

A half-hour later, he came back to the dressing room and dolled out the tips. Gloria got five dollar bills, Abigail got three. "See," Itchy said, grinning as he handed her the money, "Old Tommy Anderson took good care of you!" He shuffled out the door, still digging at his crotch.

Once he was well out of earshot, Abigail said, "You ever notice how Itchy keeps scratching his do-hickey?"

"Notice?" Gloria laughed. "Everybody's noticed! How do you think he got the name Itchy?"

It was almost three o'clock in the morning, her head was throbbing and there was a stiff breeze nipping at her back, but none of these things bothered Abigail as she walked home that night; she was busy thinking about how she was going to spend the three dollars. At the top of her list was a stewing chicken. She'd buy it first thing in the morning, boil it for an hour and then eat the whole thing—every last bit. Maybe she'd get a bag of flour and make dumplings as well—not the light as a cloud dumplings, but big doughy ones, the kind that would settle into her stomach and fill up all the cracks and crevices that had been empty for so long. Yes, she decided, flour. Coffee and sugar too!

Hostessing was never on the list of jobs she'd considered, but it was a lot better than going hungry. Somehow having three dollars in your pocket made things seem remarkably more respectable.

As it turned out, Club Lucky, a place Abigail had never before heard of, was one of the hottest night spots in all Richmond. In addition to Tommy Anderson and several more of his ilk, she met up with a young man whom she had seen at the ballet, and two ladies who were at one time members of Miss Meredith's Museum Restoration Committee. Every evening the room grew crowded with people—frivolous thrill seeking women, businessmen, jazzed up dancers, toughs looking for a brawl—people who under other circumstances would never meet, mingled at Club Lucky—they stood shoulder to shoulder, squashed together so tightly a person could barely cross the room. The music never stopped. Night after night Abigail would trudge back to the apartment with her feet aching and the strains of *Show Me the Way to Go Home* still pounding in her ears. Her sleep was restless and her dreams frenzied, full of faceless partygoers, blaring trumpets and swirling colors. She often woke in the morning with the smell of cigar smoke lingering in her nose and a purple bruise reminding her of some raucous reveler who'd given her a playful pinch.

Paul Martell seemed to be an exception. He was a Frenchman in his early thirties, not a regular at Club Lucky, but a man with fistfuls of money to spend, and a large diamond ring on his pinky. A person couldn't help but notice Paul for he stood a head taller than most of the crowd and had a rakish crop of dark curls that tumbled down upon his forehead. His green eyes were flecked with gold, a look, it was said, that drove women wild. The first encounter Abigail had with him, left her with stars in her eyes. "He's a dreamboat," she whispered to Gloria, "the kind of man I've always imagined myself *marrying*."

"Paul?" Gloria replied. "I heard he's trouble. Watch out."

"Trouble?" Abigail echoed doubtfully and then walked off.

The next night Paul Martell danced with Abigail for most of the evening and flamboyantly ordered her a second bottle of champagne while the first bottle was still half-full. In-between dances they sat at a tiny table in the darkest corner of the room, chairs pushed so close together that a breeze couldn't pass between them. He dazzled her with tales of France and she wound the image of herself through every word. When the band played *Moonlight on the Ganges*, they danced again and as Paul's large hand pressed Abigail's body to his, she snuggled into the crook of his neck. "I'm not *really* a hostess," she whispered. "This is temporary—'till I can find a writing job."

He didn't answer, just lowered his head and let his breath graze her hair as his right hand eased its way down the back of her spine.

That night Paul left a ten dollar tip for Abigail, which according to Gloria was the largest any girl at Club Lucky had ever received.

The following night Abigail took special care with her make-up; she used a pale pink lip color, less lash paint and cheek rouge that could have led a person to think it was her own natural glow. She left the dresses with fringe and sequins hanging on the rack and instead wore the ivory lace dress Miss Ida Jean Meredith had bought for her. She stepped out onto the floor looking more like one of the patrons than a hostess. Throughout the evening she kept one eye on the door as she circulated around the room, but Paul did not come. Nor did he come the following night, or the night after that.

By the time he did show up, five nights later, Abigail had lost hope of ever seeing him again and gone back to wearing a fringed dress that wriggled even when she was standing perfectly still. Sitting with an elderly gentleman from Texas and facing away from the door, she did not see Paul come in.

"Hello, love," he whispered in her ear.

"Paul," Abigail sighed and swiveled to face him.

"Miss me?" He chucked her playfully beneath the chin.

She nodded. It was strictly against the rules for a hostess to walk off and leave a customer who'd sprung for a bottle of champagne, so Abigail smiled a thin smile and said, "I'm busy right now ..." Her words trailed off as if there were something terribly important left unsaid.

"I'll be out back when the club closes." He smiled, then turned and walked over to where Francine was standing, as if she had been the one he'd come to see.

Abigail knew he hadn't come there intending to spend the evening with Francine—at least she thought he hadn't. She'd *felt* something that first night and she was pretty certain he had too. Throughout the remainder of the evening, she watched Paul's movements from the corner of her eye. "Oh, aren't you the clever one," she'd quip to her companion and laugh gaily but all the while she was thinking of how it would feel to have Paul kiss her.

It was well after two o'clock when the music died and the band started to pack up. "Have Itchy hold my tip money till tomorrow," Abigail told Gloria and then hurried out the back door. Francine was leaning against the wall and smoking a cigarette. Paul was standing beside her; he'd already removed his tie and opened the collar of his shirt. "Hello again," he said to Abigail, as though they'd somehow met up quite unexpectedly.

For an uncomfortably long five minutes they stood there chatting about nothing—the music was good, the gin was watery, the weather was cool for the season—the kind of things people drag out as points of conversation when there is nothing else to be talked about. Finally Abigail said, "I have to be going," and she turned to walk away.

Paul whispered something to Francine, something Abigail wished she could hear but did not. Then he called out, "Wait for me," and hurried along.

After they had gone almost two blocks, Abigail asked, "Did I misunderstand?"

"Misunderstand?" he replied teasingly.

"Yes," Abigail said somberly, "misunderstand that you were waiting for *me*."

He tugged her into the bend of his arm and slowed his step to match hers. "No," he answered and affectionately nudged her cheek with his nose. "You didn't misunderstand." He stopped walking and looked into her eyes as a lover might.

Suddenly she had no need for more of an explanation. Moving together like mated swans they walked the full mile and a half to her apartment building— a building that she felt ashamed for him to see and an apartment that she would *never* allow any suitor to see. "Goodnight," she mooned dreamily as they stood facing each other in the dreary vestibule.

"Goodnight?" he said, then without further words placed his lips upon hers. The first kiss was gentle, a tender touch of his lips to her mouth. Abigail felt a tinge of warmth slither down her spine. She tilted her face upward, like a baby bird wanting more. Paul kissed her again and again, first on the mouth, then at the base of her throat. Abigail felt the warmth of his breath wrapping itself around her and she wished the moment would never end; then he pushed his body into hers with such force that it took her by surprise. He wedged her back against the wall and pressed himself against her until she could feel the hardness of him.

"Please don't," Abigail whispered and made a feeble attempt to move away. Was this how love was supposed to begin? From the moment they met, she had felt a stirring inside of her, a desire to touch, to hold and be held. Now that he was holding her, the closeness made her want to pull back, it was so unfamiliar, frightening in a sense—the way new things always seem frightening. Paul was the kind of man any woman would want, and yet here he was, wanting her. She could drive him away with her Puritan way of thinking, she reasoned, when there was certainly no cause to be afraid. Sophisticated people were simply more open about showing their affection. It was life's coming of age, and after all, Paul was *French.*

He parted his lips, drew her tongue into his mouth, then slid his hands down, cupped his fingers around her behind and yanked her to his groin. Abigail's feet were dangling inches above the tiled floor. Inexperienced as she might be, she knew love was not supposed to be rough and groping. "Stop," she insisted, this time much more forcefully.

"You want it as much as I do!" was his answer—the words mean and hard-edged as the crack of her father's hand. Instead of stopping, Paul lowered his head to her bosom and suckled his mouth to her breast.

"How dare you!" she cried out. "Stop! Stop this instant!" She began beating her fists against the bulk of his shoulders. He slammed her head back against the wall, angrily ripped open the front of her dress and sunk his teeth into her tender breast. She screamed and tried to wrench herself free, but it was useless. He was bigger, stronger and driven by arousal. He jammed his right hand up beneath her skirt—to Abigail it felt more like a fist than a hand. For a brief moment the maneuver caused him to loosen his grip on her buttocks and she slid down far enough that her feet touched onto the floor. Quick as a lightning bolt she rammed her knee into his groin.

"Son-of-a-bitch," he screamed and doubled over.

Abigail ran. She flew up all three flights of stairs and didn't slow for a breath until she'd slammed and bolted the apartment door.

Still trembling, she huddled into a corner of the room and cried. Sometime before sunrise, she drifted off to sleep. When she woke in the morning she saw the large purple mass just above her right nipple and the mark of Paul's teeth edging it.

For six days Abigail did not go to work. She walked to the corner store, telephoned Itchy and told him she'd somehow gotten food poisoning. Believing the story to be true, Gloria came to call with a crock of homemade bread pudding, two bananas and a blueberry muffin. It was a full five minutes before Abigail summoned up enough courage to answer the knock.

"Food Poisoning, my ass," Gloria said when she saw the blackened eye.

"I tripped and fell on the stairs." To Abigail, a lie seemed far more honorable than the truth of what had happened.

"Yeah, sure. Was it Paul?"

Abigail shook her head side to side.

"It was him," Gloria grumbled, "I know the type." She peeled the wax paper back from the muffin and smacked it down on a plate. "You gotta wise up," she told Abigail, "lounge lizards like him ain't got no scruples. They think girls like us is dime store trash. Good time weenie-wagglers, that's what they think!"

"Paul seemed different."

"Ain't none of them different," Gloria answered.

That thought stuck in Abigail's head but it wasn't something she wanted to believe. When the bruise on her eye faded to yellow and she could cover it with face cream and a heavy dusting of powder, she returned to Club Lucky.

For a long while she shied away from the good-looking men and migrated to mild-mannered fellows, the ones who were hiding behind themselves, sitting alone and nursing a glass of whisky. She'd sit down alongside them and right away start imagining things like white roses and baby carriages. Thing was, they really weren't all that different than Paul—each of them wanted something and had nothing to give. Steven Miller ordered a bottle of champagne and then groped her bosom. Frank Something-or-another wanted to sleep at her apartment. Bobby Tollinger, who for three weeks had behaved like a perfect gentleman, eventually got so rough that Itchy had him thrown out of the club.

If it had been other circumstances, Abigail would have walked off and found another job—become something more respectable, a secretary or a governess even—but times were hard and jobs were almost nonexistent, so she stayed at Club Lucky. After a time it got so that Abigail could circulate through the crowd like the sound of a song, she was there and then gone, no trace left behind, no promises, no expectations.

She set aside thoughts of becoming a writer and rationalized that she at least had a job, was no longer hungry and was, in fact, adding money to the coffee can on the top shelf of her closet. But there were days when a sense of shabbiness worked its way into her heart and she'd wonder what her father would say of her now. Likely as not, she thought, he'd grimace. 'Daughter?' he'd say, 'I have no daughter!' Her mother would think more kindly. Livonia would understand; she'd hold Abigail close and say, 'Child, these are hard times. People do what they have to do to survive.' When the emptiness of life took root in Abigail's heart, she closed her mind to reality and dreamed of Chestnut Ridge back when she and Livonia walked together in the springtime and stopped to smell the wild roses blooming along the high road.

In time, Abigail came to accept that life was a road which traveled in only one direction—forward. There was never any going back. The following April she emptied out the coffee can and moved to the classier side of town. Abigail was making good money at Club Lucky and much as she hated being a *hostess*, the job did make it possible for her to live in a nicer place. She rented a spacious three room apartment in a brick building with azaleas lining the walkway and a uniformed porter standing at the door. The building was only six blocks from Miss Ida Jean Meredith's house—which, to Abigail's dismay, had now been transformed into a study center for aspiring poets. A crooked sign was taped to the inside of the living room window, a sign that cried out for someone to straighten it.

Nothing that once was—was anymore.

Middleboro, Virginia

The year 2000

Destiny Fairchild was the best thing that ever happened to me. I'm well aware of a tendency to repeat myself, but the truth about Destiny is a fact that bears repeating. She was the one who saw me through that last year, when things got bad. I'd mention something about my back hurting like the devil and without me even asking, she'd start rubbing those little hands of hers up and down my spine. Most folks would have chalked it up to old age and told me to take an aspirin, but Destiny was a person who believed aches and pains could come from loose worries floating around your head. "Now, close your eyes and relax," she'd say; then she'd get to talking about how we'd go one place or another just as soon as I felt better. Before you could peel a banana I'd be ready to go shopping! How could you not appreciate a person like that?

That was the year I rounded the corner on eighty-eight, and was feeling it. It got so that I'd turn on television and watch *The Today Show* just to see Willard Scott put on pictures of folks who were one hundred years old. He always told how spry they were and it was a real encouragement. Let me tell you, when a person gets to be one hundred, they *deserve* to be on television. Destiny used to say when I turned one hundred we were going to Norfolk Beach and swim naked. She claimed she was going to take a picture of me swimming naked and *that's* the one she was sending to Willard Scott. "He wants spry?" she'd say, "We'll give him spry!" That was her way; she'd start up about some little thing, maybe even something you didn't think was all that funny, but once she got to laughing and carrying on, you jumped on the bandwagon. That day she said we'd go over to the Atlantic Ocean and swim naked, I laughed so hard I wet my bloomers.

For Christmas that year, I wanted to get Destiny something really special, so I asked her what she might like to have. As good as she'd been to me, she could have asked for a brand-new Cadillac car and I'd have gotten it, but instead she tells me she'd really like this book published by the Audubon Society of America. "Excuse me?" I said, like I wasn't hearing her right.

"*The Waterbirds of Florida*," Destiny repeated.

"That's it? A book on waterbirds?"

Destiny nodded. "I saw this TV show about them. The announcer said they're the most beautiful creatures on earth."

"Waterbirds?"

"Yes indeed. They're so long-legged and graceful. Why, just watching them makes a person feel like flying." Destiny jumped up and twirled around the room flapping her arms. "Imagine," she sang out, "being a pink flamingo!"

I started chuckling at her antics.

"Try it," she said. "Just close your eyes and pretend you're all decked out in pink feathers. Picture yourself standing on one leg alongside a blue lagoon, your long neck stretched out and your head held high."

I had problems standing with both feet planted on the ground, so of course I couldn't imagine such a thing, but Destiny sure could.

That Christmas I gave Destiny a cashier's check for twenty-five thousand dollars and a first-class trip for both of us to go see those waterbirds. She gave me a pink feather boa and a nightgown to match. That day we drank eggnog and laughed till our sides hurt. Then when we run out of laughing, we watched *A Christmas Carol* on television.

Elliott can say Destiny was out for all she could get, but when I gave her that check she told me she couldn't accept such a thing and she said it like a person who was adamant about their intent. I pretty much expected she'd react that way, which is why I bought a cashier's check. "Destiny, it's money already paid out," I told her, "and, not a soul in the world but you can cash that check!" Of course, we went back and forth over it a bit, but when I got teary-eyed and started telling her how I was an old lady who had few pleasures in life other than giving a gift to someone I truly did love, Destiny threw up her hands and started laughing.

"Okay!" she said. "I'll keep the money! Just don't start torturing me with that 'I'm old and pitiful' routine of yours!" She came over and hugged me so hard I thought my ribs would split open.

We flew off to Florida two days later and when we landed in Palm Beach, Destiny rented a convertible car so we could feel the wind in our hair. We stayed in the Breakers Hotel, one of the finest you could possibly imagine, and on New Year's Eve we called room service and ordered up a bottle of champagne to celebrate while we watched the carrying on in Times Square on television. If you can believe it, Destiny brought a bottle of *hot-hot pink* nail polish and painted my toenails to match my nightgown. I got so tickled watching her brush that bright pink on my toes, I thought I'd explode. As we sat there watching the ball of lights drop down, I told her, "Destiny, I never dreamed I'd live to see a new millennium."

She said, "Maybe *this* would be the time to take that swimming naked picture!"

Of course, I wasn't about to do any such thing. So instead, she set the automatic timer on her camera and took a picture of the two of us with our hot pink toenails and a glass of champagne. After we got back home, she had that picture framed and I kept it sitting on my dresser.

Looking back, I wish I *had* gone swimming naked.

The following February was when I found out about the cancer. It's not like you wake up one morning and boom, you've got a serious case of cancer. It sneaks up on you. Ever since last summer I'd been having backaches and feeling like my stomach was aggravated. A number of times Destiny suggested that I go see Doctor Birnbaum and have it checked out, but I always pooh-poohed the idea. "A person my age is bound to have certain ailments," I told her. Then one Tuesday I woke up with my stomach feeling real bitter sour; the night before I hadn't eaten a thing outside of some chicken soup and I knew my stomach couldn't be soured over *that*! I called Destiny and told her that maybe she was right about going to the doctor.

"I'll be there in fifteen minutes!" she said and hung up the telephone.

Before she made it over to my house, I started throwing up the most God-awful stuff anybody could imagine, black and course, like week-old coffee grinds. When Destiny got there she took one look at that pasty-white face of mine and shuffled me off to Doctor Birnbaum, without even an appointment.

She marched into the doctor's office with me lolling on her arm and said, "Miss Lannigan needs to see the doctor, right now!" I thought she had a lot of nerve demanding such a thing, especially when there were a half-dozen other people in the waiting room. Cathy, who was Doctor Birnbaum's nurse, must have realized how sick I was 'cause right away she took us into the examination room—ahead of everybody else.

"I hate to be such a bother," I said, when the doctor started checking me over. He just smiled and told me that I was never a bother, then he patted my knee in the most kindly way. I always thought, if you have to be sick, you ought to do it with someone like Allan Birnbaum. He told Destiny I'd have to go into the hospital for a few tests and asked if she could bring me that very afternoon. She said yes without even a flicker of hesitation.

I was in the hospital for three days, and Destiny came to visit every day. She'd get there early in the morning, sometimes before the breakfast cart came around, and she'd stay until the bell rang at night. At nine o'clock visitors had to leave and the chimes rang out so pleasant-like, you'd think it was some kind of wonderful grandfather clock, but they were dead-serious about visitors leaving. One night I was feeling especially blue and Destiny stayed after the bells rang, but the nurse came in right away and told her she'd have to leave so I could get my rest.

I won't go on about how they did every kind of test imaginable and x-rayed me from head to toe, but I will say, I was mighty glad Destiny was with me when Doctor Birnbaum came in that Friday. He had the most somber look on his face when he sat down on my bed and took hold of my hand, right then, I *knew* something was wrong.

"I'm afraid I don't have good news," he said and shook his head like he was real sorrowful. "Those coffee grounds you threw-up, were from your liver."

Most people think you only *hear* words, but Destiny was watching the doctor's mouth like she could see the size and shape of every letter.

"It's symptomatic of pancreatic cancer."

"What's the cure?" Destiny asked. She had that kind of pick-yourself-up-and-move-on attitude because she was used to dealing with problems. Me, I'd lived long enough to *know*, there's no remedy for some things.

"Well," Doctor Birnbaum said, hesitantly, like he might have preferred to choke down the words instead of spitting them out. "Pancreatic cancer is a tough customer. In some instances, we might try chemotherapy or radiation but those treatments are difficult to tolerate and not often successful in treating this type of cancer. Given Abigail's age, I wouldn't recommend either one."

"What then?" Destiny asked.

"I'm afraid there's not much we can do."

"What's that supposed to mean?" Destiny's voice got real thin and high-pitched, nothing like the way she usually spoke.

Doctor Birnbaum coughed three or four times, then finally let go of the words. "Pancreatic cancer is almost always terminal," he said. "There's little we can do except make sure the patient is comfortable and pain-free."

"Little? Or nothing?" Destiny was beginning to get the message and her green eyes filled up with so much water they looked like the deep end of the ocean.

I always thought if I got such a piece of bad news I'd break down and cry, or holler about life being unfair, maybe even claim there had been a mistake because such a thing couldn't be true, but that wasn't what happened. I just leaned back into my pillow and let the reality of it cover me over like a heavy winter blanket. As the weight of it pressed down on me, I realized that Doctor Birnbaum was trying to tell me in the most kindly way, I was dying. Not maybe dying, but definitely dying. "How long?" I asked, trying to focus on what I needed to know.

"I can't say definitely. Three months, six months, maybe longer."

Doctor Birnbaum said he'd arrange for the Hospice nurses to come and take care of me but Destiny told him *she'd* be the one to see to my needs, whatever they might be. By the time the doctor left the room, the poor child was sobbing like her little heart was gonna break. "Hush up that crying," I told her. "I'm an old woman, Destiny. I've lived a long life and a person can't ask for more than that. Sure as a person's born, a person's gonna die!" I tried my best to console her, but she just kept sobbing. Finally, I said I didn't want to hear another word about dying and such. "Whatever time I've got, I want to enjoy!" I told her. I wasn't ready to think about the being dead part, I was busy focusing on how much more living time I had left; which I suppose was why I never got around to putting things in order the way I should have.

To be perfectly honest, my stomach was feeling a lot better by the time I left the hospital, so the two of us went out and had a plate of fried oysters for lunch. I'd already laid down the law about any talk of dying, so Destiny made a genuine effort to be her old self. She ordered us up martinis and told the waiter to bring us another round as soon as we'd finished those. She tried to pretend things were the same as always, but that happy-go-lucky laugh of hers sounded like a sorrowful echo.

That night Destiny went out to get chicken and biscuits from Popeye's— the doctor said eat whatever I felt like and that's exactly what I was doing— when she came back she brought her little valise and moved in. I had planned to tell her about the bonds after supper but we started watching *Some Like it Hot,* the movie where Jack Lemmon and Tony Curtis join a girl's band, and got to laughing so hard we about rolled off the sofa. I didn't know how many more days of laughing I had left in me, so I wasn't about to spoil this one by getting onto something serious. The thing about dying is, that even when you know it's gonna happen, you still insist on telling yourself, there's more time. Of course, I was figuring on the outside edge of what Doctor Birnbaum said, six months, maybe more. As it turned out, it was a lot less.

The very next day, Destiny called up the restaurant where she'd been waitressing and told them she needed to take a leave of absence. Six months to a year, she said. The old guy that owned the place complained and said she should have given him some notice, but in the end he told her it would be okay. I figure he went along with what she wanted because Destiny was a top notch worker and he didn't want to lose her.

That first week after she moved in, we had ourselves a pretty good time. Mostly we did silly things—like opening three different bottles of wine so we could decide which went better with Frito Lays, or driving down to Macy's to try on the most outrageous hats we could find. One day we went clear across town to the Le' Grand Salon to get ourselves a manicure and pedicure. I figured to have my nails painted some pale color, a shade appropriate for a person my age, but when we walked out of there, Destiny and I both had fire engine red nails. I felt sorry I'd never gone swimming naked, but I didn't have the least bit of regret about those scarlet colored fingernails.

The following week, I got real sick and that was the end of our running around.

A half-dozen times I started to tell Destiny about the bonds and what she was to do with them, but there never seemed to be a right time. It's a sorrowful thing to talk about what to do with your stuff when you're dead and gone— I didn't feel much like discussing it and I suppose Destiny didn't either. I could tell she was hurting; it was in her eyes, even though she didn't say a word.

That week we played cards a few times and watched a show or two on television, but mostly I slept and she sat on the chair right beside my bed. If I so much as breathed heavy, she'd jump up and ask if I wanted a pain pill. "How about a drink of water?" she'd ask, "Or, maybe a foot rub?"

Less than three weeks after I came home from the hospital, I died. It wasn't real dramatic; I just went to sleep and never again woke up.

People think dying is a painful thing, but it isn't. Sometime during the middle of the night, I simply stepped out of my old used-up body and became light as a feather. I didn't have an ache or a pain anywhere and even though I couldn't see myself, I knew I looked just like I did when I was twenty years old.

Poor Destiny was the one who found it painful. She shed enough tears to fill an ocean. I felt real appreciative that I'd been blessed with a friend such as Destiny, but hated to see her torn apart that way. I was wishing I could put my arm around her and say, *'Don't cry, honey, I'm still here.'* But of course, such a thing is not possible.

I wasn't dead more than a few hours, when I remembered about those bonds and knew I should have taken care of business while I still had the chance.

It seems to me that God ought to give a person the chance to see ahead to the terrible happenings that are gonna occur after they're dead; that way people would take greater care in settling their life properly. I certainly would have. Once you're gone, all you can do is look back and think, *Oh dear, if only I'd written that down on paper.* Of course, it's too late then.

After I died, Destiny was the one who took care of things. Thank Heaven I'd switched my bank accounts over to her name, otherwise I don't know how she would have paid for the funeral. Destiny had the little bit she'd saved from her waitressing job at the restaurant and part of what I'd given her last Christmas, but the way money slid through her fingers, even that had dwindled down considerably. There are a million good things anyone could say about a person like Destiny, but being frugal sure isn't one of them. Why, she could hold onto a greased pig longer than she could a dollar. When she was making arrangements for my funeral Destiny told long-faced Mister Panderelli that she wanted the very best of everything. She turned away from a perfectly sensible oak casket and ordered a steel coffin that Mister Panderelli claimed was vacuum sealed and guaranteed secure. Secure from what? Who in the world would want to pilfer an old woman's dead bones? From my vantage point, I could tell Panderelli was capitalizing on the poor girl's grief. Destiny spent twenty-three-thousand dollars on that coffin and then she ordered so many sprays of bright red roses you'd have thought they were laying out Tallulah Bankhead's first cousin.

She could have taken that money and crammed it into her own pocket, but instead she spent it on me, without any inkling whatsoever that I was still watching over her. Now, that's pure love, the kind most folks find hard to believe. If the good Lord Himself had ordered me up a savior, he couldn't have found a better one than Destiny.

That last year I was alive, I'd gotten pretty forgetful. I'd misplace my checkbook; forget to pay the electric bill, things like that. One time I went to the Bountiful Basket and got to the checkout with a cartload of groceries and not a nickel in my pocketbook. That very day I said, "Destiny, I need you to help take care of my finances and I'm willing to pay for your time."

She laughed that big round laugh of hers—I often wondered how such a sizable laugh could come out of such a little person—"Pay me?" she said. "Why, I'd be glad to help, but you don't need to pay me!"

"I insist!" Every time I went to give Destiny any cash money, we'd go 'round and 'round. "I'm no charity case!" I said, as if I was real insulted.

"I never claimed you were. But, I'm still not gonna take money for helping out."

"Then I'll do without your help." I could afford to talk sassy 'cause I knew full well that once I'd asked her to do something, neither hell nor high water would keep her from it.

We dickered back and forth a bit, I offered to pay five-hundred dollars a month; she said she'd take fifty. Finally we settled on one-hundred and that's when Destiny started writing my checks and taking care of whatever needed taking care of. A number of times when Elliott stopped by to tell me how down on his luck he was, I had Destiny write him out a check for five hundred dollars. "Just make it payable to *cash*," he'd usually say and she'd do exactly as he asked.

I was pleased with such an arrangement because having a trustworthy person like Destiny to oversee things was worth a lot more than a few paltry dollars. It surely made my life easier and I'm certain having that extra money was a Godsend for her. Right off she bought herself a brand new Westinghouse microwave and a red fox coat that she planned to pay off in installments. I told her, "Destiny, you oughtn't run up a bunch of finance charges, I'll buy you that coat outright." She just shrugged it off and said something about how paying on time didn't bother her one little bit. Next thing I knew, she'd gone and bought herself a twenty-one inch television set on the installment plan. I was happy to see her get the nice things she deserved. All my life, I'd pinched and saved, always worrying about the future, then before

I knew it, I was an old woman with not much future left to worry about and pitifully little to show for all the scrimping. If I had it to do over again, I'd live my life just the way Destiny does. She's one person who won't end up with a bunch of regrets about things she didn't do.

As far as the money was concerned, I had more than I could live long enough to spend. There was still well over one-hundred thousand dollars in the Middleboro Savings Bank, and that wasn't counting the bonds.

I wasn't aware of those bonds when Scott Bartell settled up Will's estate and if I hadn't gone back to sorting through the boxes a few months later they might have been shipped off to the Salvation Army along with the rest of Will and Becky's belongings. The bonds were in the very last carton, folded inside Papa's worn out Bible. United States Savings Bonds—ten of them, each one good for one-hundred-thousand dollars.

Right off I knew Will was the one who bought those bonds and I had to believe it was with the money he'd got for the farm. He claimed the United States Government was the only place a person could be sure their money was safe and if you thought otherwise he'd argue you blue in the face. Get him started and he'd go on and on about how he and Papa barely scraped through that first year of the great depression, when the Chestnut Ridge Savings Bank closed their doors and left a bunch of farmers standing in the street, wondering how they'd get the money to pay their bills. "Papa was one of those farmers," Will would say and then he'd tell how they counted up pennies and made do with the nothing more than the food they grew. "That was the year Papa did not give one red cent to the Methodist Church," Will would say to emphasize his point, for everyone knew Papa thought not tithing was as much a sin as thieving or lying.

The day I found the bonds, I counted them at least a half-dozen times. I just couldn't believe that anyone would pay so much money for a place that destroyed whole families. One-million dollars! It was a figure so big it got stuck in my throat if I tried to say it aloud but all I could think about was how Will and Becky had never gotten to take much pleasure from all those years of hard work. I cried for a long while, then I took the bonds out of Papa's Bible and hid them away for safekeeping.

After that, I pretty much willed the bonds out of my head. A wiser person would have considered their worth, but given the bitter way I'd left Papa and the farm they weighed heavy on my conscience, like an ill-gotten gain. Anyway, once Destiny started watching over my finances, I didn't have occasion to think about them. For a person who was such a spendthrift with her own money, she was surprisingly careful with mine and would count up every penny. At the end of the month she'd open the checkbook and show how she'd paid the gas and electric, the insurance, the groceries, and such. "Now, this check for five hundred dollars cash," she'd explain, "that was what we used for household spending money."

"Destiny," I told her, "You don't have to account for what you spend," but she did anyway. I don't know if anybody else would have anticipated that her signing those checks could bring the poor child such heartache, but I can tell you, I surely didn't.

I suppose there's no right time to die; when a young person's life is cut short it's considered a tragic injustice and yet it's almost as pitiful when old folks outlive their friends and relatives and are lowered into the ground with nobody to mourn their passing. I was luckier than most, I had Destiny. When somebody who was real special to you is broken-hearted because you've died, it makes you feel like your life counted for something after all. I would never have wished Destiny one minute of sadness, not as sweet as she'd been to me, but her caring so much did my heart good. After the funeral, she'd walk around my house and sniff at the clothes I used to wear, pick up a book that I'd been reading, or cry at the sight of something I'd left out of place—the same kind of things I'd do after Mama died. Why, I can still remember how I got attached to Mama's old apron and wore it till it fell apart—it was like having a piece of Mama to hold onto a bit longer.

When I got bedridden, I asked Destiny to fetch me a white tablet and I wrote out what my intentions were. I'd seen television shows where people had scratched out their last will and testament on a stretch of sand or piece of rock, so this, I thought, should do just fine. It was only one page, but shaky as my hand had become it took every ounce of strength I could muster to complete it. When it was all done, I said, "Destiny, this here piece of paper states that you are to have all my worldly belongings after I die." I folded the paper in half and stretched out my hand to her, but she acted like she hadn't heard a word I'd said. "Destiny," I repeated, "didn't you hear?"

"You're not dying!" she said, and went right on shaking a duster at the window blinds. Anybody else might have thought she was just being impertinent, but I could see how she was swiping at the tears with the sleeve of her shirt.

"Well, okay then," I answered. "But, just in case I'll leave this paper in the top drawer of my nightstand." I had planned to explain about the bonds at that time, but feeling as she did, I thought I'd just wait a while. Of course, I thought I had a lot more time to get around to such things.

With Destiny knowing that she was entitled to everything I owned, you'd think that once the funeral was over, she would have cleaned up my affairs and gotten rid of the house, but she didn't. She just kept right on paying the bills and coming over once a week to clean, same as if I was still alive. I'd watch her polishing up that old Buick like she was getting ready to take me out for a Sunday drive and the whole while she'd be brushing back her tears. I was thinking, *get rid of the old wreck if it's gonna make you cry.* At first it made me feel good to see someone so saddened by my passing, but at this point I had gotten beyond thoughts of myself and was wishing Destiny would get back to being the carefree person she'd always been.

Almost three months passed before Destiny started getting out, and even then she'd head right back to places we'd gone together. On the first Saturday of June she went back to Le Grand Salon and had her toenails painted fire engine red, after that she swung by Macy's and took to trying on outrageous hats. If there's such a thing as poking a wish through the gates of Heaven and having it land on a person, I could swear it happened at that precise moment. Destiny suddenly slapped a bright yellow straw hat on top of her head and started laughing out loud, same as she did when we were there together. Then, to my amazement, she up and bought the hat! After that she went on a spending spree, bought herself a polka dot bathing suit, a pair of red lizard skin sandals and a genuine gold watch. That was pretty much the start of her getting back to being herself. Whenever she got to feeling lonesome, out she'd go, shopping. She'd spend an entire day rummaging through first one store, then another. She'd come home with fancy dresses, matching shoes, dangle earrings, anything that happened to catch her eye; one time it was a set of crystal lamps and a blue velvet sofa for her living room. I had to laugh at Destiny 'cause she'd buy things for the pure pleasure of buying them. She was like spun cotton candy, you couldn't help but love the sweetness of her, but she wasn't the least bit practical. By August, she'd really gotten into the swing of things and that's when she traded in my old Buick for a shiny new Thunderbird Ford. It made me wish I'd done such things while I was still alive.

Even though she'd bought all kinds of new furniture and fixed her own house nice as a person might wish for, Destiny still came over to clean and take care of my place. Her being there was how this whole business with Elliott started up. It was just about six months after the funeral when he stopped by; no doubt to tell me some hard luck story about how he needed another handout. When Destiny answered the door, he didn't look any too pleased and said sharply, "Don't tell me dear old Abby isn't at home!"

Destiny gasped and just stood there with her mouth hanging wide open.

"Cat got your tongue?" Elliott said. "Or did my lovely old auntie tell you to shoo me off next time I came around?"

"Oh no. No indeed," Destiny mumbled apologetically. "Please, come in."

Elliott tromped into the living room and flopped down on the sofa. "Got anything cold to drink? Some chips maybe? Or pretzels?"

Destiny's face was as white and hard set as a plaster mask, but she hurried into the kitchen and came back with a glass of ginger ale. "Sorry," she said, "the cupboard is pretty bare, no chips or pretzels."

"Figures." Elliott took a large gulp of soda.

"I would have gotten in touch," Destiny stuttered, "but, your aunt didn't have your address or phone number in her book."

"That hurts," he said in a smart-alecky way.

"Poor Abigail was quite sick for a while." Destiny spoke with little stops and starts to her words, like someone with something to say but no will for saying it. "There was nothing that could be done. It was pancreatic cancer. The doctor…"

"Auntie's dead?" Elliott looked like he couldn't believe his own ears. "Dead?"

"I know it's terrible to find out this way…"

"Terrible?" He started laughing, it was a hearty guffaw that rose up from his stomach and echoed through the room like a roll of thunder. "Listen up, Florence Nightingale, this is the news I've been waiting to hear. That old witch has been the only thing standing between me and what is rightfully mine!"

"That's a terrible thing to say! Why, Abigail Lannigan was as generous a soul as I've ever known."

"Generous? Doling out a few hundred bucks every so often? Shit, I had to grovel just to get that!"

"She never made anyone grovel! She gave you every cent you asked for."

"Ask? Why should I have to *ask*? That old bag had no right to the money! I'm the male Lannigan heir. Me! Elliott Emerson! By all rights, I should have inherited that miserable farm, and every cent that came out of it. If my mother's stubborn-headed grandpa hadn't screwed her over, I would have had it sooner! Dear old Auntie—"

Before he had time to finish the thought, Destiny lifted her hand and whacked him in the face. "Get out of here," she shouted. "Out! And, don't ever come back!"

"Fine! Just fork over the name of the lawyer handling the estate probate and I'm out of here!"

Destiny pushed hard against Elliott's chest. "Out!" she repeated. "I'd sooner die than see you get one cent of Abigail's money!"

"You?" Elliott sneered. "*You*, Little Miss White Trash, have nothing to say about it! Your days of free-loading are over!"

Destiny punched Elliott in the chest with such force that he lost his balance, tumbled backward and landed on the coffee table with a crashing thud. "You pig!" she shouted and turned away.

As soon as he got to his feet, Elliott snatched hold of Destiny's ponytail and yanked her head back. "Just wait," he snarled, "I'll get you for this! Get you good!" He turned and stomped out the front door, slamming it so hard that the vibration caused a lamp to topple from the end table.

When you're looking at things from the other side, you can see the truth of what is in a person's heart and when Destiny started bawling like a baby I knew it had nothing to do with money or material possessions. I also knew that the poor girl was in for a rough ride, because I'd seen the meanness in Elliott's face.

Two days later, was when Elliott marched himself into the Middleboro Police Department and said he wanted to report a crime. Tom Nichols was the detective on duty that day, which is something I have come to be thankful for. One glance at Detective Nichols and a person would right off think, *now here's a man who has the look of fairness about him.*

I could tell by the expression on Elliott's face that he thought this fellow was going to be a pushover. Of course, Elliott was always misjudging a person, which was part of his problem—that and being so greedy. "I suspect this woman, Destiny Fairchild, has done away with my beloved aunt," Elliott told the detective. "Abigail Anne Lannigan, she's my great aunt on the maternal side." He lowered his head in a most sorrowful way.

"Done away with?"

"Yes indeed. This woman is a neighbor, but she's taken over my aunt's house. She claims my aunt just up and died, but before anyone could ask about what happened, my aunt was planted in the ground!"

"How old was this aunt?"

"Old. Eighty, ninety. Maybe one hundred."

"Hmm." Detective Nichols pitched his eyebrows down like he might have doubted the truth of what was being said. "Your aunt was well along in years. What makes you think her death wasn't from natural causes?"

"I think she caught this Fairchild woman stealing from her—it's likely she'd been doing it for ages! My aunt probably got wise to the scheme and ended up dead. All that money should go to blood relatives."

"Are there other relatives?"

"No, just me. But I was close, *real close*, to my aunt."

"When was the last time you saw your aunt alive?"

"Let's see now," Elliott had practiced exactly what he was going to say but he had not anticipated this particular question so he stumbled over his thoughts for a minute, then said, "I believe it was two years ago last November."

"You haven't seen this aunt for two years?"

"Um, I could be wrong about the date."

"Less than two years, maybe?"

"Possibly more."

"So, you haven't seen this *real close* aunt for two years?" Detective Nichols waited for a moment but when it appeared that an answer wasn't forthcoming, he asked, "During that time did you speak to your aunt on the telephone?"

"I can't say that I recall a specific conversation."

"When does this neighbor claim your aunt passed away?"

"As far as I can tell, it was about six months ago. Destiny Fairchild is an extremely belligerent woman and when I tried to inquire as to the circumstances of my aunt's passing, she physically assaulted me. I tell you, Detective, she's hiding something. Why, she's taken over my aunt's house, stolen her car, writes checks on her bank account—a while back the woman actually had me cashing checks for five hundred dollars, obviously, that was money she was stealing from my aunt's account. I cashed the checks, of course, but I thought the money was for poor Aunt Abigail."

That was when Elliott whipped out the typewritten list of things he claimed Destiny had stolen from my house. The detective read down the list item by item and every so often he'd stop to ask about something. "A cherry wood chest," he'd say, "you're *sure* it's missing?"

Every time Elliott answered that he was certain it was, then he'd launch into some lengthy tale of how treasured that particular thing was and how meaningful it would be to have it back. Several times he took a quick sidestep from the item in question and bounced back to whatever money might be in my bank accounts. I watched the way Detective Nichols was scrutinizing Elliott's face as he listened to the answers. It's a funny thing about lies, they stand out on a person's face like hives; anybody with a sharp eye can spot them.

After Detective Nichols finished reading the list, he jotted a comment in the margin of his pad. It read: *Complainant's concern is missing goods/money. Homicide doubtful.* He then turned the page and made note of where he could get in touch with Elliott. "I suppose that about wraps it up," he said. "We'll be in touch."

"Is Destiny Fairchild gonna be arrested?" Elliott said fighting back a smirk.

"We don't just arrest people," Tom Nichols answered. "First we investigate to find out whether or not a crime has actually been committed."

Right away Elliott started swearing up and down that it was not only a crime, but a crime of the very worst kind. "Swindling the elderly, what's worse than that?" He looked the detective square in the eye and said this with the most earnest face imaginable.

Detective Nichols nodded and said, "You're right. Taking advantage of the elderly is a terrible crime and one that is dealt with severely, but until we conduct our investigation we don't know that *any* crime has been committed." He pushed the chair back from his desk and stood in a way that signified the conversation was over.

Up until that point, I could have sworn Tom Nichols saw right through Elliott's lies. I thought the detective would stuff those notes into the back of some file drawer and forget all about them the minute Elliott walked out the door, but unfortunately that's not how it happened.

The following Monday, the detective showed up on Destiny's doorstep unannounced. He stood there for a few moments, looking around like he was taking the measure of things, then he rang the bell. Nobody answered because by that time Destiny had gone back to work at the restaurant and she was working the day shift. He waited on the front steps for a few minutes, then walked around back of the house, which is where he spotted Mary Beth McGurke, a woman who could talk the ear off a deaf dog.

"Excuse me," he called out, "Do you know when Miss Fairchild will be home?"

"No telling," Mary Beth answered, "That one keeps strange hours."

"Oh?" he said and turned to listen.

I can't say for certain that Mary Beth disliked Destiny, but she liked to gossip more than she liked anything or anybody, so it didn't take much to get her started. She walked over to the detective and started talking real low, like a person confiding something of the greatest secrecy. "She *supposedly* works at a restaurant downtown, but, no one can say for certain that's what she really does. A while back, she just up and moved in with old Missus Lannigan, didn't even bother about going to work. Now, I ask you, would a legitimate job allow a person to show up for work whenever they've a notion?"

"Lived with Missus Lannigan? How long?"

"No telling. But even before that, I saw her hauling pieces of furniture over into her own house. Big things. A lamp, a table, a huge overstuffed chair! Cartons—way more than I could keep track of! Many a time I wondered if Abigail Anne knew the girl was doing such a thing."

"Did you ever ask about it?"

"Heavens, no. I'm not one to pry into other people's business!"

"Hmm." Detective Nichols took a pad from his pocket and started to make notes. "Missus Lannigan, did she have any other friends?"

"Not a soul! I think that girl ran them all off. Abigail used to be friendly with me, not real close, mind you, but close enough that she'd stop and pass the time of day every now and again. After she got hooked up with *that one*," Mary Beth waggled a finger toward Destiny's house, "then, Abigail didn't bother with other folks."

Well, if that don't beat all, I thought. Mary Beth McGurke knew exactly why I stopped bothering with her—for the same reason everyone else on the block avoided her—she'd get hold of a person's ear and chew on it till they were about ready to scream. Of course, Detective Nichols didn't know that so he started writing down those awful things she was saying.

"By that one, you mean Destiny Fairchild?" he asked.

"I certainly do! Mark my words, she's some sort of gypsy. Pops up out of nowhere and moves in without a single stick of furniture, *cinder blocks* for a table—then all of a sudden she's living it up with poor Abigail's things!"

"Things? What things?"

"Whatever she could lay her hands on! Why, she even snatched hold of Abigail Anne's car and left the poor woman with no way to get around!"

"When was that?"

"Three or four years ago. Maybe more."

"So this has been going on for some time?"

"Yes indeed. Abigail used to drive all over the place, but after Destiny Fairchild took the car, Abigail couldn't go anywhere. She'd have to beg that girl for a ride to the market. Don't take my word; ask down at The Bountiful Basket, they'll tell you!"

"The one on High Street?"

"Uh-huh. I've heard tell that Abigail would walk up to the checkout with not a dime in her pocket and have to ask that Fairchild girl for a dab of money to pay for her groceries. Now, I ask, is that any way to live?"

Controlled money? Detective Nichols wrote on the pad. "This car of Missus Lannigan's," he said, "is Miss Fairchild still driving it?"

"No indeed. I guess that Buick was too tame for her; as soon as she got hold of Abigail's money, she bought herself a brand new *Thunderbird!* Bright red!"

I watched Detective Nichols jot down *car?*

"How about relatives?" he asked. "Did Missus Lannigan have any relatives?"

"Her brother, but he died. And a nephew or something. I can't say what his name was, a nice looking young man. He used to visit every so often."

"This nephew, he been around recently?"

"Not so far as I know."

"When was the last time you saw him?"

"I suppose it was a while after Will passed on—Will was Abigail's brother, you know, the one who died. He died not long before the Fairchild girl moved into the neighborhood and started carting away poor Abigail's possessions. Uh-huh," she said scrunching up her face like she'd given the matter careful consideration, "that's when the nephew quit coming around."

By now, Mary Beth was on a roll. Once she had someone to listen to her stories there was no stopping her.

"It's a crime," she told Detective Nichols, "A crime how some folks will take advantage of the elderly. There ought to be a law!"

"There is, Missus…?"

"McGurke. Mary Beth McGurke."

"Well, Missus McGurke, you've been very helpful." With that he closed his notebook and turned to leave.

Mary Beth, being Mary Beth, followed him all the way out to his car chattering on and on about how she'd be happy to answer lots more questions. Much as I wanted to smack her lying face, there wasn't a damn thing I could do.

I kept watch over Detective Nichols as he drove off, and when he parked in front of the Bountiful Basket, it wasn't all that much of a surprise. Had he held off and gone the following day, it would have been a Tuesday—Millicent works the register on Tuesday and she'd have been able to tell how it really was—but because it was Monday, he ended up talking to Harold. On the best of days, Harold had a hard time remembering how many dimes in a dollar, and he wasn't one to admit to a poor memory so whatever somebody said, he'd agree with.

"Did you know Abigail Lannigan?" Detective Nichols asked.

"Missus Lannigan? Sure."

"What about Destiny Fairchild?"

"Hmm?"

"She was the young woman who used to accompany Missus Lannigan, you remember her?"

"Remember? Of course, I remember." Harold held up a honeydew melon and waved it toward the other register. "Hey, Monica, how much are these melons?"

"Dollar-forty-nine," she answered.

"What can you tell me about their relationship?"

"Whose relationship?"

"Missus Lannigan and Destiny Fairchild."

"Oh, them. Well, they used to do their shopping together; but it ain't my way to carry gossip about folk's personal business. Why don't you tell me what you know and I'll say if it's true or not. Okay?"

"I'd rather not influence your opinions. How about if I just ask a few questions and you can answer to the best of your recollection?"

"Listen here, Sheriff Nichols, there's nothing wrong with my recollections."

"Detective."

"Detective? What kind of question is that?"

"It's not a question; I'm Detective Nichols, not Sheriff."

"Okay. But you'd better get to those questions; I go to lunch at twelve-thirty."

"When Missus Lannigan and Miss Fairchild came through the checkout, who paid for the groceries?"

"Say again?"

"Did Missus Lannigan have any money of her own?"

"We don't *give* food away."

"But did the money come from Missus Lannigan's purse or did she have to get it from Miss Fairchild?"

"Umm ... hold up a minute." Harold dashed over to Monica and whispered something in her ear. Monica nodded and said something that the detective could not hear. When Harold returned, he said, "It was the young one. She wrote the checks, but both their names were on the account."

I could tell Detective Nichols had more questions, but it was obvious that he wasn't going to get any meaningful answers here, so he moved on to Monica. "You recall Missus Lannigan and Miss Fairchild?" he asked.

"Sort of," she answered as she plucked a bunch of carrots from the conveyor belt.

"What can you tell me about their relationship?"

"Not much. The young one seemed to be in charge, but she was nice enough to the old lady. I never heard nothing worth repeating."

"Thanks," Detective Nichols said and left. So far it was looking like Mary Beth's story was holding up.

That evening Detective Nichols returned to Destiny's house. I don't know if he took notice of Mary Beth peeking through the slat in her blinds, but I sure did. He rang the doorbell and Destiny answered right away.

"Destiny Fairchild?" he asked. You could see by the surprise on his face that he hadn't expected someone so sweet and delicate looking.

"Yes sir," Destiny answered and smiled. Once a person got past that wide open smile of hers, those green eyes were the next thing you'd be sure to notice. I was a bit sorry that Tom Nichols wasn't a single man, but I knew for sure he wasn't because on his desk there was a picture of a pretty woman and two little blond-haired girls. A man like Tom Nichols would have been real good for Destiny.

"Were you the caretaker for Abigail Lannigan before her demise?" he asked.

Destiny's smile faded. "Uh-huh."

"Her nephew has expressed concern about some loose ends regarding her estate, mind if I ask a few questions?"

"Okay," Destiny answered and led him into the living room. "But, I have to tell you, Elliott's not actually her nephew. Miss Abigail always said he was so far removed that he couldn't be considered real kin."

"Oh, so you know Elliott Emerson?" Detective Nichols appeared to be doing nothing more than having an innocent conversation, but the whole time they spoke his gaze was darting around the room and making note of the things he'd seen on Elliott's list. "My, that's an interesting piece," he finally said and walked over to the sewing cabinet that had at one time belonged to Livonia Lannigan. "Antique?"

"I believe so," Destiny answered. "It's a sewing cabinet that Miss Abigail gave me." She pulled open the door. "See, these little spindles, that's where the thread goes. Miss Abigail treasured this cabinet, because it belonged to her mother."

"You were good friends with Abigail Lannigan?"

"Oh, yes. Very. She was a special lady."

"She give you a lot of presents?"

"Way more than she ought to, but that's how she was. Generous to a fault. Plenty of times I told her I didn't feel right about taking such expensive gifts, but she'd claim her feelings would be hurt if I didn't accept it."

"I know what you mean," Detective Nichols said and smiled like he was agreeing right along with Destiny. "I had an aunt like that, just give, give, give, never knew when to stop. What other presents did Abigail Lannigan give you?"

"Last Christmas she gave me twenty-five-thousand-dollars *and* she paid for my trip to Palm Beach, Florida."

"Man! That is really generous! Did she have had a lot of money?"

"Some. Mostly inherited from her brother."

"Oh, wealthy family?"

"I don't think so. Miss Abigail said her brother got a lot of money when he sold the family farm."

"What happened to her estate after she died?"

"Nothing."

"Nothing?" he repeated quizzically. "There was nothing to the estate?"

"No, I mean I haven't done anything with it. Oh yeah, pay bills and stuff like that, the same things I did when she was alive."

120

"Pay bills? Do you still have access to Miss Lannigan's money?"

"Yes. I can write checks, same as always."

"The accounts are in your name?"

"Uh-huh."

"What about her house?"

"I take care of that too. A lot of times I go there and spend the evening, just walking around, touching things, you know, remembering how it used to be." Destiny smiled as if she had an awareness the detective did not. "Most people don't realize it," she said, "but a person's spirit stays in a place long after they're gone."

"Wait a minute," Detective Nichols said, looking more than a bit puzzled, "are you saying you keep that house up so that you can go there and visit with her spirit?"

Destiny nodded.

"Did she leave you the house?"

"I suppose. When she was real bad sick, Miss Abigail told me she wanted me to have all of her worldly possessions. She said she didn't have any real family and I was the closest thing to a daughter she'd ever known."

"What about Elliott Emerson?"

"She didn't like him one little bit. He claimed to be a Baptist like his great granddaddy and Miss Abigail said anyone who didn't know that her papa was a staunch Methodist, was sure as the devil no Lannigan."

"I guess she specified that you were to inherit everything in her will?"

Much as I hate to say it, I could see where this was going and there wasn't a thing I could do to stop dear little Destiny from telling the truth, even though the truth would be held up as a lie. Lord help her, I thought, for it was solely up to Him, all I could do was listen.

"It happened so fast, her getting sick like that. There we were in Florida having the time of our lives, drinking champagne and painting our toenails, then next thing I knew the doctor was telling us that Miss Abigail had pancreatic cancer and was dying. She didn't have time to make up a real will, you know, one prepared by a lawyer, so she wrote her intentions on a piece of paper."

"A piece of paper?"

"Yes." A tear was sliding down the side of Destiny's cheek. "At the time I was so upset by the thought of her leaving me, that I wouldn't even look at it. 'I don't want to hear about you dying,' was what I told her."

"What did she say?"

"Nothing much. She told me that her dying was a God honest fact and whether or not I listened to what she had to say; it was still going to happen. Miss Abigail put that paper in the nightstand drawer, and said whenever I was ready to face the truth; I'd know where to find it."

"Was it witnessed or notarized, anything like that?"

"Poor Abigail was flat on her back by then, besides I didn't need any notary stamp to make me believe what she wrote. If she wanted it to be, that was good enough for me."

"You suppose I could take a look at that paper? It might help clear things up."

"Sure," Destiny said and took Detective Nichols right over to my house.

I wish Destiny would have looked at what I wrote that day. She would have seen that my handwriting had become illegible. She could have brought someone in to witness what I'd said so it would later be believed. Being dead is easy enough to deal with, but dying was a painful process that racked my bones and addled my mind. That day, lifting my arm to write felt like trying to move a mountain, not a single word came easy and time after time the pen slid from my fingers and scratched its way across the paper. I was a weary old woman looking through tired eyes and I saw only what was in my heart; although I believed those words told how Destiny should have everything I owned, the writing was nothing more than chicken scratch.

"This is it?" Detective Nichols said when she handed him the piece of paper. After that he started in with a new barrage of questions about who my doctor was, how she got hold of my car, and whether or not she had taken any other money from me.

Destiny was never the least bit devious, so she sat there and told him everything, where the bank accounts were, how she handled things and took care of my finances, and how she laid me to rest.

"Oh, so you had complete control of her money?"

"Not so much control," Destiny said, "I just paid the bills and stuff."

"Missus Lannigan made the decisions?"

"Mostly, she told me 'you decide' and I did."

Detective Nichols was scribbling away in that notebook of his. "The red Thunderbird in your driveway, that's your car?"

"Yes."

"It looks new."

"It is. I just bought it a month ago."

"Weren't you driving Missus Lannigan's car?"

"Yes. But, I cried every time I got in it, because it reminded me of how much I missed Miss Abigail, so I traded it in and bought a new car."

"Oh. So she signed the transfer papers before she died?"

"I handled the paperwork, but she told me to do it. Miss Abigail's bursitis was acting up that day—anyway, she said sign the papers for her and I did. But, she knew about it. She even gave me money for the insurance."

"Wow, that's some friend! She just *gave* you her car?"

"Yes."

"Why?"

"So I could drive her places." Destiny replied, as if this was a fact so obvious it hardly warranted an answer.

"Wow," Detective Nichols repeated and stretched his neck toward the front window to look out at the Thunderbird. "That's a great car, but I'll bet the finance charges cost a fortune!"

"I didn't buy it on time. I used to do that, buy things on the installment plan, but Miss Abigail said it wasn't practical because you end up paying almost twice the original cost. Now I pay cash for most everything I buy."

"That's great," Detective Nichols said like they were having some kind of friend-to-friend conversation. "Where'd you get enough money for that Thunderbird?"

"I took it out of what Miss Abigail left me."

"You mean according to that handwritten paper?"

"Yes. Miss Abigail's will. She wrote that so I'd get the money."

"Her estate has never been probated?"

"Probated?"

I could tell Destiny was getting in over her head because the longer she talked, the more questions Detective Nichols had. Still, I figured he was a fair man and sooner or later, the truth would find its way to the surface.

After he left, the detective drove back to the station house and started to write up a report. He took out the list of items Elliott claimed were stolen and started making checkmarks alongside those things he had seen at Destiny's house. When he sat down to work, Tom Nichols shook his head back and forth, like he was puzzling over some worrisome thing stuck in his brain.

The next morning he was standing outside the door when the Middleboro Savings Bank opened. For two hours he sat there counting up every check that Destiny had written against my accounts. He spoke to Martin Kroeger, the new Branch Manager who two years ago replaced Harvey Brown, the Manager I'd been dealing with since the day I moved to Middleboro. After that he talked to two of the tellers, both of which I had never laid eyes on—of course, they said Destiny was the one who made all of the withdrawals. "What about deposits?" he'd asked, and they told him those were made by electronic transfer.

Much as I hated it, I was starting to understand how someone who didn't know Destiny for the person she truly was, could believe there was foul play going on.

After he left the bank, Tom Nichols called on Doctor Birnbaum. The doctor, bless his heart, had nothing but nice things to say about Destiny. He told how she'd cried when he said I had cancer and how she'd been right there with me till the day I died. Still, I was worried that Tom Nichols' ears had started to close up on the good qualities of Destiny, because he zeroed in on questions about whether or not she might have exercised undue influence on me and in my state was I lucid enough to prepare a will.

"How lucid is anyone racked with the pain of pancreatic cancer?" Doctor Birnbaum asked right back at him.

I suppose it's like having a hole in a rowboat, it's hard to take notice of all the good planks in the boat when you're focused in on the one with the hole.

I'm mostly to blame for what was happening to Destiny. I should have known that after the way Elliott claimed the money from the farm was rightfully his, he'd sure as certain be standing in line like a hungry wolf once I was gone. I meant to take care of things, specify exactly what my intentions were, but I always thought I had more time. Now I look back and ask myself, *how long did I think I had?*

On Thursday morning, Detective Tom Nichols took his report, walked down the hallway and asked to speak to Morgan Broadhurst, the Assistant District Attorney.

Under other circumstances Morgan Broadhurst may have been a pleasant enough person, but on this particular morning he had a scowl etched into his face, so deep that a person could easily believe it had been there since birth. Apparently a woman driver had rear-ended his brand new Lincoln Continental and sent a full container of coffee spilling into his lap. His trousers were dangling from a hat rack that had been moved alongside the heating vent and he was crouched behind his desk in a pair of damp boxer shorts. Anyone could see Morgan Broadhurst was just waiting for someone to cross his path.

"I've got an unusual situation here," Detective Nichols said.

"Get to the point!"

"Well, the point is, I've got an unusual situation."

Morgan Broadhurst grimaced. "Either you…"

"I've got a case where a man named Elliott Emerson is accusing his aunt's neighbor of swindling the old woman. He claims the neighbor, Destiny Fairchild, exercised undue influence on his aunt in order to gain control of her assets."

"Did she or didn't she?"

"It's not cut and dry. The nephew claims the girl has gone on a wild spending spree using his aunt's money and she's made no attempt to have the estate probated. The girl, on the other hand, says she was a friend of this Abigail Lannigan and she has a handwritten document that supposedly is the old woman's last will and testament."

"Then it's a civil case."

"Yes and no. The will that the Fairchild woman produced is totally illegible. It also appears that she forged Abigail Lannigan's signature to a title transfer on the car and all of Lannigan's bank accounts have been transferred over to Fairchild."

"Fairchild got power of attorney?"

"Nothing official. But, she swears this Abigail Lannigan told her to do it."

"Stop dancing around the issue. Is there an indictable offense here or not?"

"Possibly. The nephew swears up and down that she was exploiting the old woman, but I gotta say the girl comes across as pretty believable. My gut instinct is to say kick it back and let them settle their differences in a civil suit."

"I don't give a rat's ass about what your *gut* thinks! Is there enough evidence to indict her or not?"

"Hmm. It could be a stretch."

"Tough shit, find a way to do it! If the press gets wind of a story where somebody's swindled an old fart and we're covering it up, our ass is fried!

Charge the Fairchild woman with forgery, falsifying a document and exploitation of the elderly. How much money was involved?"

"One hundred thousand give or take."

"Add grand larceny." At that point Morgan Broadhurst stood up and strode across the office in his underwear to retrieve his trousers. He turned back to Tom Nichols and snapped, "Well, what are you waiting for?"

An uneasy feeling settled into my heart and I knew that Destiny's streak of bad luck had not yet come to an end.

That afternoon Detective Nichols brought Destiny into the stationhouse and started rattling off some long-winded statement about how she had the right to an attorney and such.

"An attorney?" Destiny said, "Why would I want an attorney?"

"If you can't afford an attorney, one will be appointed to you..." Stone-faced, Tom Nichols went right on with what he had to say before they launched into the questioning. Right then, Destiny should have called for a lawyer, but she didn't. Instead she sat there and answered his questions, one by one, and she peeled off a truthful answer every single time. I can say for certain those answers were the God's honest truth because I'd been there when it happened.

"Now what exactly is your primary source of income?" Detective Nichols asked.

"I do waitressing at Aristotle's. Thursday, Friday, Saturday."

"Part-time?"

"Uh-huh."

"How much does that pay?"

"Six dollars an hour, plus tips. I've got the lunch hour so tips are pretty good."

"Good enough to afford a new Thunderbird?"

"No. I traded in Miss Abigail's Buick and bought the Thunderbird."

"They were the same price?" Detective Nichols made the question sound like some generalized point of information, but I could tell he was driving Destiny to say something she'd come to regret.

"Of course not," she replied laughingly, "The Thunderbird was a whole lot more."

"The money for the new car, where'd that come from?"

"I took it out of Miss Abigail's savings account."

"According to the bank, you've been running up quite a tally of charge accounts and paying for them with funds from Missus Lannigan's account."

"Yes. But the money is mine now. Miss Abigail gave it to me."

"Gave it to you?"

"Yes. She wrote a will stating that her intention was for me to have all her worldly possessions. That's the exact way she put it, *all my worldly possessions.*"

"What about her family?"

"She didn't have anyone but her brother and he died over five years ago."

"Doesn't she have a nephew?"

"Elliott Emerson? Miss Abigail didn't like him one little bit. Said he was a bad-mannered money-grubbing leach."

"But she did give him money on numerous occasions, didn't she?"

"Because she thought her brother, Will, would have wanted her to."

"Why would he have wanted his sister to give Elliott Emerson any money if they weren't really related?"

"It's very complicated. Will believed that Elliott was a twice removed cousin, but Miss Abigail found out he was a Baptist and she knew that never in the history of the world had there been a Baptist in the Lannigan family." Destiny shrugged apologetically, "See, the Lannigan's were staunch Methodists."

"Still, Missus Lannigan did on some occasions ask you to write checks for money she was indeed giving to Mister Emerson, didn't she?"

"Yes, but it was not something she wanted to do."

"But, you *knew* Mister Emerson was in some way related, right?"

"Yes, but…"

"Yet, you chose not to inform him of his aunt's passing?"

"I didn't have his telephone number."

"Um-hmm." Detective Nichols nodded his head in the most doubting manner.

Morgan Broadhurst, who had been watching this procedure through a mirrored window, was looking happier than he had been all day. Now, I was never a person to wish ill on others, but at that moment I was quite sorry it hadn't been a tractor trailer that smashed into Mister Broadhurst's Lincoln Continental.

After almost four hours, Detective Nichols told Destiny she could go home, but he said she shouldn't leave town as they might have more questions.

That night Destiny was sitting on the blue velvet sofa drinking her third glass of wine when the doorbell rang.

It was an narrow stick of a man with skin so black he would have disappeared into the darkness were it not for his teeth and a crop of snow white hair. "Evening ma'am," he said and smiled real wide. "Name's Elijah Blessing. I'd like to offer the word of the Lord to you in this authentic King James Bible." He held out a red leather book.

"You're selling Bibles?" Destiny asked.

"Yes ma'am, I surely am. And if I might say so, you look like a person who could take comfort in the good Lord's word. The word of God can ease a person's load, bring peace to a troubled mind, shed light on the darkest path..."

"Well, I don't think—"

"When you got troubles, you bring 'em to the Lord, He'll show the way. If you got a sorrowful heart, He'll fill it with gladness. Ain't nothing the Almighty Lord can't do when a person abides by the Good Book."

It could have been the wine or a chunk of fear settling inside Destiny's heart, maybe even the loneliness she'd been feeling ever since I died, but right there in the doorway she started bawling like a baby. Elijah Blessing dropped the red book back into the satchel he had slung over his right shoulder, then reached out and took Destiny's hand into his. He didn't look any more substantial than a winter-worn scarecrow, but I could tell Elijah Blessing was a mountain of strength.

"You got troubles, don't you Missy?" he said to Destiny.

She nodded her head and kept right on sobbing.

"I got the Good Book right here and I got two perfectly fine ears; you want a messenger of the Lord to listen for a spell?"

Destiny wiped her nose on the tail end of her shirt and nodded again.

It was a funny thing with those two, something passed between them, something that didn't require any words whatsoever. He draped his arm across her shoulder in a real tender way, like a daddy or grandpa would, and together they moved back inside the house and sat down on the sofa. *Praise the Lord* I thought, for I was pretty certain it was His doing—Elijah Blessing showing up on Destiny's doorstep this way. At first they just sat there, Mister Blessing with one arm still wrapped around Destiny's shoulder and the other hand holding onto hers. She kept right on sobbing, shaking all over and sobbing like her poor little heart was going to break. Mister Blessing told her to go right ahead and cry, get it out of her system; he said he had nowhere to go and nothing to do but share the word of God with folks who needed it. The world sure could use more men like that Mister Blessing.

When the heaving and sobbing had eased off to a trickle of tears and a puff of air that she'd suck back every so often, Mister Blessing said, "You got a notion to tell me what sort of troubles is weighing on you?"

Destiny started sobbing all over again.

"I got plenty of time," he said and patted her hand real soft.

When she was finally dry-eyed enough to talk, she poured out the whole story; she told Elijah Blessing that we'd been the best of friends, like mother and daughter she said. Then she went on to explain how I'd died without a proper will and how the police now thought she'd swindled away my car and money.

He listened to every word, not once did he interrupt or remind her that she'd already told him this or that part. Instead he sat there patting her hand and listening with every ounce of hearing he had. When she finally finished, he said, "The Good Book can show a person the pathway to righteousness, but Missy, I believe you also need a lawyer."

"Maybe it's nothing more than Elliott trying to cause trouble," Destiny replied. "Perhaps I'm making more of it than need be; Detective Nichols did say they would assign a lawyer if I needed one."

"You don't want one of *those* lawyers!"

"Why not?"

"Why not? Because you need somebody who's gonna stand up and fight them bureaucrats! Last year my boy got arrested for robbing a liquor store. He never did no such thing, but he could of been sent to prison for life if it weren't for that lawyer who *proved* he was home studying. In matters such as these, the truth needs to be dug up and aired. Now, the only person capable of doing that is an *honest* lawyer."

"You mean…"

"I ain't saying those charity lawyers are out and out no good, but they got a lot of other stuff going on and they ain't always got time to pay full attention to *your* problems. Missy, the good Lord is always willing to lend a hand, but you gotta give Him something to work with."

"Your son, did he have an honest lawyer?"

"Sure did. If it wasn't for Charles McCallum, there's no telling what would have happened to my boy."

"Charles McCallum?"

"Yes, ma'am. He'll give you the kind of lawyering you need!"

"You think he'd be willing to represent me?"

"I sure do. Mister McCallum, he's got a Christian heart. He won't stand for nobody getting railroaded by a bunch of bureaucrats."

When I saw how Elijah Blessing was reaching out to help Destiny, I had a truly joyous heart. If I was still walking the face of the earth, I'd have latched hold of Mister Blessing's skinny face and planted a kiss on it. Why, that man even gave Destiny one of his bright red Bibles free of charge; he told her that along with Mister Charles McCallum, she could trust in the miracles of the Lord, seeing as how He had parted the Red Sea for Moses.

Destiny was so touched by his gesture; she bought three more Bibles and set them on the top shelf of the new bookcase she'd purchased from Sears and Roebuck.

The morning after Elijah Blessing told Destiny she ought to have a lawyer; she called Charles McCallum's office and made arrangements to see him in the afternoon.

Thank Heaven, I thought; figuring that, at the very least, Destiny was switching herself onto the right track. With Mister McCallum being such a well spoke of lawyer, I anticipated he'd be a silver-haired man with a great big office and four secretaries typing fast as their fingers could fly. Of course that wasn't the case. He was young—to look at him you'd guess nineteen or twenty, but according to the diploma hanging on the wall, he had to be closer to thirty or thirty one—a bit gangly, rumpled hair that made you wonder if maybe he'd forgotten to run a comb through it. Right away it struck me how he was so like my brother Will—the same smile, the same loose-jointed way of moving from one spot to another as if there was no hurry whatsoever. I loved Will dearly, but I'd hoped Destiny's lawyer would be a powerful man with a booming voice, someone who could stand in front of a jury and demand that justice be done. I looked at how small Mister McCallum's office was—two rooms, him in one and a woman struggling with some hunt and peck typing in the other—and started worrying again.

Being the problem was of such a serious nature, you'd have thought Destiny would get dressed up proper; maybe wear one of those new outfits that were hanging in her closet with a price tag still dangling from the sleeve. But Destiny is just Destiny, and she's not the kind to put on airs, so she showed up at two-thirty wearing blue jeans and a real pretty pink tee-shirt. Despite the way she was dressed, Mister Charles McCallum's eyes lit up like he'd caught sight of an angel when she walked into the room.

"You must be Destiny Fairchild," he said, scrambling out of his chair and nearly tripping over his own feet.

She smiled and nodded then, when she stretched out her hand, Mister McCallum took hold like he was afraid she'd get away. "Would you like something cold to drink?" he asked." Soda? Juice? Water?"

"A Pepsi would be great."

Charles McCallum called out to the typist, "Gracie, would you please bring us a couple of cold Pepsis?"

"I didn't get *Pepsi*!" she hollered back. "It's cream soda or beer."

"Sorry," Charles mumbled, the rim of his right ear turning red.

"Cream soda?" Destiny smiled, "Why, that's one of my *favorites!*"

A few minutes later, Grace, a pair of yellow bedroom slippers on her feet, shuffled into the office and set a can of soda and a straw in front of each of them. "Here you go, honey," she said, then shuffled back out.

If Charles McCallum had known Destiny as I did, he might not have felt the need to apologize, but as it was, he said, "Please excuse Gracie, she's new to the business." What he didn't mention was the fact that Gracie was his aunt—someone he'd hired out of sympathy after her husband died, someone who couldn't type a letter without at least seven mistakes, someone who would have no reason to get up each morning if it weren't for her job. A kindness such as that was enough to make me start liking the young lawyer.

Not long after that, they got down to business and Destiny told Charles the entire story, including the part about how I wrote my intentions on a scrap of paper and stuck it in the nightstand drawer. "Miss Abigail was always doing nice things…" she said, and then she stopped talking for a few seconds and snuffled, like a person trying to hold back a river slide of tears.

When she finished the story, Charles McCallum smiled and said, "Miss Lannigan sounds like a wonderful woman."

"She really was," Destiny replied, and pulled another tissue from her pocket.

"Emerson," Charles asked, "he's the nephew who filed a complaint against you?"

"Yes."

"But, didn't you say he's not actually related to Miss Lannigan?"

"*That's* what Miss Abigail said, but…" Destiny shrugged and spread open her palms as if to signify she had no knowledge of the true answer. "Miss

Abigail was the only Lannigan I ever knew," she went on, "so how can I say for sure whether or not there were any other Baptists in the family."

"Baptists?"

Destiny started explaining how I told her Elliott couldn't be a Lannigan because he was a Baptist—and as I listened to her giving voice to such a silly thing, I felt my toes curl. Preacher Broody always said the Lord didn't hold with lying or trickery and those who did would someday suffer. Of course, it would be a lot fairer if I was the one suffering; but it was beginning to seem as though Destiny would be held accountable for my doings. See, all along Elliott was just pretending to be a Baptist to get hold of Will's money, I knew that, but never said so.

When she finished telling the tale, Mister McCallum asked, "Is *that* the only reason for believing him to be unrelated?"

Destiny shrugged again.

"What about his lineage?"

"His what?"

Charles rephrased the question. "Did he and Miss Lannigan have any common ancestors? People related to them both?"

"He claimed his great granddaddy was Miss Abigail's daddy, but she said you couldn't believe nothing that came from Elliott."

"It does sound preposterous," Charles said. "If such a thing were true it would cover an extensive period of time."

"Elliott said his grandma, Margaret Louise, was the first born child of old Mister Lannigan and Abigail Anne was the very last. Of course, they had different mamas."

"Of course," Charles repeated, but a blind person could see the confusion swirling around his brain. "Did Abigail Lannigan know Elliott's grandmother?"

"No. Margaret Louise was a whole lot older than Miss Abigail."

"Was there ever any proof that this Margaret Louise was actually a Lannigan?"

"Uh-huh." Destiny nodded. "Her name's written in the Family Bible."

"Did Miss Lannigan ever say anything about that?"

Destiny hesitated a moment and grinned—I knew she was remembering back to what I'd told her. "Yes, she said it didn't make a bean of difference where the woman's name was written, she still didn't believe Elliott was related to the Lannigans."

"This Family Bible, who has it?"

"I do. Well, at least I did. It's at Miss Abigail's house. I used to go there and tidy up once a week, but the detective said it would be better if I stayed away, until the question of ownership is resolved."

Charles McCallum was starting to knit his brows together like a man with some concerns. "Which detective?" he asked. Destiny told him it was Tom Nichols; he made note of the name then asked if she had the will Miss Lannigan had written.

"A copy of it," she answered and started rummaging through her purse. "Mister Nichols has the original." She handed Charles a folded sheet of paper.

"Hmmm," he mused eyeing it, "this didn't copy very well."

"Yes, it did," she said innocently, "That's how it looks."

"It is?"

Destiny nodded.

He angled the paper, squinted at it sideways, then glanced across the desk like a man who suspects he's the butt of a joke. Destiny wasn't laughing. He went back to the paper and studied it for a full minute trying to make sense of a page of chicken scratch—a roadmap of scribbles, not a single word legible, not even the signature. Finally he asked, "Do you have anything else? Any other documents?"

She shook her head.

"Any witnesses to her writing this?"

"Me."

"No one else, just you?"

She nodded.

Charles started jotting notes on a legal pad. "Without someone to substantiate that Miss Lannigan actually wrote this, it won't do us much good. We need witnesses to verify your relationship—people who can attest to the fact that you and she were close enough to warrant a bequest such as this."

"She didn't have any family and no close friends that I know of."

"What about people she came in contact with on a regular basis? Shopkeepers? Bankers? A nurse or cleaning lady, maybe?"

"No nurse," Destiny said, "I took care of Miss Abigail when she got bad sick."

"How about her doctor?"

"Uh-huh." Destiny nodded. "Doctor Birnbaum knows we were real close."

Charles made note of Doctor Birnbaum's address and telephone number, then he moved on to questions about friends or possibly even other relatives.

I must say, for a young fellow with such a casual look about him, he seemed to be quite thorough and Lord knows Destiny was in need of all the help she could get. I wish she knew about the letter I wrote Gloria last year, it would have helped to set things straight.

In all, Charles spent almost two hours asking Destiny questions about one thing and another, then after she left he got on the telephone and called the detective. "Shouldn't this be handled as a civil case?" he asked, but Tom Nichols indicated it was open-ended as to exploitation of the elderly and the issue of forgery.

"Actually," Tom said, "Broadhurst is pushing for an arrest warrant."

"On evidence this thin?"

"Thin? She's got a new Thunderbird, purchases up the wazoo..."

"Maybe so, but there's no priors, no obvious intent."

"You met the nephew? Tom asked, then continued on without waiting for an answer. "This guy's a real hard ass."

"Emerson? What claim has he got? There's no involvement with the deceased. Abigail Lannigan even told people he wasn't a relative."

"Well, he is."

"He is?"

"Yeah. We did a trace. The jerk's great grandfather was William Lannigan."

"Shit," Charles McCallum said. There was a few moments of silence then he suggested, "Let me dangle a carrot for the guy—suggest if he flips it over to a civil suit, he'll stand a better chance of getting the money back."

"What about the forgery? Exploitation?"

"No court is gonna go along with those charges. Fairchild has a credible story, she was taking good care of the woman and I've got witnesses that'll swear Abigail Lannigan gave her the authority to sign checks."

"Broadhurst wants her for grand larceny."

"Oh, come on!" Charles McCallum replied. "The best you can possibly hope for is fraud. With no priors, she'd get probation."

They dickered back and forth for almost a half hour and in the end agreed to a face-to-face conference, including both Destiny and Elliott Emerson.

Elliott was first to arrive at the meeting, which didn't surprise me one little bit, seeing as to how he was so fired up about getting hold of my money. When Destiny entered the room, he didn't stand as most gentlemen would, but scrunched deeper into the chair and glared across the table with the look of a man ready for a fight. Tom Nichols, who was standing alongside of Elliott, nodded and gave Destiny a pleasant enough smile, then he reached across the table and shook hands with Charles McCallum.

Once the negotiations got underway, the nastiest side of Elliott came through. "She's a thief," he shouted, "a thief! Look what she's done to my aunt—stole her house, her car, her money! She belongs behind bars! In prison for life!"

"That's not likely to happen," Detective Nichols replied in the calmest voice imaginable. "So, cool down and let's discuss some realistic alternatives."

"Realistic alternatives?" Elliott grumbled. "I suppose it's *realistic* that she won't even tell me where she's hidden the money!"

Charles McCallum's expression suddenly looked like a bonfire had sprung up inside of his head—I could tell he was on to something. He began bringing up points of law, hammering at how they'd have to first prove *intent* to defraud. "Pursuing this issue in criminal court," he said looking straight at Elliott, "would provide punishment *only* if Destiny Fairchild is found guilty of an actual crime. "However," he strung the word out as if dessert was about to be served, "if you elect to drop the criminal charges and pursue this as a civil action, my client would be required to answer interrogatory questions as to the amount and whereabouts of any assets in question."

Elliott's eyes lit up.

Now I could see where Charles was heading. "So," he continued, his face still fixed square to Elliott, "while you have the right to pursue this along either pathway, you should decide which is more important—her punishment or the restitution of any assets that may be judged legally yours."

"That true?" Elliott asked Tom Nichols. "She's gotta say where the money is?"

The detective nodded.

"Well, under *those* circumstances..." Elliott sighed, his eyes registering like cherries on a slot machine. "Although I'd *prefer* to see this criminal get her just desserts, I owe it to my dear aunt to make certain her money stays in the Lannigan family."

Lannigan Family? He meant his own greedy hands! If I was still flesh and blood, I'd have lambasted that man for all he was worth—why, the Lannigan's wouldn't wipe their feet on the likes of you, that's what I'd have told him. Destiny, who'd been forewarned not to let herself be goaded into an argument, was probably of the same opinion, because she sat there picking the polish from her fingernails and ripping her cuticles to pieces.

Detective Nichols sided with Charles McCallum. "You might want to consider that course of action," he said, glancing sideways at Elliott. "In criminal cases we've got to prove she's guilty beyond any doubt. Our exploitation case is weak to begin with, and if she's got witnesses who will swear that she was authorized to sign those checks, fraud is out the window."

"Civil court only requires the prosecution to show there's a likely probability of the crime," Charles added. "The burden of proof is much lower."

"Of course, Mister Emerson will have to drop the exploitation complaint," Tom Nichols said, "the rest of the charges can be transferred to civil court."

"But she has to tell where all the money is?" Elliott asked again.

The other two men nodded, and within fifteen minutes they reached an agreement to dismiss the criminal charges against Destiny Fairchild.

End of an Era

Richmond, Virginia 1933

Abigail and Gloria both worked at Club Lucky until nineteen-thirty-three, when the government decided to give folks the legal right to drink whisky and repealed the eighteenth amendment. It happened in December, on a day that was so cold people bundled up in wooly coats and covered their noses with scarves. Although it was rumored that there would be dancing in the streets, Abigail knew better because the moment she opened her eyes she saw that the sky was gray as a stone. Days like this, you could step outside your door and get run over by a car or trampled by a horse, if that didn't happen you were sure to catch your death of cold. Itchy had told the girls to get decked out in their best bib and tucker because Club Lucky was having a party. "A celebration to end all celebrations," he'd called it. Still, Abigail couldn't get rid of the nagging apprehension that was scratching at her brain.

After breakfast, she pulled on a pair of boots and ventured out to do some Christmas shopping. Abigail walked the full seventeen blocks to Market Street, all the while thinking how she'd buy some wonderful presents this year, now that she had the feel of money in her pocket. Other years she'd had to scrimp, looking hard at the price tag before considering a gift, settling for a scarf when she'd hoped to buy something much finer. For three hours she meandered in and out of stores, finally selecting a mohair sweater, ignoring the cost and thinking only of how handsome it would look on her brother. At five o'clock she started home, carting an armload of presents and a bright red poinsettia plant. For the first time in five years, she'd bought her father a present—a meerschaum pipe with a massive figurehead bowl. She planned to enclose a letter along with the gift, a letter asking for his forgiveness—although she knew that forgiveness did not come easy to William Lannigan. He was a man who just might refuse to read what she'd written and set the gift aside unopened. Still, she reasoned, it had been five years, long enough perhaps for even his anger to fade.

She tried to focus her thoughts on the upcoming holiday—pictured eggnog with a floating sprinkle of nutmeg, an angel atop a pine tree, presents tied with ribbon the color of cherries—but the sky was still there, ominous as a tombstone. She arranged the poinsettia in the center of the kitchen table then sat and ate a bowl of chicken soup—which Ida Jean Meredith had once said was the cure for anything—but it burned going down and ultimately gave her indigestion. It's going to snow, she thought, maybe even sleet.

At eight o'clock, when Abigail arrived at Club Lucky, the party was already in full swing. A block away from the building she'd heard the band blasting out *Happy Days are Here Again* and no sooner had she walked through the door when Gloria scooted across the room and grabbed hold of her arm.

"You're late," Gloria said, sliding a glass of champagne into her friend's hand, "the party started hours ago!"

"It feels like we're gonna get snow tonight," Abigail said, the look of worry tugging at the corners of her mouth.

"Who cares!" Gloria answered. "It'll melt by time *this* party is over."

Abigail furrowed her brows until they matched the slope of her mouth. "You know," she said, "up until midnight we could still get raided."

"Raided?" Gloria laughed, "We ain't getting raided. We ain't even selling whiskey. Tonight everything's free, Itchy said so."

"Free?" Abigail hated the thought of things running amuck of her expectations, especially on a day when the sky was so worrisome. "What about tips?" she asked, remembering the extravagant presents she'd bought that afternoon. "If everything's free, we're not going to get tips."

"We won't need to. Itchy said tonight every one of us girls is getting at least a fifteen dollar bonus. You and I," Gloria whispered, "will probably get more, 'cause we been here the longest."

"Oh." In a situation such as this, any other person might be dancing a jig, but Abigail had a stone-colored ball of worry in her head and it was weighing her down.

With the free liquor flowing every which way but up, Club Lucky didn't close its doors until the last three patrons staggered out at six o'clock in the morning. Once he'd turned out the barroom lights, Itchy came back to the dressing room and passed around the envelopes. "This is it, girls," he said, "the end of Club Lucky."

"What's that supposed to mean?" Gloria asked.

Itchy laughed. "Honey, you ain't none too swift! End is end. I'm closing down the place. We had a good run, now it's over."

"But, why?" Abigail said, her lip quivering. "Why would you close down *now* when selling whiskey is legal?"

"Because it's legal," Itchy answered, frantically digging at his crotch. "There ain't no money in selling *legal* whiskey." After that he told the girls he was real sorry, but business was business and if they wanted to take home the dresses they'd been wearing to help themselves. "I got no use for them now," he said and walked out.

That was the last Abigail ever saw of Itchy.

She and Gloria walked home together in a gray dawn, a day so bleak that you couldn't tell where cement ended and sky started, a day where you could pass by a person and believe they were a shadow. "What am I gonna do?" Gloria moaned, for although she had worked at the club for five years, she had not saved a cent.

Abigail, on the other hand, now had a shoebox of dollar bills hidden beneath her laundry basket. "Things are better now," she said optimistically, "we'll find jobs." The following morning they sat down together and started searching the help wanted section of the newspaper, but despite Mister Roosevelt's New Deal, there were still very few jobs to be had.

When Christmas came, Abigail didn't buy the pine tree she'd been wanting, nor did she splurge on eggnog, instead she settled for a small stewing hen and invited Gloria over for dinner. Although the poinsettia had already lost a good portion of its leaves, Abigail was determined they would enjoy the day, so she played Christmas carols on the phonograph and sang along as if she had not a care in the world. That night when she crawled into bed, Abigail dreamed her father had thrown away the unopened package containing the meerschaum pipe and the letter she had written. In the dream, she could see the flame of hatred still burning in his eyes and when she woke the next morning, Abigail knew that William Lannigan would never forgive her, not even a thousand years from now.

Two months after Club Lucky closed its doors; Gloria came to stay with Abigail and started sleeping on the living room sofa. "If you hadn't let me move in with you, I'd be out on the street," Gloria said. "Starving, probably."

"I'd have starved to death three years ago, if not for you," Abigail answered, then they both laughed and vowed to remain friends for as long as they lived. "Longer, even," Abigail promised, "special relationships reach beyond the grave."

"Whoooo," Gloria clowned, "that'll be us, two ghosts, sitting on our tombstones, worrying about where we're gonna find jobs."

That's how it went. Day after day they tromped downtown and asked about work at one place and then another. "I've an opening for a bricklayer, the manager at Apex said, but neither Gloria nor Abigail were qualified for a position such as that. "I'll let you know if something else comes up," he'd told them, but they never did hear from him.

The very last week in March, after the weather had turned unseasonably warm and started the daffodils blooming, Gloria burst into the apartment with her cheeks ablaze. "I got a job!" she screamed, then grabbed hold of Abigail and danced around the kitchen for a full ten minutes. "You're never gonna believe this," she finally gasped, "Sally Mae, the waitress at Chicken Castle is having a baby! I'm standing there, asking the manager for a job, when she walks up and tells him that her feet are so swollen she can't work no more."

"Just like that?"

"Yeah. Right away he starts eyeing me up, then asks if I can start tomorrow. Hell's bells, I tell him, I'm ready right now!"

"You worked today?"

"Nah. He said tomorrow would do just fine, and gave me this…" Gloria held up a wide-skirted dress with the name Sally embroidered across the pocket.

Gloria started paying the expenses and Abigail continued to plod along looking for work. Twice a week she marched herself down to the newspaper office and asked about the possibility of becoming a reporter. "You don't have any experience," the personnel manager said. "We only hire writers with *experience!*"

"I'd be willing to start in classifieds," Abigail suggested. "Obituaries, even."

"I could put you on the waiting list for a delivery boy spot—"

"Proofreading, maybe?"

Every day Abigail bought the newspaper and turned directly to the classifieds, but most times there were only a handful of listings. She'd slide her finger along the column—accountant, barber, dog catcher—a job she applied for but didn't get—electrician, jeweler, plumber, undertaker; afterwards, she'd fold up the paper and hope for better luck the following day. After a while, she quit spending the three cents to buy a newspaper and started going to the library, where she could sit in a comfortable chair and read *The Richmond Courier* for free. After she finished going through the classifieds, which usually took only minutes, the remainder of a day without purpose stretched in front of her like the Sahara Desert, so she'd stay at the library and read through periodicals that had to do with things such as raising fish or telling jokes. Once she'd gone through those, she turned to history books, then it was biographies and after that geography. She read *The Good Earth* and *Tobacco Road*, taking heart in people who overcame adversity. *State Fair* she read twice, and might have read it for a third time if it weren't for the fact that five other people were waiting for the book.

It got so that Abigail would be standing on the front steps long before Miss Spencer, unlocked the door. "Well now, aren't you the early bird," the librarian would say as she snapped on the light. As the day wore on, Miss Spencer would go to lunch and return, only to find Abigail still sitting there. When it was time for the library to close, she'd have to flicker the light on and off to rouse Abigail from her seat and start her toward the door. Miss Spencer, who had worked there for almost fifty years and never before witnessed such behavior, grew concerned. "Is there some sort of problem?" she asked.

"No," Abigail answered wistfully, but the librarian noticed that her book on the mating of alligators was held upside down.

Being a woman experienced in the art of hiding behind books, Miss Spencer said, "Well, if you've time, I'd like you to share my lunch. It seems that I mistakenly packed *two* sandwiches today." Abigail followed along to a tiny back room where they sat at a round table and ate lunch, which as it turned out, also included two apples and two cupcakes. "I see you always look at the classifieds first," Miss Spencer said, "are you in need of work?" Abigail tried to answer but the word got stuck in her throat and made it seem as though she was choking. "Oh, my goodness," Miss Spencer exclaimed, and took to patting Abigail on the back.

Three days later Abigail did mention the fact that she was looking for work. "I'm a writer," she said, "but, other than working for Miss Ida Jean Meredith, I've no experience."

"You worked for *Ida Jean Meredith*?"

Abigail nodded and said nothing of how she'd been a hostess at Club Lucky for the past three years. "Until she died."

"Why, her poetry is magical—pure genius!" Miss Spencer was suddenly aglow. "We have three of her books right here in this library. One of them autographed!"

"The newspaper said that's not qualifying experience."

"What do they know?"

"They wouldn't hire me—not even for obituaries."

"Peasants! No vision! A person of your experience shouldn't waste their time writing chit-chat destined for the trash bin!"

From that moment on, Miss Spencer took a great interest in Abigail. "We've a wonderful new book on architecture," she'd say, "now, *that's* what you should be reading!" But Abigail still grabbed hold of *The Richmond Courier* the first thing each morning and ran her finger down the help wanted columns—acrobat, juggler, tug boat captain—when she'd finally determined there was not a single job she could qualify for, she'd offer to help Miss Spencer. She spent hour after hour rolling a metal cart with a squeaky wheel through the aisles, reaching up to the highest shelf and squatting to the lowest to replace each book in precisely the right place. When the cart was empty of books, she studied the Dewey decimal system so she could sort the index cards. On several occasions Miss Spencer even allowed her to handle checkouts. Abigail loved the sound of the date stamp thunking down against a card, it seemed so sturdy, solid as a house made of bricks.

By August, the stack of dollar bills in Abigail's shoebox had grown noticeably smaller, despite the fact that Gloria was paying more than her share of the expenses. Abigail started to worry and took to considering employment listings she had previously passed by. She'd allow her finger to linger on the advertisement for draftsman, wondering precisely what such a job might entail, then she'd consider the opening for an elephant trainer, thinking, how hard could something like that be? Shortly before Labor Day, she got to feeling truly desperate and asked Gloria if there were any other openings at Chicken Castle. As it turned out, Mildred, the cashier, had developed a spur on her tailbone and could no longer sit for such long hours, so she'd given her two weeks notice.

Early the next morning, Abigail walked into Chicken Castle and asked if she might have the job. That afternoon she went back to the library.

"I missed you this morning," Miss Spencer said. "We've a number of books to be replaced in the stacks, and some overdues you can check on."

"I got a job," Abigail said despondently. "I won't be able to help anymore."

"With a book publisher?" Miss Spencer asked anxiously.

"Not exactly."

"A periodical?"

"Chicken Castle."

"What do they publish?"

"Nothing. They sell fried chicken. I'm going to be the cashier."

"Cashier?" Miss Spencer echoed, looking as if she was about to fall over in a dead faint. "A girl of your ability? A girl with aspirations of becoming a writer?"

Abigail shrugged. "At least it's a job."

"Lord-in-Heaven! A person who's worked with Ida Jean Meredith, dishing out fried chicken!"

"I won't be *serving* the chicken," Abigail answered. "I'll be the cashier."

"Absolutely not!" Miss Spencer snapped.

"I've already got the job"

"Well, you'll simply have to tell them you can't accept it."

"Why would I do that?"

"Because I need you here at the library." Miss Spencer started clacking the overdue stamp down on a bunch of books like a machine run amuck.

"But, *this* job doesn't pay any salary."

"It does now! You start today. Assistant Librarian in training."

"In training for *what*?" Abigail asked, looking as if it were virtually impossible for her to have heard what she heard.

"No," Miss Spencer exclaimed, reversing herself. "Not in training. You'll be hired as a full-fledged *Assistant Librarian!* And in November, when I retire, you'll become *Head Librarian!*"

Abigail's mouth fell open—if a person wasn't going to be a writer, the next best thing was to spend every day in a building filled with wonderful stories. She was starting to imagine herself reading every single book, not once, but twice. Maybe when she became *head librarian*, she'd stay here all night, reading until her eyes could no longer hold themselves open and then she'd fall to sleep in the back room.

"No need to argue," Miss Spencer said. "My mind's made up!"

During the month of October, Abigail propped open the library doors to catch the breezes of Indian summer. The scent of late blooming roses and fresh mown grass settled into the bindings of books, and Miss Spencer forgot to put out her bowl of Halloween candy which had been the tradition for decades. Mister Wimple, the groundskeeper took to sneezing seventeen times in a row, a condition he claimed could only be attributed to summer allergies. The balmy weather lasted through Thanksgiving, and most folks had begun to believe that winter was not going to come to Richmond that year. However, on the last day of November, the day that was to herald Miss Spencer's departure from the library, an ice storm rolled in sometime before dawn and the air turned bitter cold. When Abigail woke early in the morning, there was a crackling of ice stuck to the bedroom window and she started to worry it could be a sign. "A sign of what?" Gloria had asked, but Abigail just shrugged and mumbled something about not knowing who's at the door until you've already opened it.

"Go ahead and laugh," she told Gloria, "but just you remember when Club Lucky closed. I *knew*—first thing in the morning, when I saw the sky, I *knew* there'd be bad luck headed my way."

"Silly superstition!" Gloria laughed, and then went about ironing her uniform.

Abigail wanted to believe Gloria was right, so she focused on thoughts of how she'd start up a children's hour with nursery rhymes and fairy tales, but the image of Mother Goose flying around on a witch's broom popped into her head and she knew for certain it was going to be *that* kind of a day. "Oh dear," she sighed as she wrapped the opal pendant she'd bought as a retirement gift for Miss Spencer.

The library was still dark when Abigail arrived, which to her mind was more cause for concern since she'd never known Miss Spencer to be late. Using her brand new key, Abigail unlocked the front door and snapped on the light. She retrieved three books from the depository box then walked into the back room and hung her coat. After she had set the coffee pot on to brew, Abigail placed the box tied with blue ribbon in the center of Miss Spencer's desk and waited. By ten-thirty she was practically positive something was wrong—something drastic, for Emily Spencer would not allow herself to be delayed, especially on this day when there was to be a going away party in her honor. Abigail watched the clock tick off the minutes, each longer than the one before, then at eleven o'clock she dialed Miss Spencer's home number, even though the library telephone was supposed to be used for business calls only.

"Hello," a husky-voiced male said.

"Uh, hello," Abigail stuttered. "May I please speak to Miss Emily Spencer?"

"Who's this?" he asked.

"Abigail Lannigan, the assistant librarian."

"Oh." The man hesitated several moments before he spoke again, "I guess you haven't heard."

"Heard?"

"Emily passed away late last night," the man said, his voice sounding low as the center of the earth.

"Oh, no …" Abigail stammered, but by that time the man had hung up.

That night, after the library doors were closed and locked, Abigail took the opal pendant from its box, walked to Saint Paul the Apostle Church and dropped it into the poor box. She sat in the darkest corner of the last pew and cried for almost three hours, mostly for poor Miss Spencer who had been cheated out of her last hour of glory; but partly for herself because being the Head Librarian didn't feel anywhere near as good as she had thought it would.

Gloria had been working at Chicken Castle precisely three years on the day Fred Bailey walked through the door, sat down at the counter and ordered the fried chicken combo. She knew this for a fact because on that day the girls surprised her with a frosted cake that read *Congratulations.* Having already carved off several pieces to pass around, she was just about to stick her own fork into a slice, when he smiled at her. It wasn't as if a man had never before done such a thing—working at Club Lucky it had been a nightly occurrence—but Fred's smile was different, it made her toes curl under. She smiled back, and then stood there with a forkful of cake suspended halfway between the plate and her mouth.

"Your birthday?" he asked.

"Third anniversary," she answered.

"Your husband's a lucky man."

"Oh no," Gloria quickly clarified, "it's the third anniversary of me working here. I'm not married, not one bit married."

"Then I'm the lucky man." He locked his gaze into hers and smiled again.

It took Fred almost two hours to finish off the plate of fried chicken. He'd nibble on the tip end of a wing, then ask where Gloria was from; he'd chew a shred of coleslaw fifteen times then inquire as to what movies she liked; he'd order up another cup of coffee and ask if she liked to dance. In addition to the chicken combo, he ate two pieces of the celebration cake and drank twelve cups of coffee that afternoon. By the time he finally left, Gloria was so starry eyed she put a scoop of vanilla ice cream atop a grilled cheese sandwich and served a slice of apple pie with pickle.

That night she told Abigail, "I've met the man I'm going to marry."

"Marry?" Abigail echoed with astonishment.

Gloria nodded.

Within a month, Gloria and Fred were keeping steady company. Before the year was out, they married and moved into an apartment building three doors down.

Abigail went back to living alone. Night after night she'd sit at the kitchen table reading, forgetting to make dinner, and filling herself with the promise that someday soon she too would meet the man of her dreams. At times she'd slip off to imagining the look of him—tall, sandy-haired, eyes the color of a summer sky, a voice so melodious that birds would cease their singing to listen. He'd love children and insist they have a houseful, three or four girls and a like number of boys. They'd live in a white clapboard house on the far edge of town, a house with a picket fence and rose garden. She even conjured up a rusty-hued Irish setter that in the evening would walk to the end of the drive waiting for his master to return from work.

Each morning Abigail set aside her imaginary family and went to work at the library. She unlocked the door at precisely nine o'clock and snapped on the lights, exactly the same way as Miss Spencer had for fifty years. She spent the early hours at the circulation desk, organizing, cataloging, stamping overdue notices and watching for the sandy-haired man to walk through the door—it stood to reason that if Gloria's future husband had wandered into Chicken Castle, hers would one day show up at the library. But it was mostly older folks who came, older folks and schoolchildren. Old men with thick eyeglasses and hearing aids sat for hours on end reading *The Richmond Courier*, white-haired women browsed books on gardening and quilting, students ran in and out quickly, interested only in the book they'd been assigned to read. "You might like to try *Gone With The Wind*," Abigail suggested to a number of women, but they took a look at the thickness of the book and right away shook their head. "Why, it would take a year to read a book *that size!*" one woman commented, then she asked if the library had anything on the making of bundt cakes.

Some days Abigail sat behind the circulation desk for so long that her foot fell asleep and started prickling pins and needles—she'd shake it a few times and stomp a bit, then start off walking in and out of the stacks. At first she'd walk through Fiction, but the sight of all those wonderful stories going unread saddened her so she eventually switched over to History.

After two years of watching and waiting Abigail started to grow discouraged; she set aside tales of romance and started reading stories of women such as Amelia Earhart and Eleanor Roosevelt. She read the free-spirited poetry of Edna St. Vincent Millay and focused on the fact that women such as Pearl Buck and Margaret Mitchell had written best selling books. She resurrected the thought of becoming a novelist and bought a journal to make note of ideas for her first book. *Heroine refuses to marry man she doesn't love and runs away from home*, Abigail wrote on the very first page; but that seemed rather lame in comparison to the adventures of Scarlet O'Hara, so she crossed it out and went on to the next idea. *Heroine is dying and hero carries her outside for one final look at land she loves*—also crossed out, too similar to Wuthering Heights. After that, there was a run of ideas that went on for thirty seven pages, one thought after another, all crossed out. She was jotting down her thoughts for the story of an adventurous young girl and a wild horse, when a husky voice asked if the library had a city map.

Ordinarily she might not have bothered to look up, she might have simply gestured toward the back wall where such a map was displayed, but this voice lacked the shakiness of the old men and it lacked the high-pitched squeal of an adolescent boy, it was the rich round dulcet tone of a gentleman. Abigail raised her eyes and looked into the face of the handsomest man she'd ever seen. They stood eye to eye, him no taller than her. He had the look of Rudolph Valentino, dark eyes and slicked back hair. For a long time she stood there studying him and wondering why in the world she'd spent all those years looking for a man with sandy colored hair.

"City map?" he finally repeated.

"What street are you looking for?" Abigail asked, blatantly ignoring the map on the wall because she couldn't bear to have him walk away.

"Oak Tree Road."

"Oak Tree?" she echoed, but the thoughts running through her head had nothing to do with where such a location might be—she was busy taking note of the broadness of his shoulders. Finally, after she'd stared at him for so long that a person could easily assume the question had been forgotten, she answered, "I think that might be on the far side of town, past the railroad station."

"That sounds logical," he said. "What I'm looking for is a housing development that's under construction."

"Oh? Buying a house?"

"Afraid not," he laughed, "just here to inspect the property."

Abigail was not usually one to pry into people's business—when someone wanted information of one kind or another, she'd point to the appropriate reference section and that was that, no questions asked—this was different, she wasn't ready to let this dark-haired stranger walk away. Were it possible, she would have nailed his shoes to the floor, locked the library door and kept him prisoner. "Why?" she asked.

He tilted his head quizzically, "Why am I inspecting the property?"

Abigail nodded, and then leaned across the circulation desk as if she needed to be close to the source of sound to hear his answer. She marveled at how perfectly the curve of his neck nestled into the starched collar, how on this particular day he had chosen to wear a red necktie—red, her favorite color, the color of a heart shaped valentine, the color of roses. He told her, that he was a property inspector working for the Emigrant Savings Bank in New York City; but he could have been reciting the Pledge of Allegiance for as far as she was concerned the words didn't matter, what mattered was the rush of warmth heating up her body, making her toes curl and her fingers itch to reach out and touch his face. She could already imagine him standing before a preacher in a groom's morning suit when she said, "you'll need help finding Oak Tree Road, it's *way* across town."

He smiled and having noticed how Abigail had flung her body at him, asked, "I don't suppose you'd be…" Before he'd finished the question, she answered, saying that it would only take a few minutes for her to close up the library. "This early in the afternoon?" he asked, but by that time Abigail had turned off the lights.

"I'm John Langley," he offered as they stepped out onto the street.

"Abigail Lannigan," she answered and hooked her arm through his.

His car was parked at the corner of the block; he unlocked the door and she slid halfway across the seat to a spot that was closer to the driver than the door. When he climbed in and sat beside her, she could feel the rightness of it and started trying out the sound of *Abigail Langley* in her head.

"Which way?" he asked.

Perhaps she wasn't concentrating or perhaps it was because Abigail wanted to stretch this moment out for eternity, whichever, she directed him through every side street and roundabout route possible, and only after they'd circled through town twice, did they happen upon the spot. "This is it," John said when he saw the sign that read: Hanerman Homes—Better living at an affordable price.

The only thing Abigail saw was an endless stretch of wooden framework structures. "This is it?"

"It will be. This is the first stage." He parked the car on the side of a dirt road, got out, and started walking. She scrambled out behind him and followed along. "You may want to wait in the car," he said, "it's pretty messy back here."

"I was raised on a farm," she answered, not wanting him to think her a limp lily, "Why, I'm capable of climbing the side of a mountain."

He laughed out loud, then reached back and took hold of her hand. "I didn't mean to infer that you *couldn't*, I was just thinking you might not want to get your shoes dirty."

As they walked, he counted the structures, one hundred and twelve in all. Three times he climbed up onto the flooring platform of a particular house and each time she went along. "See," he'd say, pointing to a strip of framework, "that's the living room wall and this here will be the bedroom." Or, when they were standing in what would someday be the hallway he'd point out a tiny closet or the kitchen. Abigail thought for certain he was leading up to the part where one day they'd be living in one of these houses, which would be fine to start, but she was planning on three maybe four little ones, which meant they would eventually need a bigger house.

Once he'd finished writing up his notes, John asked if he might take Abigail to dinner to repay her kindness. "Why, of course," she answered but told him that they'd have to first stop by her apartment so she could change her muddy shoes.

That evening they went to the Tivoli, a restaurant so fine the waiters were required to dress in silk tuxedos and carry dainty linen towels across their arm to scoop away a droplet of wine if it lingered on the lip of the bottle. The moment Abigail stepped across the threshold, she wished she'd taken the time to polish her fingernails, maybe freshen her make up and change her dress as well— it would have taken half-a-minute at most, yet she'd rushed out the door wearing a cotton frock that now seemed downright dowdy. "Oh dear," she sighed.

The waiter seated them side by side on a banquette, then brought a bottle of champagne and filled both glasses. Abigail had not had champagne since the close of Club Lucky, so it spiraled to her head and caused her to flirt in the most outrageous manner. While John was explaining how the Emigrant Bank lent money to developers all along the eastern seaboard, she hooked her foot around his ankle and as he elaborated on how this building of moderately priced homes was the wave of the future, she pressed her thigh against his. At the mere mention of the fact that he expected to be in Richmond on a regular basis, she smiled and tilted her face upward in such a way that it appeared a heartbeat shy of an invitation to press his lips to hers.

Minutes later, he moved closer and wrapped his arm around her shoulder.

Abigail knew this was what she'd been waiting for, she knew just as Gloria had known the day Fred Bailey walked into Chicken Castle, and she shivered at the thought.

"You chilly?" he asked

"Not at all," she answered, settling into the crook of his arm.

At the end of the evening they kissed goodnight outside the apartment; the kiss, sweet and lingering, remained on Abigail's lips long after she'd stepped inside and closed the door. It was the kind of kiss, she told herself, that only came about once you'd found your own true love. Squinting into the mirror as she washed her face, angling a glance at the reflection until it came back just the way she wanted, Abigail could imagine the silver slick of soap to be a bridal veil dropped down over her face.

She slipped beneath the sheet, in a dreamlike state before her head hit the pillow; moments later she was fast asleep, floating on a heart-shaped cloud. She'd fallen into bed hoping to dream of the day she and John would be married, but that's not what happened. Instead they were at a train station, she was waiting for him to bend and kiss her but a puff of black smoke rolled across his face and although she could sense he was there she could no longer see him. Suddenly she spotted his figure moving toward the train; she grabbed onto the sleeve of his jacket and pleaded with him not to leave. For a moment he stopped and turned to her, then as the train started to move, he jumped aboard. *You've always known I'm a traveling man*, he shouted back, then he slid into a seat alongside a window and waved goodbye. Only then did she notice that every other window of the train was filled with babies, waving their chubby little hands and crying out *goodbye, Mama*. Abigail heard herself scream as the train pulled away and left her standing on the platform with tears streaming down her face and a ripped off patch of tweed jacket in her hand.

Abigail woke with a start, her gown soaked with perspiration and her heart galloping at a thousand beats per minute. It took her a full minute to grab hold of herself and come to the realization that it had been nothing more than a dream. No, she thought, not a dream, a nightmare! But it was enough to set her thinking about the fact that John had kissed her, then turned and walked away, saying nothing about when they might be together again. Maybe he'd never come back, never even call. He'd have no further need of the city map now, so he'd move on to some other town, some other map, some other librarian.

She sobbed and wailed until the sound of anguish filled the room and spilled out into the airshaft. A neighbor called across that he was trying to sleep and banged down his window, but Abigail continued to cry. When the wailing eased off to a steady flow of sniffles, she started to shiver like a person who'd been hauled up from a frozen lake. In the middle of July, on a night so warm that every window in the building was left open, she took a wool blanket and covered herself. She buried her face in the pillow and curled her body into a ball of desperation. "I should have changed my dress," she sobbed, "worn something with glitter." She told herself that she was the picture of plainness and it was no wonder he'd not fallen in love with her. She bolted to a sitting position and raised her hands in an airborne gesture, "No man can love a woman like me," she shouted, "I'm a *librarian!*" Someone across the airway called out that it was three o'clock in the morning and two more windows slammed closed. Again drenched in perspiration, she threw off the covers and stripped away her gown. Before the sun peered over the horizon, Abigail had washed herself down with ice water twice, drank three cups of tea with honey, one cup of warm milk and a half glass of whiskey, but not once did she again close her eyes.

By morning her eyes were swollen, dark as an overripe plum, and there was a red blotch of hives circling the side of her face. Even though the temperature was forecasted to hit ninety-five degrees by mid-afternoon, she pulled on a black dress with long sleeves and did not bother to add a single speck of jewelry. She drank a glass of water for breakfast, then stuck an apple in the pocket of her skirt and left for work. The desolate drag of her feet gave Abigail the look of mourner as she shuffled along in the rising heat.

Arriving at the library fifteen minutes after the scheduled opening time, she unlocked the door, then went and sat behind the circulation desk—not filing, or cataloguing, not stacking books or stamping overdue notices, but just sitting. Although her brow was slick with perspiration, she didn't remember to turn on the fan until well after ten-thirty. And, even after she finally did turn on the fan, she neglected to turn on the overhead lights, so from the outside the library appeared to be closed.

About one-thirty a boy of fourteen or so, poked open the door and called out, "Anybody here?"

"I'm here," Abigail answered in a weary voice. "You need a book?"

"No ma'am, I got a delivery." He pushed his way through the door with a large bouquet of red roses. "Miss Abigail Lannigan?"

She nodded and he handed her the bouquet. "For me?" she exclaimed.

"You're Abigail Lannigan, right?"

She reached out and took hold of the roses; in the center of the bouquet was a folded note. With the roses nestled in the crook of her arm, she started fishing through her purse. "Wait a minute," she said, "I'll get you a tip."

"The man already gave me fifty cents."

"What man?"

"The man standing out there." The boy pointed to the far corner of the street.

Abigail stretched her neck and followed the line of the boy's finger—she could see someone standing there, someone who looked to be the size and build of John Langley, but with the sun behind him she couldn't for the life of her make out the face. "What did he say?" she asked.

The boy shrugged. "Nothin' much. Just I should bring these to you."

"Was he tall? Dark hair? Very handsome?"

"I think he had brown hair," the boy started backing away.

"Very handsome?"

"Handsome? He was old—old as my dad!" The boy inched further back.

With a trembling hand Abigail pulled the note from the bouquet, by the time she started to read the boy had fled out the door.

> *Dear Abigail,*
> *I hope you are not hiding out in a darkened library to avoid me. I greatly enjoyed your company last evening and would love it if you would join me for dinner again tonight.*
> *If the answer is yes, please turn on the light.*
> *Fondly yours,*
> *John Langley*

Abigail darted across the floor and clicked on the interior lights, every one of them, including the far back reference room which had been closed off for the past six months. After that she turned on the outside lights, despite the fact that the sun was shining bright enough to blister a person's eyeball. Lastly, she switched on the flagpole light. "That should do it," she sighed.

When the glass door swung open Abigail caught sight of her reflection. "Oh no!" she screamed.

"But," John stuttered, "you *did* turn the lights on."

"Of course I turned them on, but look at me, I'm a fright."

"Not a fright," he laughed, "a bit tired, maybe."

Abigail was not about to tell how she'd worried herself into a frenzy—a thing such as that would make her seem all the more pathetic—so, she said, "Someone in the apartment building kept carrying on all night long, the most God-awful noise, why I couldn't sleep a wink."

"If you're too tired, we could wait, have dinner tomorrow night."

"Me, tired?" Abigail saw him smile and for a moment she thought a star had dropped down from heaven. "I'd *love* to see you tonight—of course, I do have to go home first to freshen up."

That evening Abigail stepped out looking as she did in the days of Club Lucky.

The vase of roses sent by John Langley sat on the front shelf of the circulation desk until the leaves turned brown and fluttered to the floor. Wilbur Atkins, a man who was considered legally blind and seldom said anything more than good morning, squinted at the vase and told Abigail he thought those flowers were dead. "Not quite," she answered, with a breathy sigh that sent several petals cascading to the floor.

"Not dead, huh?" Wilbur cleaned his glasses and took another look.

Two days later, Bunny Pence, offered to cart the flowers out to the garbage can if Abigail was busy. "Why, I'm not the least bit busy." Abigail answered, then explained that she simply wanted to continue enjoying the flowers. "I adore the smell of roses," she exclaimed as Bunny stood there looking bewildered.

When there was just one rose petal left, Abigail plucked it from the stem and pressed it into a book of Elizabeth Browning's poetry. She then wrapped the bare stems and a dry sprig of baby's breath in pink tissue paper and placed the package on a shelf usually used for overdue notices. That entire summer, not one person in all of Richmond received an overdue notice. There was frost on the ground when Amelia Cooper remembered to return a book on the planting of daffodils, but Abigail told her to just forget about the fine.

Every other week John Langley spent two days in Richmond and on those nights he courted Abigail as she had never been courted before. They ate in the finest restaurants, danced at the rooftop pavilion, saw movies, went to the opera, walked in the park and kissed. When they were alone, John whispered words of love into her ear and kissed her so ardently that Abigail truly believed her body would burst into flames. Her happiness would have been complete were it not for the fact that John always left. "I'll be back," he said, and after a while Abigail came to understand that he was true to his word.

It was easy to know when John was in town, for Abigail's feet never touched the ground. She'd float into the library looking radiant as a movie star and click on the radio, despite the *Silence Please* sign she'd put there herself. Old men got tickled behind their beards and boys were told how handsome they were growing to be. Bouquets of flowers appeared at the reading tables and there were dishes of chocolates set out on the circulation counter even though Halloween was almost two months off. Abigail's cheeks blushed scarlet, not only while John was in town, but for weeks afterward.

"You're in love!" Gloria said and Abigail nodded. "But," Gloria stammered, "you don't know a thing about this guy."

"I know he makes me happy," Abigail answered. "Just, look at me!"

Gloria had to admit she'd never before seen Abigail looking so good—her cheeks were blossoming, the curve of her face full and round, her mouth upturned and tinkling with the sound of laughter. "Does he feel the same about you?" she asked.

"Of course!" Abigail giggled. "He said I make his head spin."

"Yes, but did he say he *loves* you?"

"Maybe not that exact word. He said he's crazy about me."

Gloria, a skeptic to start with, frowned and left it at that. After all, it had only been a few months. Abigail was surely smart enough to insist on a commitment when the time was right.

Abigail never knew a summer to fly by as that one did. One morning she noticed Wilbur Atkins wearing a wooly sweater instead of his straw hat, which prompted her to check the date on the calendar. Much to her surprise, both Labor Day and Halloween had slipped by without notice. She didn't want such a thing to happen with Thanksgiving, so then and there Abigail decided to fix a roast turkey for John; she planned on sausage stuffing, candied sweet potatoes, cranberry sauce and a raspberry trifle—he could bring a bottle of wine. Two nights later, she told him of her idea; but he heaved the saddest sort of sigh and said he'd be up in New York that week. When her face fell into a look of disappointment, he suggested that they have their own Thanksgiving celebration a week early—which is exactly what happened. On November seventeenth, a Tuesday, Abigail hired a substitute librarian and stayed at home to cook.

Although she'd not had much luck with the trifle and had at the last minute rushed out and bought an apple pie, the dinner, John claimed, was wonderful. Afterward, he gave her a cameo locket to commemorate their first holiday together, even though it wasn't really the actual holiday. After he fastened the chain around her neck, John kissed Abigail clear down to her bosom all the while whispering how he was absolutely crazy about her. With his mouth suckling the hollow of her throat, Abigail swooned into his arms and when she finally came to her senses, she was lying on the bed.

"You fainted," he explained.

"Oh," Abigail sighed, locked into the pleasure of his face hovering above her.

On Thanksgiving Day, Abigail anticipated a call from him—John did things like that; telephone at odd times, send flowers when she least expected it, poke his head in the door on Tuesday when he wasn't due back till Thursday—so she got up early and sat beside the telephone. She waited for seven hours, but the telephone never rang. At three o'clock she began to think there was something wrong with her line, but just as she started downstairs to inquire about a repairman, the phone rang.

"Hi," Gloria said and Abigail's heart slid down past her knees. "Can you come over?" Gloria asked. "We've got something special to tell you."

"Well, actually, I'm expecting John to call." Abigail answered, trying to hide the greatness of her disappointment. "Tell me on the phone."

"That would spoil everything. Come on over. *Please?*"

Abigail, still hoping John would call, said she'd be there a bit later. She hung up, waited another five hours then went to Gloria's apartment.

The moment Fred opened the door; he called out "She's here!"

Judging by the glow on his face, Abigail thought he might be a bit tipsy.

"You want champagne?" he asked, "Mince pie, maybe? We still got turkey…"

Abigail hadn't eaten all day and she was just about to say that some of the turkey sounded pretty good, but Gloria cut in. "Don't anybody don't want that left-over stuff," she laughed, "but we could all use a Coke-cola."

Abigail saw something new in her friend's face—something impossible to put a name to, a softness around the eyes, a half-smile curling the corner of the mouth, an at-peace-with-the-world look of gentleness. Long before the words were said, she knew Gloria was expecting a baby.

"In June," Gloria said, "and we want you to be the Godmother."

Abigail was so pleased; she told Fred she'd have the champagne, after all.

With Christmas now seeming just around the corner, Abigail began shopping—she bought her forthcoming godchild three yellow baby buntings and a rocking horse and she took to telephoning Gloria most every day to check on how she was feeling. "Do you have any cravings?" she'd ask, "Want some ice cream? Pickles, maybe?"

Gloria would usually laugh and say that Fred was taking very good care of her. "Oh," Abigail would answer, with a tinge of jealousy because she wanted to be more than a Godmother, she wanted a part in the pregnancy.

The more Abigail thought about Gloria's baby, the more she longed to become John's wife and grow fat with her own child. She went to Blumgarten's, the finest men's shop in all of Richmond and bought John a pair of leather slippers lined with fleece, the kind of slipper any man would look forward to at the end of a hard day. She also bought him a fine briarwood pipe, even though she'd never known him to smoke. She wrapped both gifts in Santa Claus paper and fixed a sprig of holly atop the packages. On Christmas Day she planned to feed him a hearty dinner, and then insist that he sit in the easy chair to relax with his pipe and slippers. That, she thought, would be the right time to drop a subtle hint about marriage.

On Christmas Eve John called, at a time when she'd already slipped a roast of beef into the oven and was expecting him to be knocking on the door. "Sorry," he said, "I'm tied up with some emergency inspections in Philadelphia and won't be able to get there for another week."

"It's Christmas," Abigail moaned.

"I know," he sighed, "But, what can I do?"

"I've already started dinner."

"Could you maybe invite some friends over?"

"On Christmas Eve?" she sniffled.

"I'm sorry, sweetheart," he said, "I promise I'll make it up to you."

Abigail heard the contrition in his voice and ached to feel his arms around her no matter the cost. "I'll come to Philadelphia," she offered.

"Oh no," he answered almost a little too quickly, "I couldn't let you do that. I'm out at the site all day, every day. It's terrible. Muddy. Cold. Dangerous even."

"Dangerous?"

"These are industrial buildings, steel scaffolding and such. Way too dangerous for a woman to walk around." As Abigail sat there crying into the telephone, he went on to say he missed her just as much as she missed him and that he'd see her as soon as he could finish up and get to Richmond. Then he hung up.

Abigail threw herself across the bed and cried for three hours, completely forgetting about the roast beef in the oven until a curl of black smoke wafted through the apartment. She didn't eat at all Christmas Eve and on Christmas Day she ate a bologna and cheese sandwich.

John did not get back to Richmond until the third of January, by which time Abigail had decided that she was going to return the pipe and slippers to Blumgarten's and ask for her money back.

"I don't care much for roses," she grumbled when he came through the library door carrying a bouquet the size of an oak tree.

"You've always liked them before," he answered.

"That was before..."

"Before what? Before I disappointed you? Before I ruined Christmas?"

Abigail mumbled, "Yes." She looked down at an overdue notice she'd already stamped seven times and didn't allow her eyes to meet his.

"Don't you think I was disappointed too?"

She shrugged and whacked the overdue stamp.

"Damn you," he shouted, "Look at me!" He reached across the counter and tilted her face to his. "I love you, Abigail! Can't you understand that I was just as disappointed as you?"

Abigail was going to tell him that such a thing wasn't possible, but before she could push the words from her mouth, a tear rolled down her cheek.

"Yell at me, scream at me," John pleaded, "but, please don't cry." With that he leaped across the circulation desk and took her in his arms.

Before that happened, Abigail was set on saying she wasn't interested in a boyfriend who bounced around like a rubber ball, but once he started smothering her face with kisses, whatever resolve she had was forgotten. Right there, in full view of library patrons, she slid her arms around his neck and pressed her lips to his. The kissing continued for a full five minutes and may have lasted through the afternoon, were it not for the fact that Gertrude Fishman asked for a book on tropical rain forests.

That night John took Abigail to dinner in a French restaurant, a romantic place with lights so low, you couldn't know for sure what you were eating. He ordered a bottle of champagne tucked inside a silver bucket, and every time she took a sip, he quickly refilled her glass. He sat alongside of her, close enough that she could feel the pulse of blood in his veins. He whispered how missing her had driven him wild with desire, then slid his hand over her thigh and drew her closer still. Abigail knew that even if the building suddenly burst into flames, or the sky came tumbling down, she would be helpless to pull herself away.

Later that evening, at her apartment, they celebrated their own Christmas, despite the fact that Abigail had already taken down the small pine tree in the parlor and ripped the Santa Claus paper from John's presents. "I'm sorry this isn't wrapped," she murmured handing him the shoe box. He claimed it didn't matter, then removed his shoes and slid his feet into the slippers.

John opened the suitcase he'd carted up to the apartment and pulled out a small box wrapped in silver paper. "This is for you," he told Abigail.

When Abigail peeled back the paper she found a solid gold watch sprinkled with diamonds, a watch so delicate a person would have to squint to actually see the time on the face, a watch so perfect, it could only come from a man in love. "It's beautiful," she squealed, throwing her arms around his neck so enthusiastically that they both toppled over. She then leaned into his chest and covered John's face with kisses.

When he was finally able to catch his breath, he handed her a second box— pearl earrings. After that it was a bottle of lavender bath salts. The last gift was a large box from Macy's Herald Square. "This came all the way from New York?" she asked.

He nodded.

Abigail knew she'd been wrong about John not caring. Obviously, he was every bit as much in love with her as she was with him.

Inside of the box was a pink satin nightgown with thin straps tied at the shoulder, beneath the nightgown was a matching robe—the most beautiful lingerie set she'd ever seen, elegant enough perhaps to be considered an evening gown, something that a movie star or debutante would wear, something that could only come from New York City or maybe, Paris, France.

"Try it on," he said.

"A *nightgown?*"

"Wear the robe overtop, that's perfectly decent." When Abigail seemed as though she might be considering the thought, he added, "You ought to make sure it fits."

She hesitated a moment then moved into the bedroom; when she came back she was wearing the nightgown. The romantic sound of ballroom music was coming from the radio and John was pouring a second glass of champagne.

"You're a vision," he said and gave a long low whistle.

Never before had Abigail known herself to be the object of so much admiration, it was an aphrodisiac that seeped through her skin and settled into her bones.

"A beautiful woman should always have beautiful things," he whispered; then swept her into his arms and started swaying to the strains of *Beautiful Dreamer*. The room was tiny, crowded with furniture, too small to do a waltz or fox trot even, but Abigail closed her eyes and imagined that they were at the Rainbow Room, high above the world. She hardly noticed when the music stopped and an announcer started telling listeners that Duz is the detergent that does everything.

"Merry Christmas," John said, and handed her the glass of champagne.

Although December twenty-fifth was long gone and the calendar hanging on her kitchen wall had already been switched over to 1938, it was the best Christmas Abigail had ever experienced, so when John wrapped his arms around her and pressed his body to hers, she offered no resistance. Nor, did she object when he slid his hand beneath the robe. When he whispered, "I love you," and cupped her breast in his hand, Abigail was long past remembering that she'd planned to bring up the subject of marriage.

Only once, when John untied the shoulder straps of her gown and watched it drop to the floor, did she feel afraid of what was happening, but as she offered up the feeblest of protests, he worked his way into her body.

That night she dreamed of Preacher Broody pounding on the pulpit and hammering home the message that an adulteress will forever burn in Hell's pit of fire. Abigail could see herself standing naked in front of the congregation, her body and her sins exposed. But when she woke in the morning and found herself wrapped in John's embrace, the dream was quickly forgotten.

That January John remained in Richmond for eight days, surreptitiously slipping in and out of the apartment building's side door to save Abigail's reputation, but it was she who ultimately gave rise to rumors of romance. A rosy glow settled onto her skin like summer sunburn, she'd arrive at the library late and leave early, she'd find herself wearing one black shoe and the other brown, she'd be scribbling page after page of the name *Abigail Langley* and forget about the patrons standing in line to check out a book.

"Isn't your name *Lannigan?*" Melissa Cooper asked, after she'd been waiting for a full fifteen minutes.

"It's going to change," Abigail answered with a smile.

Pretty soon, the word around town was that the librarian was in love and about to be married, but to whom people asked each other.

Abigail figured it was only a question of time until John proposed, so she set about demonstrating the kind wife she would be. She'd lock the library door on the dot of three and rush home to bake pork chops, or set a beef stew to simmering. The moment he walked through the door, she'd bring his slippers and the day's newspaper. "Sit in the easy chair and relax," she'd say, then start massaging his neck so he'd be certain to do so. After dinner they made love, and she held back nothing.

On January eleventh, as he was packing his things into the suitcase, she brought up the subject of his traveling.

"That's my *business,*" he answered with a grin. "*Traveling.* I've got to go where buildings are being built. The bank depends on me."

"Oh," she sighed, making her disappointment obvious.

"Don't frown," he said, tracing his finger along the slope of her nose, "you'll get wrinkles on that pretty forehead." He turned and walked out, promising only that he'd be back at the end of the month.

John had been there for only eight days, but once he was gone the apartment seemed so empty that Abigail was forced to walk from room to room making certain the furniture had not also disappeared. Everything was as it had always been, except for the pair of slippers left alongside the living room chair.

Abigail, feeling very much in love, floated through January and February. Although a winter storm stacked three inches of snow on the ground, she swore the lilacs were getting ready to bloom. A smile settled onto her face and refused to leave. She'd walk down the street greeting passersby as if they were lifelong friends, or stopping to tickle the chin of a snowsuited baby. John was coming to Richmond every other week, sometimes he'd stay a few days, other times it would be just one night, and then he'd be gone before Abigail could rub the sleep from her eyes. When he was there, her skin itched with the desire for him to touch her, hold her, be inside of her again. Once they'd eaten supper, she'd stretch her arms above her head and start yawning, which was her way of suggesting the need to go to bed early.

When he wasn't there, she'd be thinking of when he would be. On Valentine's Day, forgetting that he wouldn't be back for another six days, she roasted a large round of beef. That night she claimed to have heard the newspaper rustling in the parlor and John calling for a cold glass of beer, even though he was hundreds of miles away. Night after night she'd fall asleep imagining herself in his arms; but on nights when there was a full moon, she'd wake and start wondering what city he was in at that moment.

On a March day when the wind was whistling through the window and Abigail was dreamily recounting how John had given her a satin slip with lace sheer as spun glass, Gloria asked, "What about getting married? Has he said anything about that yet?"

"Not exactly," Abigail answered.

"He ought to have asked by now."

"He will," Abigail sighed, "in time, he will."

Gloria started shaking her head side to side, "Don't be too sure," she grumbled, "some men just ain't the marrying kind."

"John's not one of those!" Abigail answered indignantly, then she went on to tell about how he'd telephoned her long distance from New York City.

"Long distance ain't the same as being there," Gloria said, and it was a point with which anyone would have had to agree.

That night it was all but impossible for Abigail to fall asleep because when she tried to picture John lying beside her, the only thing she could see was a carved out indentation he'd left in the sheet.

The same thing happened the next night and the night after that. After she'd gone without sleep for three straight nights, Abigail found herself walking right by people she'd known for years without giving them so much as a nod. When Bobby Granby inquired about a book of nursery rhymes, she ignored him completely. She tossed Alice Flynn's eyeglasses into the trash basket instead of the lost and found bin. And when Gloria called to say that she'd decided to call the baby Belinda if it turned out to be a girl, it took Abigail a full minute to remember what baby she was talking about.

By the time John arrived back in Richmond, Abigail had worked a conversation through her mind, a conversation that would lead him onto the subject of marriage. "Did you miss me?" she asked.

"Of course!" He pulled her body to his and kissed her so ardently that she almost forgot the thing she was leading up to. After he planted a row of kisses from her mouth down to the valley in her bosom, he asked, "What's for supper?"

"Well, actually," she smiled in what she thought to be a most alluring manner, "I thought we could go out for dinner. Someplace fancy. Maybe that French restaurant, the one with red velvet wallpaper…"

"Not tonight. I've been on the road all day."

"But, we haven't been out in such a long time," Abigail moaned.

"I thought you enjoyed cooking for me."

"Oh, I do!" she exclaimed. "But someplace romantic would be…"

"This isn't romantic?" He came up behind her and brushed his lips across her shoulder. "Me and you, alone together? Nothing to do but make love?" As he spoke he slid his hand beneath her skirt.

"But," she sighed, "I thought maybe we could talk."

"About what?" His fingers were working their way into her panties.

"A more permanent relationship," she answered.

He pulled his hand back like he'd suddenly discovered a patch of poison ivy. "Permanent? I'm here every chance I get. I go miles out of my way. I'm supposed to be in Arlington but I drive to Richmond to be with you. That doesn't mean anything?"

"Of course it does, but you're away so much of the time."

"You think I *like* it?" he growled angrily. "I have to do it! It's my job. My territory is the *entire* eastern seaboard—you knew that when we met."

"Well, yes…"

"What did you expect?"

His voice was hard edged, so cold it caused Abigail to shiver. "I just thought…"

"Thought what? That I'd quit my job? Let you take care of me? No!" he said emphatically, "That will never happen! I've got my pride!"

His hurt settled like a stone in Abigail's heart. "I never meant to infer," she said tearfully, but by then he'd turned and walked off to the parlor. She swallowed back the rest of the conversation she had planned and went to fix supper.

When they went to bed that night he turned his back to her and Abigail could sense the falling apart of things. Nothing was going the way she'd planned. Tomorrow morning he'd probably leave and never again come through Richmond. Never again send flowers or whisper about how much he loved her.

Abigail reminded herself over and over again that he did indeed love her—he'd told her so a thousand times, maybe ten thousand times. It stood to reason that he'd balk at the thought of giving up his job. A man's job was the measure of his merit, everyone said so. Fred proposed to Gloria, but then he was an electrician who could *still* go to work each and every day. In time, she and John would be able to work it out; they'd find a way to be together, people who were in love with each other always found a way. He wouldn't have to quit traveling, she could move to New York, maybe even ride along in the back seat of his car; but if he left with a wedge of anger stuck in his throat it could be the end of everything. She reached out her hand and touched his shoulder, "John," she whispered, "I'm sorry."

He turned to face her. "I'm sorry too," he said, then eased his arm around her body. "I shouldn't have flown off the handle that way."

She shushed him with a kiss and then they made love as if no anger or hurt feelings had passed between them. "I love you, Abigail," he whispered, "I never meant to fall in love with you, but I have."

Abigail didn't hear the sound of sorrow muffled beneath his words; to her ear it was simply a declaration that he'd found her irresistible. "I always meant to fall in love with you," she answered, "I knew the day you walked into the library, that you would be my one true love." She kissed him again, softly, sweetly, with her heart soaring on wings wider than an eagle's.

"I suppose it was meant to be." He breathed a sorrowful sigh that rose into the air and splintered like frozen teardrops. At that same moment, a chill touched down on Abigail's shoulder and she moved deeper into his embrace.

By time they woke in the morning, John had slipped into an unusual mood of seriousness. He braced his hands against her shoulders and once again told Abigail of his love. "I only wish I could make you happy," he said, then disappeared out the door.

Abigail sighed—deep inside she *knew* everything would work out fine, he needed time, that's all, just a bit more time.

She waited two days before calling Gloria again. "You're wrong," she told her friend, "John is *very* much in love with me."

"He proposed?"

"Well, it wasn't exactly a proposal—but, he said he loves me and wants to make me happy. Sooner or later we're gonna get married, but with his job it's impossible for him to settle in one spot, right now."

Gloria groaned. "What hogwash!"

"No, it's not. He's on the road seven days a week."

"Nobody works seven days a week."

"Oh really? And just how many property inspectors do you know?"

"None. But I do know that when a man wants to latch onto a woman, he puts a wedding ring on her finger, job or no job!"

After Abigail hung up the telephone, she decided that although Gloria was her best friend, she had no understanding of John, so they didn't speak again until almost two weeks after baby Belinda was born and when they did, the issue of John's intentions was never again brought up. Once they resumed their friendship, Abigail went to visit most every day, except of course, when John was in town. "Look at that sweet smile," she'd coo and jiggle Belinda in the air even when it was long past the baby's bedtime.

The first time Abigail noticed the difference in her face was the day before Halloween, as she looked into the mirror and considered what type of candies she'd set out on the circulation counter. Such a thing wasn't possible she thought and wrinkled her brow. She turned to one side and the other, then leaned in so close her nose touched upon its reflection; but regardless of how she turned or angled herself, the look was still there—the same look she'd seen on Gloria's face last Thanksgiving. Her skin was the color it had always been, but glowing. Her eyes sparkled like a prism shot through with sunbeams. Her mouth was fixed into a smile and even when she tried to reconfigure it into a frown, such a thing could not be done.

"Impossible," she muttered and turned away from the mirror. She'd not missed a monthly and John had been diligent about the use of a condom. Abigail shrugged off the thought then sat at the kitchen table with her breakfast of tea and a muffin; before she'd taken a single bite, she was back at the mirror. The look was still there.

On her way to the library, Abigail bounced along the street as if she were dancing on a trampoline. Each step felt as though the next would send her soaring skyward, to pluck loose a cloud the size of a baby pillow. Pots of chrysanthemums were already lining the walkways but Abigail saw roses and daffodils, she caught the fragrance of jasmine and felt the warmth of a summer sun when the sky was drizzling rain. She imagined John tenderly touching his hand to her stomach and stating that although he'd still have to do some traveling, they ought to be married right away. Suddenly it struck her that even though she'd seen *the look* on her face, there was no other indication that she was pregnant. It would be a terrible thing, she decided, to tell John that he was going to be a daddy and then disappoint him if she'd made a mistake. It would be far better to wait—wait until she was absolutely certain.

But uncertainty didn't stop Abigail from dreaming and by the time she reached the front door of the library, she'd decided if the baby was a boy, she'd name it John, after his father. A girl, she'd name Livonia. "Livonia," she sighed as she switched on the lights, "a pretty little girl who will grow up to be just like Mama." Prompted by nothing but *the look* she'd seen on her face, Abigail spent that day and the remainder of the week reading about the care and feeding of babies; after which she went on to nine books on lullabies and seven on nursery rhymes.

The following week John came to Richmond for an overnight stay and although it was all she could do to hold back the news, Abigail said nothing. Her monthly was only two days late and twice before it had been a week late.

In the morning John kissed her goodbye and told Abigail he'd been assigned to cover Georgia and the Carolinas for the next month. "But," she moaned, "that's *so far* from Richmond."

"I know," he answered. "I'll try to get back a time or two, but please understand if I don't." After seeing the disappointment in her eyes, he added, "It's only temporary, and I'll be thinking of you every minute."

If he hadn't had one foot out the door, Abigail would have told him the news right then and there, but hollering out to the back end of his coattail wasn't the way she'd pictured it happening. He stopped for a moment and called back, "I'll bring you something special," then he disappeared down the stairs.

"I'll have something special for you too," Abigail whispered into the emptiness he'd left behind.

As it happened, the month that John was to spend in the southern states stretched into three. The weather turned cold and an unusual series of sleet storms hit Richmond, leaving the streets so icy that even the most sure-footed people were hesitant to walk anywhere. Driving was no better. In December there were a record number of car crashes and the emergency room of Saint Elizabeth's Hospital was full from morning to night. One newspaper report claimed there were thirty-two broken legs in a single day.

After Abigail missed her second monthly, she was absolutely certain of the baby growing inside of her. She started to picture a dark-haired girl curled into a comma, her face sweet as an angel's dream. Although the books said it was too soon for such a thing, she could feel the movement of the baby's tiny hands and feet. On nights when the sky was black and cold, she'd hear its whisper thin voice calling out *Mama* and she'd wish with all her heart that John could be there to enjoy the moment. "Daddy will be home soon," she'd coo over and over again to her stomach.

John telephoned eleven times during the month of December and each time he assured Abigail he'd be back soon. "I miss you more than you can possibly imagine," he told her, but it seemed small consolation for the nights of loneliness. On the twenty-third of the month, she received the red velvet dress he'd sent from Sears and Roebuck. It didn't fit because her waist had grown wider and her breasts had blossomed to almost twice their original size, but she hung it in the closet and thought about how she'd wear it for the next Christmas, when they were together as a family.

On the coldest day of January, a day when a snowstorm had buckled the telephone poles and cut off electricity to most of the city, John showed up at the door. "I tried to call," he said, "but the wires were down."

Abigail, who'd been in bed for three days with a cold worse than any she'd ever encountered, sprung to her feet and danced around as if he was the Maypole. "Oh," she sighed, "If I'd known you were coming, I'd have dressed up fancy."

"You look beautiful," he said, and kissed her.

"I'd have made a roast turkey, stuffed zucchini, a chocolate cake." That was the meal Abigail had planned for his homecoming, for the night he'd learn that he was going to be a father—everything was supposed to be perfect. Unfortunately, he'd shown up when her nose was red as a springtime tulip and there was no electricity but after three months of missing him, she didn't care. Abigail dabbed on some lipstick and hurriedly slipped into the pink satin nightgown; her swollen bosom rose up like an armload of ripe melons.

"Whew-eee," John said, "Get a load of you!" He reached over, untied the shoulder strap and started suckling her nipple; before five minutes had passed he'd slipped inside of her. Abigail wanted the intimacy as much as he did, but she'd hoped it would be slower, more stretched out and lasting.

It was hours later when Abigail whispered that she had a wonderful surprise for John. "Oh?" he answered quizzically.

She sprang from the bed and stood before him, in profile, naked, with her stomach pudged out as far as she could push it. "Notice anything?" she asked.

John's eyes widened and for a moment he seemed unable to speak.

"Well?"

"You're not..." he gasped, pointing a limp finger at her stomach.

She nodded. "I am. Isn't it wonderful?"

"Wonderful?"

Abigail had been practicing this moment for so long that the dream had settled into her head as reality and now she was blind to the look of despair on John's face, deaf to the mournful tone of his voice. "Yes," she sighed, "we're having a baby!"

"How?" he asked angrily, "how could such a thing happen? You know damn well, I used a condom. I used a condom every time."

"I suppose it was God's will," she answered.

"God's will, my ass!"

Suddenly feeling ashamed of her nakedness, she reached into the closet, pulled out a cotton dress and slipped it over her body. "You shouldn't talk that way," she said. "We may not have planned this baby, but once we're married it will be—"

"Married?" he shouted. "I told you—"

"Don't worry, I'm not asking for you to quit your job. I'll move to New York. The baby and I can travel with you from time to time. Wouldn't that be nice?"

"Are you out of your mind? I already told you we're not getting married."

Abigail was going to say she thought having a baby would change that, but the words got turned sideways in her throat and she started to sob.

"Please, don't cry," John pleaded, and took hold of her hands. "I love you Abigail, I honestly do, but I just can't marry you."

She took her hands from his and turned away, sobbing so hard that her words became almost indistinguishable, "Why not?" she moaned, "Why not?"

For a long time he said nothing, then when he finally spoke, the words were as weighted as a body dredged up from the ocean. "I have a wife and two boys in New York," he said sadly.

"No!" Abigail screamed. "That's impossible! You love me!" She whirled to face him, but by then he had turned his eyes toward the window.

"Yes," he answered, "God forgive me, but I do."

"Look at me!" she screamed, "Damn you, look at me! Tell me how you could do such a thing. I trusted you. I gave you everything I had to give." As she spoke, he continued to stare into the blackness of night, a night so cold that a latticework of ice crusted the inside of the windowpane. "How," she sobbed, "can you do this? Leave me? Leave our baby?"

"I've no desire to leave you, Abigail. We can go on as we always have. I love you but I can't marry you."

"What about the baby? Do you want your baby to be born a bastard?"

"Of course, that's not what I want." He walked across the room and placed his hands on her shoulders. "Listen," he said, "it's early in the pregnancy; you could do something. The child in your stomach is not formed yet, it has no eyes, no brain, no feeling, why, it's barely more than a seed. Get rid of it and we'll go on as we always have, just the two of us, in love with each other."

"Get rid of it!" she screamed and broke loose from his grip. "Never! Never in a hundred thousand years! I would sooner die than harm my baby!"

"Well, have it. Then, give it up. Let somebody else adopt it."

"No! Never! This is my baby and I'm going to—"

"Abigail! I love you but I cannot marry you. I cannot!"

"Then don't!" she screamed. Abigail grabbed hold of a spring coat hanging in the hall closet, the first her hand touched upon, then she ran from the apartment.

Abigail stumbled along the staircase in a blinding haze of tears. Halfway down she missed a step and would have tumbled all the way to the landing, had she not been clinging to the banister. When she ran from the apartment with her bedroom slippers still on her feet, she'd thought only of escape—were it possible, she would have willed herself to vanish, disappear into the blackness of night and drift off to another place where she could pretend the baby's father, her husband, had died a tragic death. As it was, all she could do was run—run away from the shame of a baby called *it*.

It, not son or daughter, not baby, just *it*—a *thing* to get rid of. The woman in New York was a *wife*, those babies were *sons*, but this baby was *it*. Get rid of *it*. Give *it* away.

As soon as Abigail stepped onto the sidewalk her foot skidded on a patch of ice and she went down hard; her back hit the frozen ground with such force that it set her ears to ringing and created a dizziness which made her forget where she was going. When she felt a sharp pain shoot across her stomach, she remembered the need to run, so she pushed herself up and continued moving forward, sliding each foot up a bit and steadying it before daring another move. Never had there been a night black as this, no moon, no streetlights, window after window dark, nothing but a faint candle glow in some distant building. She inched along the walkway until she caught the smell of the bridal path that cut through the park; she then made her way across the path and stepped into the frozen grass. Walking in the grass was easier, it was icy cold, it brushed against her ankles and made her shinbones shiver, but it was not as slick and treacherous as the sidewalk.

Once she had turned into the park Abigail started to feel an ache in her back and her legs grew so heavy, they had to be pushed along with lumbering lunges. Streams of tears had frozen upon her face and turned the skin raw. She was cold to the very core of her bones. She wanted to go home, crawl into her own warm bed, pull the comforter up over her head and hide for a month, maybe two months, maybe a year. But, she couldn't—not with John there. Abigail headed for the one place she could go—Gloria's apartment. It was only five minutes away if she cut across the park, ten at the most. She'd curl up in the rocking chair beside Belinda's crib and breathe in the sweet smell of a baby girl. In the morning she'd go home, after John had gone back to his wife and sons in New York.

How could he think she'd give this baby away, Abigail asked herself. How could he possibly think she'd consider such a thing? He said the baby wasn't formed yet, but he was wrong, he had to be wrong. She'd seen the baby in her dreams—a sweet little girl, dark-haired like him. A thought suddenly shivered down Abigail's spine, a thought more bone-chilling than the wind. What if John, like her father, wanted only boy babies? What if he could tell by the look in her eyes that this baby was a girl? Was that why he wanted her to get rid of the baby? "God have mercy!" Abigail screamed in a voice so shrill that it caused the ice to splinter and fall from the branches. As her cry echoed across the sky Abigail could hear the sound of her father saying he'd sooner have a three-legged pig than another girl baby.

Lost in the blackness of thought and night Abigail turned herself around and wandered in circles. On any given day she could have walked the path from her apartment to Gloria's blindfolded, she would have listened for the sound of traffic, sensed direction by the sun on her back, touched her feet down upon a stretch of flagstones and been there in less than ten minutes. But on this night, she'd walked for what seemed hours, at times losing sight of the bridal path, then finding it again but uncertain which way to turn. Her feet, she believed, were frozen and it was probably only a matter of minutes until the toes would start to drop off one by one. When she became too weary to walk a single step further, Abigail sat beneath a tree and prayed for morning. She cradled her stomach in her arms and promised baby Livonia that she would always be loved.

As soon as Abigail closed her eyes she slipped under the warmth of her comforter, downy soft, cozy as a baby bunting. She could feel herself floating on a cloud of feathers, the chill in her bones melting, her blood turning from blue to orange and then red, a blazing red, hotter than the center of the sun. When the wind tore loose a chunk of ice from the branch directly above her, Abigail never heard the crash, she never felt the shower of crystals that landed in her lap, because by then she was dreaming. She could see the baby growing into a toddler with chubby arms and legs, a smear of oatmeal on her chin. Then she saw the child as a girl, her cheeks pink as rose petals, her laugh melodious as the song of a white-throated sparrow. She saw herself sitting alongside of John, both of them with hair of silver; a flock of grandchildren gathered around, all clamoring to sit on grandma's lap. Abigail could hear God calling and she was ready to go, for she'd lived the life she'd wanted.

"Miss," the voice shouted. "Are you alright?" Angelo Lucci shook the lifeless body for a second and third time, before he heard the woman moan. That's when he knew she was still alive. He pulled the overcoat from his back and covered her with it, then he ran from the park and called for an ambulance.

That night, there were very few people in Richmond who dared venture out—a few policemen bundled in wool scarves and layered overcoats, a nurse making her way to Saint Elizabeth's Hospital for the midnight shift, a dark-haired man walking through a maze of unfamiliar streets calling out Abigail's name, and Angelo Lucci. Angelo hated the cold weather and would never have stepped foot out the door if it weren't for Lucifer, a Labrador Retriever black as the night itself, a dog that howled and clawed at the back door when he didn't get his nightly outing. "Alright, alright," Angelo had moaned as he hooked a leash to the dog's collar. He was wishing he'd listened to his wife and bought a smaller breed, a poodle maybe, or a miniature dachshund, anything that wouldn't drag him out on a night like this. Angelo pulled on two pair of wool socks and four sweaters, then he squeezed his arms through the sleeves of his overcoat. "Damn dog," he mumbled as they left the house. He tried to coerce the dog into relieving himself on the front lawn, but Lucifer was accustomed to the park and so he tugged at the leash until Angelo crossed over the street and headed down the bridal path. That's where he found Abigail; sound asleep under Lucifer's favorite tree.

John, who figured Abigail would never leave the building on a night when the temperature was well below freezing, had waited for twenty minutes, and then gone in search of her. He'd walked for an hour, up one street and down the other, calling her name, hollering out that he was sorry for the things he'd said. When frostbite wrapped itself around his feet, he turned back to the apartment building. He was standing in the kitchen and scratching his head as to where she might have gone, when the distant sound of a siren screamed through the night.

By morning, John guessed that Abigail's intention was to stay away until after he was gone, so he sat down at the kitchen table and wrote her a letter, then pulled on his coat and left.

Abigail did not wake for three days. From time to time she'd sense the coming or going of a nurse or doctor, but they floated at the edge of her world and appeared as people other than themselves. Caught up in a dream Abigail told Nurse Osterly, a woman with snow white hair and six grandchildren, to sit down and get her hair twisted into pigtails. "You can't go to school with fly away hair," she said. Nurse Osterly shook her head sadly and noted the rambling on a chart. Abigail told the orderly collecting bedpans that she could smell the roses on Ridge Road and three times she mistook the doctor for Preacher Broody. "I know," she said, "you've come to punish me for sinning."

On the fourth day, when Abigail finally opened her eyes, she had no recollection of Angelo Lucci or the ambulance ride to Saint Elizabeth's Hospital. "Where am I?" she asked the bearded face looking down at her.

"Saint Elizabeth's," Doctor West answered. He frowned at the rattling of breath coming through his stethoscope. "You've got pneumonia." He stuck a thermometer into Abigail's mouth and told her to hold it under her tongue. "I guess that was your intention!" he grumbled like a man with little patience left, "Sleeping outside in zero degree weather, it's a wonder you're not dead!"

"I didn't mean to sleep," Abigail tried to explain. "I got lost and—"

"Why didn't you have boots on? A proper coat?"

"Something happened. Something awful. I ran out not thinking—"

"Not thinking of your baby," the doctor grumbled, "that's for certain."

"My baby!" Abigail gasped. She slid her arm beneath the blanket and placed her hand on her stomach; it felt different—knotted and hard like an elbow or a knee—and, the image of a dark-haired baby curled into a comma was gone form her head. "My baby!" she screamed, "Someone's taken her!"

"Your baby's still there," Doctor West said, his voice softening to a sympathetic tone, "but, I'm afraid we will have to take it, because there's no heartbeat."

"No," Abigail moaned, "You're mistaken; you've got to be mistaken!"

"I wish I were," the doctor answered, but by then Abigail had started tearing at the bedclothes as if she'd gone mad.

She lashed out at the doctor with her arms and legs flailing. "Nobody is taking my baby away from me!" she screamed, "Nobody! Stay back or I'll tear your heart out!" She heaved a carafe at the doctor and knocked a picture from the wall. She then knocked over a washbasin full of soapy water and toppled a tray of dishes to the floor. Eventually the ruckus grew so loud that four nurses were called to restrain her long enough for Doctor West to administer a sedative.

She was given sedative after sedative for the next two days, but each time she woke up, Abigail started in sobbing all over again. The nurses, women accustomed to dealing with people in pain, agreed that they had never seen a woman so distraught as Abigail. One after the other, they'd come into the room to massage her back, adjust her pillow, or slide a spoonful of Jell-O into her mouth. On the third afternoon, when Nurse Parker discovered a pool of blood on the sheet, Abigail was wheeled into the operating room without further delay.

After they'd taken the baby from her, Abigail didn't speak a single word for five days. The doctors and nurses began to speculate that she'd suffered brain damage from prolonged exposure to such severe cold. On the sixth day, Abigail asked Nurse Bolinski if she'd be kind enough to call Gloria and see if she could come for a visit.

Despite their friendship, Abigail had never before mentioned that John slept in her bed, nor had she said a word about being pregnant. A thousand times she'd started to, but whenever the words came into her throat they turned sour, like bits of rancid food rising up. Now, Gloria, who had every right to say she'd warned against just such a thing, listened to the story without a word of reproach.

"I murdered my baby," Abigail sobbed. "That's what it comes right down to…"

"Hush," Gloria said and held Abigail to her chest tenderly as she would hold Belinda. "Blaming yourself won't bring that baby back. Sometimes awful things happen; nobody knows why."

Abigail dropped back onto her pillow, "I know why," she moaned tearfully. "That baby died because of me. Instead of thinking about her, I was thinking about myself. I killed my poor innocent baby, because I couldn't stand the hurt of hearing John say he'd never intended to marry me."

"He's the one you ought to blame," Gloria answered, but by that time Abigail had cemented the last brick into a wall around her heart with the guilt sealed inside.

Four days after Abigail came home from Saint Elizabeth's Hospital, she heard the scrape of a key unlocking the apartment door. It happened early in the evening, but she was already half-asleep and so believing it to be Gloria with yet another pot of soup, she didn't bother to get up until she heard the footsteps, familiar footsteps, heavier than Gloria's. Footsteps that stopped for a moment, then sounded in the hallway leading to the bedroom. Abigail bolted up and swung her feet to the floor but before she could reach for her bathrobe, John was standing in the doorway with a look of great concern. "Are you alright?" he asked, then without a moment's hesitation crossed the room, sat beside her on the edge of the bed and took her hand in his. "I've been out of my head with worry," he said.

"Worry?" Abigail echoed absently, "about me?"

"Of course, about you!" He gave a sigh of exasperation, "Not answering the telephone, was that your way of punishing me? Didn't you read the letter? What more can I say?" He stood and began pacing the room like an expectant father. "I've apologized every way possible. I've said keep the baby. I promised we'd find a way to make it work. I don't know how yet, but we will. I love you too much, Abigail. I love you too much to ever walk away."

"It's too late," she answered, turning her eyes from his face.

"Aren't you listening? I'll be a father to the baby, whatever it takes."

"It's too late," she repeated.

"Don't say that," he pleaded, "I've told you I'm sorry and I am—truly, from the bottom of my heart. The whole thing, you being pregnant, saying I ought to marry you, it came as such a surprise—I know I reacted badly. I'll make amends. Get a divorce, if necessary." When Abigail didn't reply, he took hold of her shoulders and turned her face to his. "Please," he begged, "don't turn away from me, think of what we mean to each other, think of what it would mean to the baby, having both parents."

"She's gone," Abigail said, her voice wavering on the edge of tears.

"What?"

"I killed our baby."

"You had an abortion?" John gasped, but upon seeing the sadness in Abigail's eyes, he, himself, answered the question. "No," he said, "you'd never do that."

Abigail spoke in a voice so melancholy it seemed to be that of a dead person. "God, forgive me," she said, "I was so wrapped up in my own hurt that I didn't stop to think about my baby. A baby, tiny as she was, couldn't survive in that awful cold. She froze to death. Froze to death inside of me. The doctor wouldn't say that's what caused her to die, but I know."

"Oh, Abigail," John sighed. He wrapped his arms around her but it was like trying to embrace a curtain or a towel, a thing that hangs limp and lifeless. "We'll start over," he said. "It can be just as it was, me and you, together. Only this time I'll be more considerate, I'll find a way to make things right."

"Right? How can you possibly make things right?"

"We'll get married. Not immediately, of course. I'll have to divorce Kathleen, and she's probably not ready for this, so it's gonna take time, but eventually—"

"What about your boys?" Abigail asked. "Will you divorce them too? Get rid of them, the way you would have gotten rid of our baby?"

"That's not fair!" he snapped, "I'm only trying to please you!"

"Please me? Please me by hurting other people?"

"Jesus Christ, Abigail," he moaned, "what do you want? Tell me. I'll do whatever you ask; just tell me what will make you happy."

She pulled herself from his grip and turned toward the window. The sky was already darkening, but far off on the horizon she could see a glimmer of lingering sunset. How greedy the red ball of sun seemed, clawing at the sky, refusing to step aside and allow the moon its rightful due. Abigail wanted to cling to John as the sun clung to the day, she wanted to feel his arms around her, feel his lips pressed to hers, and know that he'd be beside her year after year until they both grew old and silver-haired. From where she stood, Abigail saw the entrance to the park, the stone archway, beyond which was the bridal path. Nothing would ever drive out the haunting memory of that icy cold night. Theirs was a love born of sin and strewn over with lies and heartbreak, a love for which she had suffered an unjustly cruel punishment.

"Go home, John," she said without turning back. "Go home to your boys."

"Abigail, please. Can't you see I'm trying—"

"Don't. What kind of life would we have together? Do you think there's ever any joy for people who carve their happiness out of someone else's hurt? And what about your boys? You gonna have them grow up with no daddy?"

"I'll visit the boys often as I can."

"The way you do me? When you're passing through some nearby town?"

"Abigail, you know damn well, I came to see you every chance I got!"

"It was never enough. You've no idea how often I cried myself to sleep missing you. Sometimes I tried to picture the way you'd look coming through the door, but there was always a piece of you missing—an eye, an ear, an arm, always something. Now I realize it was because the whole of you never did belong to me."

"Things will change. I'll ask for a smaller territory, I'll be here more often."

"It's too late," Abigail said, "way too late."

John pleaded with her throughout the night but she stood firm in her resolve. When he said that he loved her more than life itself, Abigail turned her face to the wall so he couldn't see the flow of tears coming from her eyes. Just as the first light of dawn flickered across the sky, he pulled on his overcoat and walked out the door. Abigail stood at the window and watched him cross the street, he didn't turn back, didn't look up at the window to see if she was there. He climbed into his car and started the motor. For several minutes he sat there like he was thinking maybe he'd forgotten something, and then he drove off.

"I'll never let myself fall in love again," Abigail sobbed as she watched him go, then she threw herself across the bed and cried more tears than she'd ever dreamed a person could have. Hours later, when she staggered into the kitchen for a drink of water, Abigail found the door key she'd given John lying on the table.

That evening Abigail gathered up the fancy dresses, slips and nightgowns that John had given her and packed them in a valise along with the pair of worn slippers and a pipe he had never smoked. She could not bring herself to get rid of the things, so she closed the valise and slid it beneath her bed. Two years later, she deposited it on the doorstep of the Salvation Army.

For years after she'd seen the last of John Langley, Abigail would stretch her neck or turn full around to catch a glimpse of some dark-haired man passing by on the far side of the street. On those occasions when she'd encountered someone who walked with his swagger, or spoke in his teasing tone of voice, she'd lie awake all night, looking at the moon and wondering if she'd done the right thing in sending him away. In the dark of night, her bed seemed to grow larger, and the space that John had once occupied felt barren as the inside of her body. When morning came, Abigail would gather herself together and recall her reasons for turning him away. *Thy shalt not covet thy neighbor's husband. Thy shalt not steal. Thy shalt not lie.*

It was one thing to lay claim to the love of a man free to give it, it was quite another to steal someone from his family. Forbidden love was a sin for which Abigail had paid dearly—she had lost both her baby girl and the only man she'd ever love.

Abigail filled the years of emptiness with other children; toddlers who'd gather round in a circle as she read nursery rhymes or fables of fairies and flying elves, little boys she'd introduce to swashbuckling stories of pirates and princes, teenage girls longing for tales of romance. "Just remember," she'd say with a smile, "true love seldom comes riding in on a white horse." The girls would nod politely, but Abigail could tell, their heads were filled with the same foolish fantasies as hers had been.

In nineteen-eighty-four Abigail retired from the Richmond Library; she'd been there for forty-eight years and was hoping to make fifty as did Miss Spencer, but at seventy-two her knees were beginning to ache and her eyes no longer focused in on the clarity of words.

Four-hundred and twenty-six people crowded into the library for her retirement party—many were parents who came to the library as youngsters and then returned with their own children, so that they might also listen to the magical tales of Miss Abigail. The Mayor came along with two City Councilmen, one of whom was a woman.

Abigail, who by that time had to rely on a pair of spectacles to distinguish one face from the other, searched the room, still hoping to catch a glimpse of a tall dark-haired man lingering at the side of the crowd, waiting for a chance to step back into her life. Although she knew that by now, his hair was probably silver and his shoulders stooped as hers, Abigail still pictured him as he had been the day he walked through the library door and asked to see a city map.

In all the time they'd been together, there had been only one photograph of the two of them together—a grainy souvenir photo taken by the girl at the Tivoli Restaurant. In it, John's arm was draped over Abigail's shoulder and they smiled at each other like lovers with no fear of the future. That photograph was on Abigail Lannigan's bedside stand the day she died.

The Blind Eye of Justice

2001

erbert J. Hoggman, the lawyer Elliott retained to prosecute the civil case, was wide as a house and constantly belching—but a man rumored to be cutthroat in matters of litigation. The interrogatories started six weeks after the civil complaint was filed in Dalton County Probate Court. From the moment Mister Hoggman opened his mouth, you'd know whether he had eaten pastrami, pizza or banana blintzes for lunch because a rolling burp came with every question. "Do you have the account number for Abigail Anne, burrrrp, Lannigan's savings account?" he asked, but before Destiny could answer she had to fan the odor of fried onions from beneath her nose.

Destiny offered up the account number, but before the smell of fried onions floated off, he burped a blast of strong coffee and asked for the dollar value of the account. Elliott, who wasn't allowed to ask anything, passed a note to Mister Hoggman. *There's more money* he wrote, *ask about other accounts.* "Did she have a household fund?" Hoggman asked. "What about a Christmas Club?" It was a sorry sight to watch them badgering Destiny over nickel and dime accounts, especially since she didn't even know I had the bonds, let alone where they were hidden.

"It's my understanding," he said, "that Miss Lannigan's, burrrrp, brother realized a sizeable profit from the sale of the family farm, burrrrp, now can you detail where exactly that money has gone to?" She answered that to the best of her knowledge, the money was in my account at the Middleboro Savings Bank—then Hoggman asked the exact same thing all over again, just switching the words around.

"It's in the bank," Destiny told him over and over again, "almost one-hundred thousand dollars in the Middleboro Savings Bank!"

"The Lannigan farm sold for over a million dollars, and, burrrrp, you want us to believe a paltry one-hundred thousand is all that she had left?"

Destiny started to answer but before she could say yes, he burped again—directly into her face. She finally asked for a break so that she could go out into the hallway for a breath of air.

Once Mister Hoggman found out where my money was he went running to Judge Kensington and filed a motion to freeze the bank accounts. "Those funds belong to the Lannigan estate," he argued, "and should be held in escrow until a settlement decision is reached." It was ironic to note that when Mister Hoggman was standing before Judge Kensington, he spoke on and on without a single burp.

Two days later, Charles McCallum received a notice indicating that Judge Kensington had granted the motion. "But," Destiny exclaimed, "I won't have enough money to pay you." She suggested she could take on the Saturday dinner shift, which usually meant pretty good tips, "I'll pay on the installment plan," she said. "Twenty-five dollars a week?"

Charles laughed, "Why, that would take *years!*"

Destiny, completely oblivious to the twinkle in his eyes, sighed. "I suppose," she said, "I could sell my car."

Charles laughed again, then reached across the desk and took her hand in his. "First, let's concentrate on proving you're innocent," he told her, "then we'll worry about the money." That afternoon, after they finished reviewing the interrogatory transcripts, he took her to lunch. He hooked his arm through hers and strolled past the luncheonette, past the pizza parlor and into Stephano's—where they sat at a linen clothed table and shared a bottle of wine.

"I owe you so much," Destiny cooed in that sweet-voiced way of hers and I watched Charles McCallum's face melt into a boyish grin of satisfaction. Anybody with half an eyeball could see what was happening, and I'd already noticed that he didn't have any woman's picture sitting on his desk nor was he wearing a wedding ring. Back when I was a young woman very few men wore wedding rings so you couldn't tell if they were married or not; and I can certainly bear witness to all the heartache that causes.

The second day of depositions started off with a barrage of questions. Where was this, where was that, what about the silver coffee service which, in all honesty, never existed. Elliott was insistent that there was much more money and probably a bunch of valuables his lawyer had yet to uncover, so he continued writing notes to Mister Hoggman. Each time a slip of paper was unfolded, the lawyer would ask about another far-fetched thing. "Diamonds, maybe? Gold Bullion?"

Destiny swore that, far as she knew, I had no other assets. Elliott, making no effort to control himself, gave a loud facetious snort and Charles suggested that he be removed from the proceedings. Mister Hoggman claimed such an action wouldn't be necessary as his client had just been excising a frog from his throat, and, he assured, it wouldn't happen again.

After that they went back to the questioning and Mister Hoggman got onto Destiny's relationship with me. "Exactly *when* did you meet Abigail Anne Lannigan?" he asked and belched up the odor of pickled herring.

"Let's see now," Destiny mumbled, obviously trying to come up with an honest answer. "Six years ago. I know it was six years ago, because I met her a few months after I moved into my house." She started to tell how the newspaper was stuck on the roof, but right off Charles whispered in her ear that she should stick to the shortest possible answers, and so she left the rest of the story untold.

"And, you were employed by Miss Lannigan for that entire period?"

"I didn't work for Miss Abigail," she answered. "We were friends."

"Ah," he sighed in the most gratified manner, "so you charged one hundred dollars a month to be her *friend?*"

"I didn't charge for being her friend!" Destiny snapped.

Before she could finish what she'd started to say, he was back at her. "Then it wasn't a salary? You just used her account to arbitrarily write yourself a check for one hundred dollars every month?"

"That's not it at all. I took the money because she insisted on paying me."

"Oh, really?" He let go a rolling belch that rumbled up from a place so far down, it brought back the odor of kosher hot dogs he'd eaten two days ago. "Did Abigail Lannigan ever sign those checks made out to you?" Without giving her time to answer, he repeated, "Ever? Even one time?"

Destiny's lip started quivering. "Well, no," she answered. "That's what Miss Abigail had me do—write checks, take care of her financial affairs."

"Judging from these," he slammed a stack of bank statements down in front of her, "You took care of yourself!"

Charles jumped out of his chair so fast that at first I thought he was going to take a swing at someone, but instead he growled, "That's *not* a question!" He told Herbert J. Hoggman to stick to asking questions and keep his opinions to himself, then declared it was time to break for lunch.

"But," Hoggman stammered, "I've got more questions." However, by that time Charles had taken hold of Destiny's arm and they'd started out the door.

After lunch Hoggman picked up where he'd left off. "In December of last year," he snarled, "you were the recipient of a twenty-five thousand dollar cashier's check that was purchased with funds from the Lannigan account. Explain that!"

Destiny could tell he'd had fried chicken for lunch. She waited for the smell to pass by, and then said, "It was a Christmas present from Miss Abigail."

"Christmas present? You already stated Miss Lannigan gave you an all-expense-paid trip to Palm Beach for Christmas. Have you forgotten you told me that? Or, was it a lie?" He slammed his hand against the table. "Why don't you just tell the truth—you helped yourself to that money, didn't you?"

"No!" Destiny shouted. "I did not! It was a present from Miss Abigail!"

"Oh, really? And just what Christmas gift did you give her?"

"A silk nightgown and a feather boa."

"How generous!" Hoggman sneered as if he'd proven a point. He then stretched his jaw open and gurgled up a burp with a stench that caused the stenographer to pause and wave it from beneath her nose.

"Excuse me," the stenographer said, "could you repeat that last statement."

"How generous!" Hoggman roared sarcastically. "I was making a point of how generous this little swindler was to her victim!"

"Okay! That's enough!" Charles handed Hoggman a roll of Tums. "Either you restrain yourself from such unprofessional behavior, or this deposition is over. As a matter of fact," he said eyeing his watch, "I think my client has had enough for today—we'll stop right here."

Hoggman didn't challenge the statement, but walked out and left the Tums lying on the conference room table.

"I could use a glass of wine," Charles said, as he and Destiny left the building. "How about you?"

She nodded. She would have answered, told him that she'd like nothing better, maybe even mentioned something about how she was hoping he'd ask, but there was a tremor stuck in her throat, a squashed down moan of exasperation.

They walked east on Charter Street and before they'd gone a block, Charles linked his arm through hers. "Don't worry," he said in the most comforting manner, "you're doing fine. Depositions are always difficult. Especially with Hoggman—he works at being obnoxious."

The tremor in Destiny's throat grew larger and caused her words to sound wrinkled, folded over, stacked on top of each other. "I'm not," she mumbled, "not what he said. I never, never, ever swindled—she was...we were..."

Charles stopped walking and loosened his arm from hers. "Why would you think," he said, taking hold of her shoulders, "you need to tell *me* that?" With the gentlest touch of his fingertips he tilted her face upward so their eyes met. For a long moment it seemed as though he was going to kiss her. "I knew *exactly* what you were, the moment you walked into my office. Miss Lannigan was lucky to have you for a friend. Anybody would be lucky..." His voice trailed off, then he smiled, hooked his arm back through hers and continued along Charter Street.

It was late October, the time of year when a cool wind blows and darkness comes early, but Destiny felt the heat of summer rising to her cheeks and she could swear a sunbeam was focused on Charles McCallum's face. *Anybody would be lucky*...the words kept running through her brain, words spelled out in bright lights like a Times Square sign, a message circling around and around, a message with the tail end missing. "You said," she started to ask, and then backed off.

"I said," Charles repeated, "you're doing fine. There's nothing to worry about."

The next day Hoggman attacked Destiny on issues of where she'd gotten the money for her car, red fox coat, big screen television, and any other thing a person could possibly imagine. "I understand that you've a brand new velvet sofa," he said. "Now, just where did the money for *that* come from?"

Destiny began to wonder if maybe there was a peeping Tom outside her window, someone taking inventory of everything she owned. "Miss Abigail said it's better to pay for a thing straight out rather than on the installment plan," she answered. "So, with that in mind, I figured—" She was on her way to telling the whole story of the conversation when Charles leaned over and whispered in her ear again. She listened to what he had to say, then responded curtly, "The money came from the bank account which was given to me by Abigail Lannigan prior to her death." From that point on, she gave the same answer to almost any question Hoggman asked.

"What about the fur coat?" he repeated, and she started rattling off her statement saying that the money was given to her by Abigail Lannigan prior to death. It was like a rubber stamp, smacked down after each question.

When Hoggman finally got tired of listening to Destiny repeat the words that Charles had whispered into her ear, he switched over to asking if Abigail Lannigan had ever given her a Power-of-Attorney document.

"Why would she do that?" Destiny asked. "I wasn't her attorney,"

Elliott snickered at the answer, but when he caught sight of the mad look on Charles face, he stopped immediately.

"I know," Hoggman sneered, "that you are not an attorney, that much is *obvious!* But did you have legal authorization to make financial decisions and distribute funds from Abigail Lannigan's account?"

"Miss Abigail changed her accounts to both our names 'cause she wanted me to be able to sign checks—how much more authorization did I need?"

Charles gave her a wink of confidence, and smiled.

"Yes," Hoggman shot back, "but, did she do so of her own free will or did you, taking advantage of the fact that she was elderly and in poor health, coerce her?"

"It was her idea! She asked me to help out because she was getting forgetful."

"Was it also her idea for you to help yourself to whatever you wanted?"

Charles set his hand on Destiny's arm—his intent being to hold her back from responding to such a statement—but the silkiness of his fingertips sliding around her wrist prompted Destiny to stare at him, dreamy-eyed, like there was not another soul in the room. For a moment he lost track of himself, forgot what he'd intended, forgot, in fact, where they were or what they were there for. Not until she smiled, was he able to shake free, then he snapped, "That's an improper line of questioning!"

Hoggman, of course, claimed it was no such thing. He huffed and puffed like a boiler on the verge of exploding, but shied away from belching and eventually pulled back on the manner of questions he was asking.

His deposition of Destiny went on for another five days, the same questions over and over again—restructured, rephrased, reworked and twisted around to make them sound different, but always circling back to the issue of where the remaining money was. I had to admire the way she handled herself—not once did she tell Hoggman to take a royal crap in his hat, which is something I might have said. Instead, she sat there answering questions she'd already answered five times over, generally smiling like a person who couldn't think of a better place to be, of course more often than not, that was because Charles was squeezing his knee close to hers, or hooking his foot around her ankle.

As the days went by, Elliott convinced himself that her smile was a result of having stashed a million dollars in some offshore bank account, and he started to regret that she wasn't being tried in criminal court.

When he finished with Destiny, Hoggman hauled Doctor Birnbaum in for interrogation. At first he tried to phrase the questions in such a way that a positive answer could be construed as negative, but Doctor Birnbaum restated almost every question and thereby eliminated any doubt as to the meaning of his answer. "Well then," Hoggman blustered, twisting the doctor's words, "you're saying that Fairchild was capitalizing on Miss Lannigan's helplessness!"

"I never said that!" the doctor answered. "I said that Destiny Fairchild was a helpmate to Miss Lannigan. She acted as her companion, friend and caregiver."

"Acted! Ah-ha. So she was pretending to play the part!"

"No," Doctor Birnbaum answered, by now starting to get a bit agitated. "She was Miss Lannigan's primary caregiver, and a very good one at that."

"Miss Lannigan was quite feeble-minded at that point, wasn't she?"

"Abigail? Feeble-minded?" The doctor laughed aloud. "Obviously, you didn't know Abigail Lannigan. She could keep *you* on your toes."

"But she was forgetful, had memory lapses, right?"

"No," the doctor answered shaking his head. "No more than anyone else."

"She was taking morphine, wasn't she?"

"Only for two weeks prior to her death."

"Wouldn't that impair her judgment? Make a rational decision impossible?"

"Possibly. But, Abigail—"

"Possibly? When the woman died, she couldn't sign her own name, how could she make a decision regarding the disbursement of her estate? *Unless*," Hoggman stretched the word out as far as it would go, then he shoved his chair back and stood like the statue of liberty, "unless," he repeated, "someone coerced her!"

"You're pontificating again," Charles complained, "stick to the questions."

"The question as I see it," Hoggman said, "is—did Destiny Fairchild fabricate this entire story and did she force a dying woman to hand over her life's savings."

"Save it for opening argument," Charles moaned. "It's not a valid question."

For almost three hours Hoggman badgered Doctor Birnbaum with the same questions over and over again—was Abigail Lannigan incapacitated by drugs, was she incapable of making a decision, was she too weak to resist.

"Resist what?" the doctor asked. "She was well cared for by Destiny, and, knowing Abigail Lannigan as I did, I'm certain that any decision making she had to do was done long before the morphine became a factor."

Finally the doctor informed Mister Hoggman that his questions were ridiculously redundant and then he stood up and marched out of the room.

When he finished with Doctor Birnbaum, Hoggman called four different people associated with the Middleboro Savings Bank. The first was Martin Kroeger, the branch manager, a man so mild-mannered he'd wait five minutes before answering a question so he wouldn't be perceived as interrupting. "Isn't it true that Destiny Fairchild dragged Abigail Lannigan into the bank and forced her to transfer those funds into a joint account?" Hoggman blustered. He asked most of his questions that way—flip-flopping facts to make it sound as if Destiny *actually did* something underhanded. If the person he was badgering at that particular moment wasn't quick-witted, they'd end up nodding yes to an answer the exact opposite of what they'd intended to say.

Martin Kroeger shrugged. "I can't rightly say," he stammered. "Those accounts were changed over before I came to Middleboro. If there was wrongdoing I certainly had nothing to do with it."

"During the two years you were at the bank, did you ever *once* know Abigail Lannigan to come in alone and withdraw money from her own account?"

"Alone? I really can't say. You'd have to ask Donna Watkins or Sally Klein, they worked the teller stations."

"Did Abigail Lannigan appear to be confused, not in control of herself?"

"Confused?" Martin Kroeger himself looked confused. He twisted his mouth to one side, then removed his glasses and set about polishing the lenses, a task which took the better part of five minutes. Once he'd set them back onto the bridge of his nose, he answered, "I don't know." After that Hoggman dismissed him and went on to the tellers.

He asked Donna Watkins if Destiny Fairchild appeared suspicious, but she answered no. "Not even," he raged, "when she wrote one check after another on Miss Lannigan's account?"

Donna shook her head. "What was there to be suspicious about?" she asked. "Most of the checks were to the gas company, water company, telephone company, supermarket, ordinary places like that."

"But," Hoggman steamed, "you could see Destiny Fairchild was taking advantage of Miss Lannigan, right?"

"Advantage? Not at all. Abigail Lannigan seemed to be genuinely fond of that girl; they'd come in laughing and holding to each other like best friends."

Hoggman snorted and told Donna Watkins he didn't have any more questions. He then called on Sally Klein but as it turned out her story was pretty much the same as Donna's. By the end of the day the hairs on the back of Mister Hoggman's neck were stiff as porcupine quills.

Harvey Brown, a man who'd been the branch manager at Middleboro for fifteen years, but had two years ago moved on to the more prestigious York Federal, was the first to be deposed the next morning. Perturbed because he'd had to take time away from his job and spend four dollars for downtown parking, he'd stated, "I doubt that I can be of any help," before even taking a seat.

Hoggman ignored the comment and jumped right in. "You were the person responsible for the conversion of Abigail Lannigan's accounts to joint ownership," he growled in an accusatory tone. "Were you aware that Destiny Fairchild planned to swindle her out of everything she owned?"

"What!" Brown snapped. "You called me down here to ask bullshit questions like that? I'm a busy man!"

"Sorry," Hoggman mumbled, sensing he'd stepped across the line.

"I did my job," Brown said. "Abigail Lannigan *asked* that Fairchild's name be added to those accounts. It was *her* decision, hers and hers alone."

"But, did she seem confused, under duress at the time?"

"No. She seemed quite happy—told me it was a relief to have somebody trustworthy taking care of things for her."

"Did she know that Fairchild was going to use that money herself?"

"How would I know what she knew?" Brown glanced at his watch impatiently. "Is this going to take much longer?"

"I'm finished," Hoggman moaned. "I'll be in touch if there are any more questions."

"I'm a busy man!" Brown repeated.

There were two more days of interrogatories. Hoggman called in several clerks from the supermarket, a man who owned the local dry cleaners, and the attendant who worked in an Exxon station close by. No one offered anything that was of use to Hoggman, so he moved on to three of Abigail Lannigan's neighbors—the first two claimed they knew nothing of the relationship, except that from all outward appearances it seemed pleasant enough. The third was Mary Beth McGurke, a woman willing to say whatever Hoggman wanted to hear, for the pleasure of being in on some gossip.

"So," he said, "you actually saw the Fairchild girl removing Miss Lannigan's possessions from the house?"

"Oh, yes!" Mary Beth said, then she launched into a story detailing hundreds of different things she'd seen Destiny cart off—almost all of them pure fiction. "A six-foot tall coat rack, a three-tiered tea cart, some dishes, a soufflé pan…"

A soufflé pan? I wondered if Mary Beth was losing what scrap of common sense she might have once had. Why, I never even owned a soufflé pan—besides, anyone who knew Destiny would have realized she'd have no need of such a thing because she only made frozen dinners and chocolate chip cookies. The only truth about Mary Beth's statement was the part about the overstuffed chair and, of course, my car.

By the time she ran out of things to lie about, Hoggman was puffed up as a frog and grinning ear to ear. "Well, I suppose," he finally said, "I guess that wraps it up for me."

That night Charles took Destiny to dinner. She wore a black crepe dress that molded itself to her body as if she'd been born in it, when in truth she'd clipped the tag from the sleeve just moments before slipping it over her head. The earrings she'd chosen were the color of emeralds and made her eyes appear greener than the make-believe stones. She'd hesitated in the middle of dressing, thinking that perhaps a person who usually wore jeans would appear foolish in such an outfit, but the hour was late and rushed as she was, she stayed with the dress. She was sliding her foot into a black silk sandal when the doorbell chimed.

"Whoa!" Charles said when she opened the door. "You look great!"

She smiled.

"Really great! Fabulous, in fact!"

He'd had in mind a little Italian restaurant just minutes from the house, but as it turned out they drove back to the downtown area and ate in Trumbull Towers, a restaurant which looked down on the city—a restaurant that had music and dancing and tables lit with the tiniest of candles. He'd planned on discussing the things he'd be asking about next week when it was his turn to question Elliott, but instead he wound his fingers through hers and stared like a schoolboy. After dinner they danced to waltzes, rumbas, fox trots, and even a tango that forced them to laugh at their own clumsiness. They danced until the music stopped, then long after the trumpet player had disappeared down the elevator, they remained in the center of the floor still swaying to the strains of something only they could hear.

On the way home, Charles mentioned that next week, he'd start deposing the plaintiff, but, try as she may, Destiny couldn't imagine him belching in Elliott's face.

It's always been my belief that a no good lying snake will slither out into the open if you give it enough room—apparently that's what Charles McCallum thought also, because when he started deposing Elliott he sounded so pleasant and polite you could start to wonder whose side he was actually on. "Are you comfortable?" he'd ask, "Do you want a glass of water? Soda, maybe?"

"I understand you were very close with your aunt," Charles said in a sort of sympathetic way. "You saw her pretty often, didn't you?"

"Not real often. That one," Elliott pointed to Destiny, "wouldn't let blood relatives near Aunt Abigail. She didn't want to lose control of the old lady's money."

"When was the last time you tried to see your aunt?"

"About eight months ago."

"What happened at that time?"

"That bitch attacked me. Jumped on me like an animal—sent me flying over the living room coffee table and damn near broke my back."

"Oh, so you were *inside* Abigail Lannigan's house when this happened?"

"I don't know anybody who keeps their coffee table outside."

"Miss Fairchild didn't prevent you from entering the house?"

"No, but Aunt Abigail was dead by then."

"On earlier visits, Miss Fairchild prevented you from entering?"

"Her? Shit, she couldn't stop a dog from getting fleas. No, what she did was poison Aunt Abigail's mind—turn her against her own blood relative. I shouldn't have been begging for handouts, I was entitled to the money."

At the far end of the table, Destiny, who'd been forewarned not to say a word, kept twitching and twiddling like a nervous tick. I wanted to whisper in her ear that she ought to relax a bit seeing how Charles McCallum seemed comfortably in control of things, but being dead has a number of disadvantages, not the least of which is the inability to speak your mind.

"In what way did Miss Fairchild poison your aunt's thoughts?" Charles said.

"Ask her!" Elliott rolled his eyes and waggled a finger at Destiny again. "All I know is that when I asked Aunt Abigail for a drop of the money that rightfully should've been mine, she acted like I was trying to pick her pocket."

"You asked Miss Lannigan for money?"

"I was forced to—financial reverses and such."

"At that time, did she give you anything?"

"Not much to speak of. The old lady dolled out a measly five hundred bucks every now and again."

"So, you asked for financial assistance on more than one occasion?"

"Yeah. But I never got more than five hundred bucks. Five hundred! I should've had it all! Me! A direct descendant of William Lannigan's *first* born. My aunt didn't deserve one cent of that money, she was the tail end of the line—female, at that!"

"Why would her being a woman affect the inheritance?"

"Are you kidding? I'd have every cent of the money if my grandma's father hadn't been hung up on having a son inherit the farm."

"Then how did Abigail Lannigan get control of the estate?"

"From her twin brother! Him getting it, I could maybe understand. But her?"

"Are you then," Charles said, "contesting Abigail Lannigan's right to the estate she inherited from her brother?"

At that point, Mister Hoggman belched up the smell of pastrami and while people were fanning the odor from beneath their nose, he whispered something into Elliott's ear.

Charles had to repeat the question, then Elliott, who likely as not had been instructed on the way to answer, said, "I don't question Aunt Abigail's right to the money, but now that she's gone it ought to be passed on to a Lannigan descendent."

"And you are the only descendent?"

"Yes," Elliott answered.

"Of *all* those twelve children William Lannigan sired, you alone are the *only* surviving descendent?"

"I suppose it's possible," Elliott said, "that there could be others. Of course, there's no one who's close to the Lannigan family like I am."

"Then I take it your grandmother and your mother maintained an ongoing relationship with William Lannigan Senior?"

"Not exactly. You know women, too busy to stay in touch. I was the one who called Will Lannigan." Elliott said proudly, "The son, of course. Old man Lannigan was long dead by that time."

"So after all those years of separation, you suddenly took the initiative and called Will Lannigan?" Charles gave the question the sound of confirming an admirable trait. "What could have prompted such action—a death? Family reunion?"

"Something I saw in the newspaper."

"What was it?"

"A story about how some development company was gonna build a tract of houses in the valley on what used to be the Lannigan farm. Paid over a million dollars for the property. Part of that was rightfully mine."

Hoggman erupted like a volcano, hollering how Charles was trying to make it seem that his client had done something unscrupulous, and belching in-between every fifth or sixth word. After the fourth belch, the stenographer requested a fifteen minute break saying that she had to go out for a breath of air.

When they returned to the deposition room, Charles stated that he had every right to question the complainant about his relationship with the Lannigan family and if Mister Hoggman disagreed, he'd seek a ruling from Judge Kensington. Hoggman fumed and fretted a few minutes longer but, knowing the Judge to be a man of short temper, he eventually sat down and allowed Charles to resume the questioning.

Almost immediately, Charles went on the attack and started asking questions that got Elliott squirming around in his seat like a man with hemorrhoids. "Wasn't money," he said, "the primary reason for your establishing contact with the Lannigan family?"

"I should've been in on it," Elliott growled. "I'm blood."

"Isn't it true that you hardly ever visited Abigail Lannigan?"

"I knew she didn't want me there!"

"Wasn't that because you were always asking her for money?"

Elliott turned to Hoggman and asked, "Do I have to answer that?"

"No," Hoggman answered. "Not unless you're a mind-reader and *knew* what Abigail Lannigan was thinking!"

"Let me rephrase the question," Charles said, "How many times *did* you ask her for money?"

Elliott hesitated a long time, like he was trying to recollect the accurate number, finally he said, "Not more than a half-dozen."

"And you visited her house, what—ten times?"

"Maybe not that many."

"Eight? Six, perhaps?"

"I can't recall the *exact* number."

"How many times did you visit in the year preceding her death?"

Elliott sat there looking like a man who'd lost his memory.

Charles waited a moment then said, "Let me help you, Mister Emerson, the answer is none. And the year prior to that? Once. When you wanted money."

Hoggman, who by now was sweating like a politician on judgment day, smacked his hand against the table and said that Charles was answering his own questions. "My client doesn't have to sit here and listen to your insinuations!" he shouted.

"Your client *does* have to answer my questions," Charles snapped back, "and so far he has not been forthcoming as to the nature and depth of his involvement with the Lannigan family."

"Maybe he honestly can't remember," Hoggman grumbled. Then he grudgingly told Elliott to answer to the best of his recollection.

The rest of the afternoon was pretty much a back and forth of questions about things Elliott claimed Destiny had stolen from my house—mostly things that never existed, silver this and that, jewelry, sculptures. Lord God, I thought, *sculptures*?

"How is it," Charles asked, "that you can so accurately inventory your aunt's belongings when you were at her house only a few times?"

"I just happen to have a very good memory," Elliott answered.

"Good memory?" Charles repeated incredulously.

Hoggman suggested they break for the day. Then as soon as Destiny and Charles walked out the door, he stuck his nose into Elliott's face and started yelling that such a remark was downright stupid. Elliott didn't answer back, but he had this evil eye look, and I was hoping he'd sink his teeth into Hoggman's neck. Not much about a situation like this can make a soul happy, but seeing those two go at each other came real close.

It was easy to see that Charles was smitten with Destiny—the way he'd watch her every little movement, brush back a strand of hair from her face, smile when there was nothing to smile about—I may have become a sorry-faced old spinster, but I sure do remember how it feels to have a man look at you that way. When the two of them left the building, Charles suggested he walk Destiny to her car. He seemed to be trying to stay on the lawyerly side of himself, talking about how the deposition had gone and what-all he was planning for the next session, but before they'd gone three blocks, he had his arm snuggled around her shoulder. "Maybe we should discuss this further," he said, "are you free for dinner?"

"Uh-huh," she nodded and smiled as if that invitation was the very thing she'd been waiting for. "I was hoping you'd ask."

They walked fourteen blocks to an Italian restaurant that was so dimly lit, I'd have needed a seeing-eye dog to get to the table. It wasn't real hard to figure out that they didn't have a whole lot of working on their minds. He ordered a bottle of red wine right away, but they didn't get around to deciding on food until nine o'clock at night.

After dinner they got onto the subject of Elliott's deposition. "We should insist on a jury trial," Charles said, "he's not a credible witness, comes across as shady at best. I can show the only contact he's had with the Lannigan family was for the purpose of obtaining money. Right off, that makes him seem dislikable."

"He *is* dislikable," Destiny replied. "But he's right about Miss Abigail not wanting him around. She used to say he was a greedy man with about as much Lannigan blood as her big toe and the less she saw of him, the better."

Charles laughed, "Repeat that on the stand." He poured the last few drops of wine into Destiny's glass, then took hold of her hand. "It's not going to be all that difficult to discredit Elliott," he said, "but we're light on evidence to establish you as the legitimate heir. Our character witnesses are solid and we've got enough to prove the validity of your relationship but the lack of an actual will is going to hurt us."

"But Miss Abigail wrote—"

"Honey," Charles sighed, "that piece of paper is chicken scratch."

Destiny looked at him and smiled; she focused in on the word *honey* and ignored the rest of his statement, which to her mind were only leftover words.

The following morning Charles resumed his deposition of Elliott by asking to see the documentation establishing that he was indeed a Lannigan descendent. Hoggman had come prepared and offered up the birth certificates of both Elliott and his mother. The lineage of Margaret Louise, his grandmother, was established with a baptism certificate issued by the Chestnut Ridge Methodist Church and a copy of the handwritten entry in the Lannigan Family Bible. Hoggman spread the documents across the table and smiled. "Satisfied?" he said, his fat lips curled like overcooked sausages.

Charles asked to see the actual Bible, which Hoggman agreed to produce the following day. Shortly after, he said he was finished with Elliott and called for a fifteen minute break.

For the remainder of the day Hoggman paraded in a string of character witnesses, all of who had little or nothing to do with the case. They attested to the fact that Elliott did indeed bank at their bank, or shop at their store, and was a fine upstanding person.

"How long have you known Mister Emerson?" Charles asked the banker who seemed the most credible of the lineup.

The man answered, "Three, maybe four months."

"In that short time, you've determined him to be an upstanding citizen?"

"I've had no reason to think otherwise."

Charles shook his head wearily and dismissed the witness.

On the third and last day of depositions, Hoggman produced the Lannigan Bible. Charles spread it open and methodically copied down each and every entry.

"Do I need to make note of those names?" the stenographer asked.

"Uh-uh," Hoggman said, "he's just wasting time."

The final witness was Elliott's mother, a woman nearing ninety and so hard of hearing that Charles had to bellow to make himself heard. "Do you believe that either you or your son are entitled to a portion of the Lannigan estate?" he shouted.

"Hell, no," the woman shouted back. "Were it up to me, I'd tell that miserly old skinflint to stick his money where the sun don't shine! He wasn't no kind of grandpa, never so much as laid eyes on my face. Rot in hell with your money, old man—that's what I'd tell him."

"Are you aware that your son Elliott is filing a suit against Abigail Lannigan's estate? He claims to be the rightful heir."

"Abigail? I don't know no Abigail."

"She was the last of William Lannigan Senior's children."

"Oh. Well, if she got anything out of that miserable bastard, I'd say she deserves to hang on to it."

"Unfortunately," Charles said, "Abigail Lannigan is deceased."

"Well then," the woman sighed, "she don't have no use for the money and I suppose Elliott's as good as any to get it,"

The depositions ended at three-thirty and Judge Kensington was advised that both sides were ready to schedule a trial date.

In the months prior to the start of the trial, Charles saw Destiny two or three times a week. He'd call and say he had this or that to discuss, but more often than not they'd end up going out to the movies or some cozy little restaurant and never mention word one about the case.

When Destiny went back to working full-time at the restaurant, Charles started coming in for lunch every day and waiting on line to get a table in her section. "I've got a single at the counter," Hilda, the hostess, would say but he'd shake his head and hold onto his place in line. Once he was seated, he'd order one thing at a time to keep her coming back to his table. First it would be a soda, after she'd brought that, it would be some sort of sandwich, next he'd ask for another pickle, then a piece of pie or a single scoop of ice cream. By the time he got around to ordering coffee, he'd usually been there almost two hours.

"Aren't you tired of this food?" Destiny asked, but he just looked at her with a goofy-eyed grin and said she had the prettiest smile he'd ever seen.

About three weeks before the trial was scheduled to start, they did have an actual conversation, not so much about the case, but about the outcome. Destiny had made a home cooked dinner of spaghetti and meatballs, and then they'd settled down on her living room sofa. Charles slipped his arm around her shoulder and asked, "Not that I'm expecting it to happen, but if the judgment should go against us, will that change your feelings for me?"

She bolted to a straight-backed position, "Are you saying I *could* end up in jail?"

He laughed, "Absolutely not. This is a civil trial, it's only about the money—who's entitled to what. There's no aspect of criminal prosecution."

"Thank heaven," she sighed and cuddled herself back into the arch of his arm. "For a moment you frightened me."

"Well? Would it change our relationship?"

She looked at him with a puzzled expression, "Change it how?" she asked.

"Say you didn't get Abigail Lannigan's money, would you be angry enough to maybe stop seeing me?"

"Oh, Charlie," she said, an echo of sadness in her voice, "How *could* you think such a thing? I wasn't a friend to Abigail Lannigan because of her money; we were a tiny little family. Two people with one thing in common—neither of us had anyone else to love. It wouldn't have mattered if she was poor as a church mouse. I needed her just the same as she needed me. When I did the least little thing to make her happy, it gave me a good feeling about myself. You think *that's* about money?"

"No," he mumbled sheepishly, "but leave it up to a fool lawyer to ask."

"Don't misunderstand," Destiny said, "it's not that I don't appreciate having the money, but it's not important as having someone to love. If the judge decided to take the money and flush it down the toilet bowl, I wouldn't give a fig; but I hope Elliott Emerson doesn't get his hands on it. Miss Abigail hated the man; the thought of him having her brother's money would probably make her rise up from her grave."

I watched as he leaned over and kissed her. The look in his eye was that of a man head-to-toe in love. Believe me, I know. Being dead wipes away a bunch of heartaches but it doesn't stop a soul from remembering the good parts of love. You might think a woman my age was too old and withered to be dreaming of romance, but up until the night I died, I was still wishing John Langley would come knocking at my door.

Ten days before the trial started, Charles called Destiny and said that he had to see her right away, that very day. She twiddled the telephone cord through her fingers and smiled, "Sure," she said, "how about coming here for dinner?"

"No," he answered, "this *really* is about the case. I need to see you soon as possible. Can you get to my office this afternoon?"

"Office?"

"Yes," he answered. "Afterward we can grab a bite."

When she arrived at four-thirty, Charles was at his desk with his nose pointed toward a computer screen. "Tell me something," he said without turning around, "did you really mean what you said?"

"What did I say?" she asked.

"You said you'd rather see the money flushed down the toilet than have Elliott Emerson get hold of it." He swiveled to face her. "You mean that?"

"I suppose I do. Of course, I'd rather keep the money. If Judge Kensington decides I'm not entitled to the inheritance, it'll take me thirty years to pay off your fee."

"My fee?" Charles chuckled, "*that's* what you're worried about?"

"Yes," she answered indignantly. "Did you think our relationship was about me trying to freeload some legal services?"

"No," he laughed, "I never thought that. But," he stood, walked around to the front of the desk and took her hand in his. "I thought you knew, I took this case on a contingency basis."

"Contingency?"

"Yes. The only fee I'm entitled to is a percentage of what the court awards you. If you don't keep Abigail Lannigan's money, you don't owe me a cent." Charles was telling a lie, because he'd taken her on as a client facing a criminal charge, but he didn't want to wonder if her affection was just a feeling of obligation.

"That hardly seems fair," she sighed, "after all the work you've done?"

"That's the way lawyers work." He kissed the tip of her nose, and then moved back to his side of the desk. "Well," he said, "how about it? If the jury does find in the complainant's favor, could you live with losing the money if it doesn't go to Elliott?"

"I suppose so," she answered. "Although it would mean that you don't get anything either and that would make me feel pretty bad."

"Forget about it," he said, then he swung over to talking about the differential in the estimated and actual value of Abigail Lannigan's estate. "Hoggman claims that the Lannigan Farm sold for one point three million, and of that, almost one million dollars is unaccounted for—"

"I didn't take it!"

"I'm not saying you did. As a matter of fact, I've gone through Abigail Lannigan's accounts and can't find a trace of there ever being such an amount. You don't know of any other holdings—right?"

Destiny shook her head.

"Any bank accounts outside of Middleboro?"

"Not that I know of."

"Do you know the name of the lawyer who probated her brother's will?"

Destiny pressed her fingers to her forehead and stretched her lips into a straight line. "I think so," she answered pensively. "I remember Abigail mentioning him several times—a fine gentleman, she said, who'd done right by her. His name was, um, Culpepper! No," she corrected herself, "he came from Culpepper. His name was Bartholomew, something like that."

"Culpepper, huh?" Charles turned back to the computer and started a search of lawyers registered in the state of Virginia. He zipped ahead to Culpepper. "Babcock? Baguchinski? Bartell?"

"That's it!" Destiny shrieked.

"Scott C. Bartell?"

She nodded. "I'm almost positive, that's him."

Charles reached for the telephone. "Okay," he said, "let's see if he knows anything about this supposedly missing million."

As it turned out, Scott Bartell had gone for the day, but once Charles explained what he was looking for, the secretary promised to pull the file and have her boss return the call first thing in the morning.

The following morning, while Charles was in the middle of working up a list of Lannigan descendents, the phone rang. "Scott Bartell," the caller said, "you wanted to talk to me about the William Lannigan estate probate?"

"Yes, indeed," Charles replied, then he explained the situation and asked if Mister Bartell could detail the contents of the estate that was passed on to Abigail Lannigan.

"Hold on, I'll take a look," Bartell said.

Charles heard a click, then found himself listening to a particularly loud rendition of *Send in the Clowns.* That eventually changed over to *Pretty Mary* and finally Scott Bartell clicked back onto the line. "Sorry," he said, "it took me a while to locate this."

"Well?"

"Everything in William's estate went to his sister Abigail. There was a cash account valued at one-hundred-sixty-seven thousand and a bunch of personal effects."

"That's it?"

"Far as I can tell."

"Any securities? Bonds? Real estate holdings?"

"None listed."

"Thanks," Charles said, a smile curling the corners of his mouth. "Please send me a certified copy of the transfer."

Shortly after that, Charles placed a call to the Blackburn County Courthouse and asked to speak to the Property Registration Office.

The telephone rang seven times before a woman answered, "Justine Tyler."

"Miss Tyler," Charles said, "I'm trying to ascertain the details of a property transaction that took place in Chestnut Ridge, Virginia. The seller was William Lannigan and the buyer a land development company."

"What was the date of sale?" she asked.

"Sometime within the last ten-fifteen years."

"You want me to search fifteen years of records!"

"It's quite important," he said.

After a fair bit of grumbling, she agreed to research the transaction, but warned that he shouldn't expect a call back before late afternoon.

When Charles hung up the receiver, he went back to the list of Lannigan descendents—which now totaled one-hundred-forty-seven. One by one, he called them and asked about their relationship with the late William Lannigan, Senior. He found forty-six grandchildren, eighty-three great grandchildren, seventeen thrice removed cousins, and one elderly gentleman who could recall that his grandma's maiden name was Lannigan, but couldn't say for sure that she was a *direct* descendent of William. Charles added his name to the list anyway—what was one Lannigan more or less when they were already stacked up like firewood.

It was almost five o'clock when Miss Tyler called to inform Charles that the property in question had been sold to Malloy Brothers Development in nineteen-seventy-nine for a price of one-million and three-hundred-eighty thousand dollars. Charles made note of the purchaser's name, the date and the amount, then he sat there doodling a picture of a million-dollar bill with wings. It seemed highly unlikely that Abigail Lannigan's brother, a man who by all other accounts lived rather conservatively, could run through a cool million in nineteen short years.

From on high, I was watching as Charles sat there scratching his head and puzzling over where the money had disappeared to. Pity, I thought, my leaving behind such a mess. Here, I'd spent biggest part of my life filing things away in their exact proper spot, and then I leave with something as important as this hanging like a loose garden gate. I knew exactly where those bonds were, but

I was the only one, which didn't do anybody a speck of good since I was dead and buried.

The trial started six days later, in a small courtroom at the far end of the hall on the second floor of the County Courthouse. During the process of jury selection, Hoggman, who was no longer belching, rejected nine potential jurors, eight of those women, five young enough to perhaps be sympathetic to Destiny. The lone man rejected by Hoggman had once been robbed by a visiting nephew.

Charles rejected a grandmother who didn't think it possible for a young person to be friendly with an older woman without some ulterior motive. He also rejected an accountant who was firm on things being either black or white. His third and final rejection was that of a man who claimed his mother had been swindled out of her entire life savings by an unscrupulous nursing home attendant.

After twelve jurors and two alternates were seated, the trial began in earnest. The Judge addressed the jury first and clarified, item by item, the written instructions they had received. The plaintiff's side then presented their opening statement. Hoggman strutted back and forth in front of the jury box for almost an hour, huffing and puffing about how he could *prove* that Destiny Fairchild had embezzled funds which should rightfully belong to Elliott Emerson, the Lannigan heir. "Almost one million dollars," he said, waving his arms about as if to demonstrate the vastness of the amount, "is missing from the original estate of William Lannigan, and we will show ample cause for believing it to be in the possession of the defendant, Destiny Fairchild."

Charles McCallum's opening statement took just over fifteen minutes. He told the jurors that this was a case of a greedy relative crawling out of the woodwork and trying to take over that which was never intended to be his. "Had Miss Fairchild been callous enough to leave Abigail Lannigan's bedside to have the dying woman's hand-written will notarized," Charles said, "I would not be standing here."

At that point Judge Kensington called for a recess for lunch.

That afternoon Elliott was the first to get to tell his side of the story. Of course, he laid it on thick about how he'd been devastated because Destiny didn't let him know that his favorite aunt had become bedridden. Ha, I thought. If he'd known I was on death's door, he'd have come to call with a bottle of arsenic in his pocket. Anyway, he sat on that stand and lied so convincingly that even I almost got to believing him. Several times, he buried his face in his hands and shook as if he was sobbing, but knowing Elliott, he was yanking a hair out of his nose to produce some crocodile tears.

Hoggman's questions were not the did-you-or-did-you-not variety; instead he prefaced everything with a preamble which pictured Elliott in the most favorable light. "As a devoted nephew," he'd say, "interested only in your aging aunt's welfare, did you suspect that the defendant was interfering with your family relationship?"

Of course, Elliott swore up and down that such was the case. "Why, I'd have been at my aunt's bedside night and day, if it weren't for her!" he said, pointing to Destiny. "She kept dear Aunt Abigail in that house and wouldn't let me visit!"

"I see," Hoggman would say, stroking his chin thoughtfully. "And, as a devoted nephew, a true descendent of Lannigan blood, interested only in the wellbeing of your aunt, did you repeatedly try to visit, only to be turned away?"

"Oh yes," Elliott swore, "repeatedly!"

"And, as a devoted nephew, concerned only with..."

Pretty soon, everybody in the courtroom had grown weary of hearing the same thing over and over, so the tenth time Hoggman started, Charles jumped to his feet and exclaimed, "Your Honor, this rambling is preposterous, a waste of the court's time!"

"I agree." Judge Kensington fixed a firm eye on Hoggman and told him to stop pontificating and get on with whatever questions he had left."

Hoggman then moved on to the issue of Elliott Emerson's lineage and introduced into evidence copies of birth certificates, baptismal certificates and the Lannigan Family Bible. After that, Charles McCallum started his cross-examination.

"Isn't it a fact," Charles asked, "that neither you nor any member of your family had any contact whatsoever with William or Abigail Lannigan until you learned that the family farm had been sold for over one million dollars?"

"I suppose we might have lost touch there for a while," Elliott answered.

"When you spoke to William Lannigan, just after the sale of the farm, didn't he say he'd never before heard of you?"

"Well yes, but he was still happy I'd come around to make his acquaintance."

"Did he ask what prompted you to contact him at that particular time?"

Elliott nodded sheepishly.

"Mister Emerson, please give an audible answer for the court record."

"Uh, yeah," Elliott mumbled.

"What reason did you give William Lannigan?"

"Um, I didn't know his whereabouts until I saw his name in a newspaper article." Elliott squirmed in his seat as if he'd suddenly discovered himself sitting on an anthill.

"What exactly was the context of that article?"

"I don't recall. I've got a rather poor memory."

"Mister Emerson, didn't you in the interrogatories state that you had an exceptionally good memory?"

"I don't know if I did or not." Elliott swiped his hand over the line of sweat that had popped up on his forehead.

"Would you like me to read that discourse back to you?" Charles asked.

"It's not necessary," Elliott answered, "I think I remember saying such a thing."

"Can you also now recall the article that prompted you to contact William Lannigan or would you like to see a copy to refresh your memory?"

"It's coming back to me now. It was, uh, something to do with houses being built over in the Valley, where the Lannigan farm used to be."

"Didn't the article state that the Malloy Brothers Development Company had paid William Lannigan one point three million for that land? And, didn't you say in the interrogatories that part of that money should have been rightfully yours?"

Elliott nodded but he was starting to look green as a man with food poisoning.

"Please give an audible answer for the court record," Charles repeated.

When Charles finished hammering home the fact that Elliott was only interested in his Lannigan heritage after the family had come into some money, he moved on to Elliott's claim of trying to visit me. "Approximately how many times in the past three years have you visited Abigail Lannigan?" he asked.

"I've lost count," Elliott grumbled.

"How many times in the year prior to her death?"

"I can't remember."

"It appears," Charles said, turning to the jury, "that Mister Emerson has a somewhat selective case of amnesia."

Hoggman immediately jumped to his feet, "I object!" he shouted, but by then several jurors had already taken to snickering.

Charles said, "I apologize, Your Honor," before Hoggman had a chance to pursue the issue any further. He turned back to Elliott and resumed his questioning. "Mister Emerson, may I remind you that in the interrogatories you stated that you had visited Abigail Lannigan's home only six or eight times and on each occasion it was for the purpose of obtaining money. Was that a true statement?"

Elliott sensing the weight of his words swinging back to punish him, mumbled, "I suppose so, as best I can remember."

"And isn't it true that Miss Fairchild never once interfered with those visits?"

"That is not true!" Elliott shouted. "Last time I was there she knocked me over the coffee table and almost broke my back."

"Why did she attack you on that occasion, when she'd never before interfered?"

"Maybe I caught her on a bad day."

"Could it have been," Charles asked, "because you said the news of Abigail Lannigan's death was what you had been waiting for? And, didn't you also refer to your aunt as the old witch who prevented you from getting what was rightfully yours?"

"I never said that!"

"What if I told you the defendant has a recording of this very incident?"

"Well, I might have said the words, but I didn't mean it the way you're making it sound." Elliott's face was as hot and puffed as a boiled dumpling.

At that point, Charles told Judge Kensington that he was finished for now, but would like to reserve the right to recall the witness for additional cross.

As they left the courthouse for the day, Destiny looked at Charles with a bewildered expression, "It's true that Elliott said those things about Miss Abigail," she confided, "but I never had a recording of it."

He smiled sheepishly. "Oh, no? Well then, I must have been mistaken."

The second day Hoggman called Albert Friedlander, the chief accountant for Malloy Brothers Development. "In nineteen-seventy-nine," he asked, "did your firm purchase a parcel of land in Chestnut Ridge, Virginia, from William Lannigan?"

Albert Friedlander, a timid man with frightened eyes peering from beneath an overhang of grey brows, answered, "Yes, sir."

"What was the purchase price?"

"One million, three hundred thousand and eighty dollars, sir."

"That was the amount of the check that William Lannigan received?"

"Yes, sir."

"Was any part of the purchase price designated as the payout for an outstanding mortgage on Mister Lannigan's property?"

"No, sir."

"So," Hoggman took a deep breath and hiked his shoulders up another inch, "far as you knew, William Lannigan was entitled to keep every cent of the money."

"I'm sorry, sir," Friedlander apologized, "But, I can't honestly say. I've only been with Malloy Brothers Development for three years. What a person did with the money we paid for a property is not something that would be written in our books."

Hoggman gave the man a disgusted grunt then turned him over to Charles for cross.

"No questions," Charles said, and Albert Friedlander hurried from the courtroom.

Hoggman's next witness was Martin Kroeger, the Branch Manager at Middleboro Savings and Loan. He showed up carrying an armful of file folders and testified that he was indeed familiar with Abigail Lannigan's accounts and knew Destiny Fairchild. "Miss Lannigan added Miss Fairchild's name to her accounts three years prior to her death. She submitted this request." He pulled a slip of paper from the topmost folder and handed it to Hoggman. "See, it directs the bank to add Miss Fairchild's name to both of the accounts and restructure them so that either party could write checks or withdraw funds."

"An old woman suddenly signing her accounts over to someone who was in no way related, didn't that make you suspicious?"

"I didn't handle the transaction; I've only been at this branch for two years."

"Since the conversion almost every check drawn on the account was written by Destiny Fairchild, are you suspicious now?"

"Objection!" Charles declared. "Whatever suspicions Mister Kroeger may or may not have, has no bearing on the facts of this case."

Judge Kensington rapped his gavel once. "Sustained."

"Let me then ask," Hoggman huffed, "who wrote the majority of checks on this account?"

"Miss Fairchild." Kroeger handed a thick folder to Hoggman, "Here's a master printout and a copy of every check. Miss Fairchild wrote almost every check, but there were a few written by Miss Lannigan."

"And to whom were the checks written by Miss Lannigan, made payable?"

"Mostly, Miss Fairchild."

"Ah," Hoggman said with the greatest of pleasure, "So, Miss Fairchild was taking the money out with both hands."

"Objection!" Charles shouted.

Judge Kensington instructed the jury to disregard the statement, then turned to Hoggman and told him to watch himself.

The admonished Hoggman turned back to his witness, "Please tell the court," he said, "what is currently the remaining balance in Abigail Lannigan's accounts."

"Both accounts, checking and savings, total one-hundred and fourteen thousand dollars and seventy-six cents."

"Have you any idea what happened to the one million dollars that is presently unaccounted for?"

"Me?" Kroeger's eye started to twitch.

"Yes. Six years ago, Abigail Lannigan inherited her brother's estate, which according to all indications should have been worth substantially over a million dollars and now you are telling the court that the total of her accounts is a mere one hundred and fourteen thousand. Can you explain that?"

"Not me." Kroeger said nervously. "I've only been at the bank for two years, and there's no record of such an amount ever being in Miss Lannigan's account. I've got all the files, and there's no record of anything close to that amount."

"Is it possible that Miss Fairchild got it away from Miss Lannigan before she had a chance to deposit it?"

"Objection!" Charles shouted, "Your Honor—"

"Sustained." Judge Kensington rapped his gavel twice. "Mister Hoggman," he said, "persist in this line of questioning and I'll find you in contempt of court."

"I'm finished with this witness," Hoggman said and sat down.

Charles stood and approached Kroeger, who by now was blinking like a firefly. "Mister Kroeger," he said, "You've obviously come here well-prepared."

Kroeger nodded and the blinking slowed a bit.

"I see on this master printout," Charles said, opening the folder which Hoggman had introduced into evidence, "that you have recapped the checks, not only by date, but also by the payee to whom the check was issued. Quite thorough."

Kroeger smiled and nodded again.

"For the court's edification, please read off the names of the payees who were the most frequent recipients for the checks written by Miss Fairchild."

Kroeger took the folder and read down the list. "City Gas; Public Utility Electric; Bell Telephone; Bountiful Basket Market; Hartford Insurance Company; Doctor Allen Birnbaum; Drug Emporium; want me to continue?"

"I think we've heard enough," Charles said. "Judging by this list, would you say the checks written by Miss Fairchild were basically standard household expenses?"

"That's pretty much what it appears to be." By now Kroeger wasn't blinking at all. "Except," he said for the checks made out to Elliott Emerson and Destiny Fairchild."

"Tell us about those."

"Emerson got one for two-thousand dollars, signed by Miss Lannigan and he got six for five hundred, signed by Miss Fairchild. She got a monthly check for one-hundred but those were mostly signed by Miss Lannigan. Of course, they were written before Miss Lannigan's death."

"Since Miss Lannigan's demise, has there been a drastic difference in the nature of checks drawn against the account?"

"Not a whole lot," Kroeger answered. "Miss Fairchild did issue a check to the Panderelli Funeral Home for twenty-eight thousand and another one to Loony Louie's Automobile Dealership for thirty-two thousand; then there were a dozen or so to various department stores, those were for much smaller amounts, other than that, it was pretty much the same as always."

"Thank you, Mister Kroeger," Charles said, and sat down.

For the remainder of the afternoon, Hoggman introduced a string of character witnesses, who paraded in and out of the courtroom without testifying to much more than the fact that they knew Elliott Emerson. By ten minutes after three, Hoggman had run through his list of witnesses and informed the Judge that he was ready to rest. "Very well," Judge Kensington said, "we'll adjourn for the day. The defense can start their presentation tomorrow morning at ten."

When Destiny left the courtroom, she looked frazzled as a person who'd stuck a finger in a live light bulb socket; Charles on the other hand had the grin of a man without a care. There they were, her with her forehead wrinkled as a washboard and him whistling a tune. At first, I thought he was being awfully callous about the whole thing, then I realized what he was up to and the smile on my face could have set the sun to shinning if it wasn't already.

"I'm really nervous about testifying tomorrow," Destiny said.

"Don't be," Charles told her, "just tell the jury what you've told me."

"But Mister Hoggman…"

"He's a tub of hot air."

"Maybe so, but he'll make it look like I'm lying."

"He'll try, probably. But, trying and doing are two different things. Hoggman's arrogant, pushy—if he leans on you too hard, the jury will see him as a bully."

"I'm still nervous."

"Don't be," Charles repeated. "The only thing this trial can decide is whether or not you get to keep Abigail Lannigan's estate. If you don't, you don't." He traced two fingers across her forehead. "Get rid of that frown," he laughed and began talking about how they were going to the fanciest restaurant in town for dinner.

The Palace Garden was the sort of place where husbands took wives to celebrate special anniversaries or to make amends for some unforgivable thing they'd done. The room was lit only by candlelight and tuxedoed waiters swished in and out so discretely that people would sometimes wonder how a piece of cake or glass of wine had come to be in front of them. "Ah yes, *Mister McCallum*," the maitre de said knowingly, and then he led the way to a table nestled in the corner, a table where a scarlet rose was artfully angled across one plate. "Please," he said, and slid the chair out for Destiny.

"Oh my," she sighed, apparently forgetting her concern over the trial.

Charles sat, then stretched his arm across the table and twined his fingers through hers. "The luckiest day of my life," he said, "was the day you walked into my office."

"I'm the lucky one," she answered.

I do believe a circus monkey could've started dancing a jig in the middle of the table and they'd never have taken notice, they were just too wrapped up in each other. Charles began talking about how he was thinking of taking a trip to visit his folks in Atlanta and asked Destiny if maybe she could come along to meet them. Hearing that did my heart good, because an ill-intentioned man such as John Langley never mentions meeting his family, he mostly talks about how hungry he is for your kisses. Looking back, such a thing is easy to see, but at the time I was so crazy in love, I wouldn't have believed The Lord God Himself, if He'd told me I was headed for a lifetime of heartache.

Over the years, I cried a million tears for my lost baby girl and, wrong as it might have been, I loved John till the day I died, which I suppose was my punishment for having loved him in the first place. Pastor Broody used to say the Lord was a forgiving God and I believe that's the truth; although I did a lot of suffering, He sent me Destiny who was as close to a daughter as I might ever wish for. John was never mine to be had, and nothing on earth would have changed that, but seeing Charles so much in love with Destiny gave my heart the happiness I'd missed out on. *Thank you, Lord,* I whispered, knowing the words would find their way into God's ear.

After dinner, Charles asked if Destiny had given any thought to what she might do after the trial was over. "It's hard to say," she laughed, "if I lose my house and the Thunderbird, I'll be riding the bus and trying to find an apartment."

"I don't mean right after the trial," Charles said nervously, "I'm talking about the rest of your life. Have you given *that* any thought?"

"Rest of my life?"

"Oh hell," Charles moaned as he fumbled to open the box in his pocket, "I'm trying to propose, but obviously doing a terrible job of it." He clumsily pried the ring from the box and reached out for her hand. "Destiny, I love you with all my heart," he said, "It would make me the happiest man on earth if you'd marry me."

"Oh Charles," she sighed, looking down at the ring but not offering her finger. "I love you too—more than words can say—but this isn't the right time. I think when the jury sees Miss Abigail's will, they'll believe I'm telling the truth, but what if they don't? What if they decide Elliott should get everything? He's claiming I've got a million dollars hidden away—that's more money than I can ever hope to repay. I can't say I'll marry you with the threat of that hanging over my head."

"Marriage is for better or worse," he answered, "whatever happens, happens. It's important that we talk about this now, because I don't want to ever question whether or not your answer was predicated on the outcome of the trial—and, more importantly, I don't want you to ever wonder whether I wanted you or Abigail Lannigan's money."

"But, what if I lose?"

"Will that change the way you feel about me?"

"Of course not!" she answered. "It's just that…"

"Better or worse," he repeated.

She smiled a smile that sent a glow of happiness clear up to heaven, then she extended her left arm across the table and offered him her finger. "There's nothing in the entire world," she sighed, "I want more than to be married to you."

The following morning when Destiny promised to tell the whole truth and nothing but the truth, there was a gleam in her eyes that out-sparkled the diamond on her finger. A person blind from birth could have seen she was in love and paying way more attention to her lawyer than the questions he was asking.

Charles on the other hand, was trying to pull from her the story as she'd told it to him. Finally, he said in desperation, "Please, Miss Fairchild, in your own words, tell the court the nature of your relationship with Abigail Lannigan." As it turned out, that was the right thing to ask, because Destiny opened up like a daisy in sunshine.

"We were close as sisters," she said. "There wasn't anything I wouldn't do for Miss Abigail and nothing she wouldn't do for me. When I moved into the house with not a nickel for furniture, she gave me a whole bunch of stuff."

Knowing what her answer would be Charles asked, "You mean she *bought* the furniture for your house?"

"No. It was mostly things she didn't use. We hauled them up from the basement, the two of us. I carried most everything, but Miss Abigail helped with the table and recliner—you know, big things that were hard to maneuver around the corner."

"Did you pay for any of this furniture Abigail Lannigan gave you?"

"Not with money," she answered, "but, I cleaned her house, ran errands, took her places she had to go, things like that." Destiny gave the most nostalgic sigh, and then said, "That's how we became friends." After that she didn't need a lot of prodding to tell about things we'd done. When she went on to tell how we'd planned to swim naked in the ocean, Eleanor Farrell, a housewife sitting in the front row of the jury box, was grinning like a person who might have considered doing such a thing herself.

Eventually Charles moved on to the issue of my will. "When Abigail Lannigan wrote what was intended as her last will and testament," he asked, "couldn't you see that the handwriting was totally illegible?"

"No," she answered. "Miss Abigail put it in the drawer; I never saw it."

"Weren't you curious? Here, she'd indicated that you, not a blood relative, were to inherit her entire estate—didn't you want to safeguard that inheritance, check to make certain the document was legal, maybe have it notarized?" Charles' question sounded almost harsh, but he was pushing her to tell the story as he'd first heard it.

"She tried to show me what she'd written, but I wouldn't look," Destiny finally said, her voice thin and weighted down with sorrowful memories. "I told her I wasn't interested in seeing it, because I didn't believe she was going to die."

"What was Miss Lannigan's reaction to that?"

"She put the paper in the nightstand drawer and told me when I was ready to face the fact of life and death; it would be there for me."

Then Destiny started sobbing like her poor little heart was going to break, so Judge Kensington called for a fifteen minute recess. When they returned to the courtroom, Charles focused on questions about household expenses, various checks that had been written, bank accounts, and whether or not she had any knowledge of the money that was allegedly missing. Of course, Destiny said she'd never known me to have that much money, and if I had, she'd no idea where it could have gone to, which I assure you was the absolute truth.

After Destiny had adequately accounted for every dime she'd ever spent, Charles went on to asking about my relationship with Elliott. When, straight-faced as a judge, she started telling how I'd said nobody who claimed to be a Baptist could ever be a Lannigan, the jury snickered—all except for Herman Cohen, a crotchety old fart who'd insisted on being the jury foreman. Once Destiny finished going over the rest of what I'd had to say about Elliott, Charles told the judge he had no further questions and asked if that might not be a good time for a noon recess.

After lunch, Hoggman started an antagonistic cross-examination of Destiny. "Do you honestly expect this jury to believe," he sneered, "that you and eighty-eight year old Abigail Lannigan were like *sisters*?" Before she could answer, he thundered on, "That you had *no* designs on her money? That your intention was *not* to swindle Elliott Emerson out of his rightful inheritance? That you—"

"Objection!" Charles said. "Your Honor, he's badgering the witness, pounding her with suppositions and not allowing time for an answer."

"Sustained," the judge said and gave Hoggman a hard glare.

"Sorry, Your Honor," Hoggman mumbled and then went back to his questioning. After almost an hour of picking at every aspect of our relationship, he asked, "Miss Fairchild, before you sought out Abigail Lannigan you knew that she had come into a sizeable inheritance, didn't you?"

"No."

"There is reason to believe you did. In fact, Elliott Emerson believes that you not only knew about the money, but worked to turn Miss Lannigan against him so that you alone would inherit the entire estate."

"That's not true, I never—"

"After Miss Lannigan's demise, did you try to sell the house or probate the handwritten will to claim your inheritance?"

"No."

"Of course you didn't, because you knew that so-called will would never hold up in court! In fact this entire story is nothing but a giant fabrication, isn't it?" Hoggman turned to the jury and gave the smug grin of a man who had proven his point. Herman Cohen, the self-appointed foreman nodded as did two other men sitting in the front row.

"That's not why," Destiny answered tearfully, "keeping Miss Abigail alive was more important to me than having her money. If I cashed in the accounts and sold her house, she'd be gone from my life. So, I kept the house and made believe she was asleep in the bedroom." She twisted the left side of her mouth into a sad sort of half-smile, "Sometimes I'd forget it was just pretend and make two pork chops for supper or hesitate to turn on the television set because it might wake her."

"Oh, please!" Hoggman sneered with an air of disbelief, but by then, Eleanor Farrell and Francine Walker—a woman with two kids and a deadbeat husband at home—already had tears rolling down their cheeks.

Seeing the jury's sympathy slide over to Destiny, Hoggman moved on to questions about the money and where exactly the million dollars had gone to. After she'd said a number of times that she knew nothing of the money, had never seen it, nor had ever known Abigail Lannigan to have it, Hoggman exclaimed, "Are you asking this jury to believe *all that money* just disappeared, vanished into thin air?"

"Objection!" Charles said but right away Hoggman jumped in, claiming that Destiny was a hostile witness and he had the right to treat her as such.

"I'm not the least bit hostile!" she snapped back at him.

"Enough!" Judge Kensington said and rapped his gavel. "The objection is sustained, now move on Mister Hoggman."

"You claim to know nothing of the money, but since Miss Lannigan's death, you've purchased a new car, new furniture, extensive amounts of clothing, where did the money for those things come from?"

"Out of Miss Abigail's account, but she'd said that money was mine."

"Oh really? Well, if you believed that money to be rightfully yours, then why didn't you at least present the will for probate so a court could verify it?"

Destiny shrugged.

"You have no answer, do you? That's because you knew all along that the money should have gone to Elliott Emerson, a true Lannigan heir!" When Hoggman saw six nodding heads in the jury box, he said he had no further questions for the witness and court was adjourned for the day.

The next day started with a lineup of witnesses testifying as to the nature of Destiny and my relationship. Dear old Doctor Birnbaum was first and he told how she was right there by my side every time he saw me. "I've never known a more dedicated caretaker," he told Charles. Then when Hoggman tried to twist those words around and make it seem that Destiny was a person who did little more than drive me to and from his office, Doctor Birnbaum told how she'd cried like a broken-hearted baby the day we found out I had pancreatic cancer.

They say if you live long enough, you'll have seen it all, but I was pretty amazed when the four Bountiful Basket clerks, three Middleboro Savings Bank tellers and Harvey Brown, the Branch Manager I used to deal with, all showed up to tell the truth of how things were. Every one of them put their hand on the Bible and swore to God that I treated Destiny like she was my own child and that she took care of me as kindly as any daughter would have. When they finished up, Scott Bartell, the lawyer who'd helped me settle up my brother's estate told exactly how much I'd gotten. "One-hundred and sixty-seven thousand dollars," he said. Of course, he never knew about the bonds Will had hidden in Papa's Bible—thank heaven for that, I thought.

At one o'clock Judge Kensington called for a lunch recess.

Destiny was trying to force down a chicken sandwich when Charles told her he thought Herman Cohen and the two men sitting alongside of him were sympathetic toward Elliott. "I'm pretty sure we've got five jurors on our side," he said, "but the other four, I'm not sure about. We could be looking at an even split, which would mean a mistrial."

"Then what?"

"We do it all over again."

"Oh no," Destiny moaned.

"There's one other alternative—a strategy that can probably prevent Elliott Emerson from getting the money, but it doesn't do anything to help your case."

"Do it," she answered, willfully. "Do whatever you can to keep Elliott from getting his hands on Miss Abigail's money."

At two-fifteen when the court reassembled, Charles said he would like to recall Elliott Emerson to the stand for additional cross. The bailiff reminded Elliott that he was still under oath, then Charles started his questioning.

"You've petitioned the court to name you as beneficiary to Abigail Anne Lannigan's estate based upon the fact that you are a direct descendent of her father, William Lannigan Senior, is that true?"

"Yes," Elliott answered apprehensively.

"The great grandson of William Lannigan?"

"Yes."

"If being a direct descendent gives you a legal right to the estate, then may I assume that other relatives—children, grandchildren, great grandchildren would have the same right?"

"Do you see any other relatives in this courtroom?" Elliott answered angrily. "There's only me. I'm the one who ought to get the Lannigan money."

"You've made certain that there are no other relatives in this courtroom," Charles said, "but there *are* other Lannigans. Your sister, Felicia, for example; fourteen first cousins who went to high school with you—including yourself, there are one-hundred and forty-eight Lannigan descendents alive today."

"I object!" Hoggman shouted.

"To what?" Charles asked, "The fact that William was such a prolific man?"

Everyone in the jury box, including Herman Cohen chuckled.

Judge Kensington banged down his gavel. "Approach the bench," he said. "Now just what is it, that you're objecting to?" he asked Hoggman.

"This wasn't mentioned in discovery."

"He's your client," the judge growled, "it's up to you to find out the facts. Objection overruled."

"Back to the Lannigan descendents," Charles said, "there are forty-six grandchildren, eighty-four great grandchildren, one of whom is Felicia, your sister. There are also seventeen cousins. Are you planning to share the Lannigan estate proportionately with all of them?"

"They don't deserve to get anything," Elliott said, "they were never close with Abigail Lannigan."

"Judging by the testimony given here," Charles replied, "neither were you." He then turned to the judge and said, "The defense rests, your Honor."

Judge Kensington rapped his gavel, "The court will hear final summations at nine-thirty tomorrow and I would strongly recommend that both sides limit themselves to forty-five minutes."

Hoggman began his summation bellowing like a cow in labor; he claimed the facts had proven beyond a doubt that Elliott Emerson, the great grandson of William John Lannigan, was indeed the rightful heir to Abigail Anne Lannigan's estate. He made sweeping gestures with first one arm then the other as he ticked off item by item every fragment of testimony that was marginally favorable to Elliott. He focused on discrediting Destiny and never once mentioned that there were one-hundred and forty-seven other Lannigan descendents. "The scrap of paper which the defense would have you believe to be Abigail Lannigan's will is laughable!" he said. "Why, the defendant herself could have scribbled those lines in an attempt to give credence to the preposterous claim of being the sole beneficiary. Then, there is the issue of the missing money—*one million dollars*—which she claims to know nothing of. I don't for one minute believe that such a huge amount of money just vanished into thin air. Nor do I believe that Abigail Anne Lannigan intended that scrap of paper to be her last will and testament! The truth of this matter is that Abigail Lannigan died intestate, and without the existence of a duly executed will, therefore, her estate by law belongs to surviving relatives."

After the summation had rambled on for close to an hour, Judge Kensington coughed loudly and pointed a finger at his watch. "Ladies and gentlemen of the jury," Hoggman quickly concluded, "I trust that you will see through Destiny Fairchild's scam and award Elliott Emerson, the estate to which he is legally entitled."

After a fifteen minute recess, Charles started his summation in a voice which, in comparison to Hoggman, seemed outright friendly. He thanked the jurors for their time and attention, then promised to keep his summation short which brought smiles from several members of the jury and a favorable nod from Judge Kensington. "We've all had special relationships in our life," he said, "relationships that are not according to bloodline, but born of the heart. Such was the type of relationship that existed between Abigail Lannigan and Destiny Fairchild. This is a fact attested to by the people who saw them together day after day—grocery clerks, tellers, and Miss Lannigan's own doctor. The two women loved each other like mother and daughter, not because of a predestined family relationship, but because of a special bond that grew to be stronger than an umbilical cord. On her deathbed, Abigail Lannigan scribbled out what she intended to be her last will and testament; now Miss Fairchild could have rushed out for a notary to witness the document and insure that it would hold up in court—but she didn't. She chose to stay by Miss Lannigan's bedside and take care of her. That's not the behavior of someone who's eager for the money—that's the behavior of a woman who is distraught by the impending death of her closest friend."

Charles lowered his voice and took on a hard-edged tenor. "On the other hand," he said, "Elliott Emerson had no interest whatsoever in Abigail Lannigan. His only interest was in her money. He never once went to see his aunt without asking for money. In fact, his visits were so infrequent that he didn't learn about her death until almost eight months after it happened. Abigail Lannigan disliked Elliott Emerson because she saw him for what he was—a man with a greed for money. Greed, so overwhelming that he covered over the existence of one-hundred and forty-seven other Lannigan descendants, one of whom is his own sister. Mister Hoggman would have you believe that Miss Fairchild is a person looking to benefit from the death of her friend; in fact, he has insinuated that she somehow managed to hide away one million dollars. Yet, we've heard testimony stating that the actual amount of the estate Abigail Lannigan received was nowhere near such an amount. If that money was never in Abigail Lannigan's possession, it stands to reason that Miss Fairchild could not have taken it."

Charles hesitated for a moment, letting the thought settle in with the jurors, then he continued. "Ladies and gentlemen of the jury," he said, "I ask you to do as Abigail Lannigan would have wanted—award her friend and companion, Destiny Fairchild, the estate as was intended. Please do not allow this plaintiff to profit by his greed. His right to the Lannigan estate is no greater than the one-hundred and forty-seven other descendants, none of whom are seen here today. You cannot, in good conscience, award Elliott Emerson the Lannigan estate, without decreeing that every one of the other descendants is likewise entitled to a share. "

Judge Kensington then told the jurors that they were to consider the facts in evidence and render a decision for either the plaintiff or the defendant. "You may," the judge said, "make monetary recommendations for distribution of the estate assets, in total or in part, and you may also make a recommendation for any restitution you deem appropriate."

How ironic, I thought, twelve people who didn't know a thing about me, were going to decide whether or not Destiny could keep the money I'd given her. I could tell that three or four women on the jury would say right off that she ought to have every last cent, but I was also pretty sure Herman Cohen would argue the point. Now that Destiny was engaged to Charles, I wasn't worried about her anymore, so when the two of them left for lunch, I stayed behind and listened to the jury argue about who ought to get what.

Herman Cohen claimed that since he was the foreman, he should be first to state his opinion. "I say Mister Emerson should get the whole ball of wax," he told everyone emphatically. "He's a blood relative and that's good enough for me."

"Well it's not good enough for me," Eleanor said, and several others echoed the same sentiment. They went round and round for a good twenty minutes, nobody agreeing on anything, then the blond woman in the polka dot blouse spoke. "That Emerson fella is a phony," she said. "I'll bet my dog's ass there ain't a word of truth in what he's said."

"Oh yeah? Herman Cohen grumbled, "And, you're an expert?"

"Yeah, I'm an expert!" Blondie snapped back. "I been tending bar for fifteen years and can spot a phony before they stick a foot through the door."

"He has got shifty eyes," one of the men conceded.

"He's also got a birth certificate that *proves* he's a Lannigan!" another argued.

"So what!" Eleanor said. "It proves he's a Lannigan, but it doesn't prove that he's entitled to one red cent of the money." Three women, including Blondie, agreed with Eleanor, then she continued on. "I think we ought to do what the old lady wanted, and give everything to the Fairchild girl."

"I agree," the housewife said. "A lot of people swore that she and the woman were real close, and Destiny Fairchild acts like a person telling the truth."

"Acts?" Cohen growled. "We're not here to judge her acting ability; we got a responsibility to see justice is done. That thing, she's been waving around ain't nothing but a scribbled on piece of paper, it sure ain't no will. Emerson's lawyer told us when a person dies with no will, the estate is supposed to go to the next of kin."

"Automatically!" a plumber, who up until now hadn't said a word, added.

"He ain't the only kin," Blondie argued. "Apparently, there's one-hundred and forty-seven other Lannigans. Like her lawyer said, if this guy gets the estate, every one of them relatives ought to get their part."

"Okay," Cohen said begrudgingly, "we make the girl pay back everything she's spent, then we'll give the whole ball of wax to all of the Lannigans and let them divvy it up. How's that sound?"

"Absolutely not!" Eleanor snapped. "I'll not go along with making that girl give back one nickel!"

"Me neither," Blondie said.

"Nor will I," a woman who'd been filing her fingernail echoed.

"We ought to give Destiny Fairchild everything," the housewife repeated. "That's what the old woman wanted and that's what we ought to do."

"The law says if there's no will—"

"Law-schmaw," Blondie sneered. "If there wasn't no question about what ought to be, then there wouldn't have been no trial!"

They argued it back and forth for another two hours, and then sick of hearing what one side or the other thought, they worked out a compromise and sent word to Judge Kensington that they were ready with a verdict. I have to say, I really did admire the way Eleanor stood up for things, in fact the way several of those women argued and argued for what they thought was right. I didn't much agree with their final decision, but I suppose under the circumstances, it was the best they could do.

"Ladies and Gentlemen of the jury," Judge Kensington said, "have you reached a verdict?"

"We have, Your Honor," Herman Cohen answered. "Assuming that this petition has been filed on behalf of all Lannigan descendents, we find for the plaintiff, and award the remaining assets in Abigail Lannigan's estate to be divided proportionally among the one-hundred and forty-eight eligible relatives. We also find that the defendant has acted in good conscience, and therefore, no restitution of assets is warranted."

Destiny asked Charles, "Does this mean Elliott will get her house?"

"Not him," Charles answered. "The estate. The house will be sold, and the money in the estate divided among all one hundred and forty-eight Lannigans.

The good news is that you don't have to make restitution for anything, and you're rid of Elliott."

She looked at him teary-eyed, "Thanks," she said, "for everything." As they walked down the courthouse steps, Destiny said, partly to Charles and I believe partly to me, "I know Miss Abigail's happy that Elliott didn't get everything."

"She'll be *very* happy," Charles replied, "because by time they probate those holdings and pay out lawyer's fees, he'll probably get less than one thousand dollars."

"Honestly?" Destiny squealed.

"Honestly," Charles repeated, then he wrapped his arm around her shoulder.

Lord Almighty, I thought, *I certainly do like this young man!*

Three Months Later

fter the trial Judge Kensington allowed that Destiny could select three things from my house to keep as personal mementos, nothing valued at more than three hundred dollars, he told her and a sheriff's deputy would have to escort her through the house to make certain of the fact. I, of course, was hoping she'd take the picture of Will that was hanging on my bedroom wall, but she passed it by and took the tiny little snapshot of me and her with our painted pink toenails. After that, she rummaged through my jewelry box and scooped out my mama's wedding ring—she remembered how much I'd treasured it. The third thing she took was the little leather pouch I'd kept under my pillow all the days of my life. The leather was dry and crackled, worn thin as a piece of parchment paper, but the yellow tie was still knotted tight. When I was sick in bed and waiting to die, I told Destiny the story of that pouch. "It's the heart of a she wolf," I said, "a woman of magical powers gave it to me on the day I was born and I've carried it with me ever since. It gives a person the courage to get through some mighty rough times."

When the sheriff's deputy saw Destiny reach under my bed pillow and take that little pouch, he said, "Wait a minute, what's that you have?"

I suppose he figured the purpose of him being there was to make certain that she didn't take something real valuable.

"It's the heart of a she wolf," Destiny answered.

"Yeah, sure." He had the look of a man who figured himself being played for a fool. "Let's just have a look."

"It's not supposed to be untied."

"If I don't check what's in there," he said, "you can forget about taking it."

Destiny reluctantly handed over the pouch and watched as the deputy tugged loose the leather tie. Despite its years, the tie unfurled as easily as a satin ribbon.

All my life, I'd believed that pouch contained the heart of a she wolf, and many a time when I felt so worn down that I thought I couldn't get through another day, I'd remind myself that some brave wolf gave up that heart for me. I'd go to sleep thinking about that, and then the next morning I'd get up and move on with my life. When the deputy opened the pouch and poured out a handful of Shenandoah Valley sand, I laughed so loud it sounded like the thundering of a rain storm.

"You sure *this* is what you want?" the deputy asked, and Destiny nodded. He poured the sand back into the pouch and handed it to her.

Those three things surely weren't the most practical choices, but my heart was truly touched by the love that went into picking them.

Mister Hoggman refused to waste any more time arguing an appeal—it was a decision he made as soon as he learned that there wasn't any million dollar inheritance and his thirty-percent fee would be fifty thousand dollars instead of the four-hundred-thousand he'd been expecting.

Elliott, on the other hand, never could accept that there was no million dollars to be found. While Destiny and Charles were on their honeymoon, he, acting as executor of my estate, came and cleared out my house. He tore through things like a sore ass bull, yanking stuff out of drawers and closets, shaking loose every towel and blanket in the linen closet, ripping the linings out of coats, still looking for some lost bankbook or safe deposit box key that would lead to the missing million. I always knew that man didn't have a bit of love for anybody or anything, except maybe the money, and he certainly proved me right. Without giving a second thought, he threw my personal belongings in plastic garbage bags—perfectly good clothes that should have gone to the Salvation Army for poor folks to get some use out of, but he wadded them up and tossed them out. He ripped open every garment bag and suitcase he could find, the entire time cussing and ranting like a man gone crazy. "Son-of-a-bitch," he'd yell and bust up some little knickknack that I'd had for fifty years or more. He even sliced a big hole in my mattress and box spring, figuring the money might be hidden in there. Not one thing of sentimental value did he set aside. My good dishes, that for years and years I'd washed by hand so they wouldn't get the least little chip in a cup or saucer, he threw into a garbage pail and shattered into a million pieces. I can't say it didn't hurt to see him treating my things in such a manner, but I kept watching because I wanted to know what would happen to the picture of Will I had hanging on my bedroom wall. Elliott walked right by it a half-dozen times, then he finally yanked it off the wall and tossed it into a garbage bag along with two photo albums and my picture of John Langley. Well now, I thought, that's that.

Elliott had always let on like he was real fond of my brother, but when it came down to it, Will was just another chunk of garbage to him. They say God works in mysterious ways, and I for one believe it. If Elliott had honestly cared about Will, he would have held on to the photograph—and who knows, maybe sooner or later he would have found those bonds hidden behind the picture.

Elliott—well, after they sliced up the money from my estate, he got five-hundred and eighty-seven dollars—the exact same amount as went to Lannigan Families up and down the Shenandoah Valley. Housewives who barely recognized the name Lannigan would open up the envelope and gasp at a windfall they'd never expected. Emma Mulberry bought a new washer and dryer; Albert Bennigan had his tractor repaired and splurged on a gold locket for Mary, his wife of thirty years; Susan Carter bought her daughter a wedding dress, some pearl earrings and a blue garter. All in all, I'd say spreading that money around brought a lot of happiness to a lot of people—well, all except Elliott. He kept looking for that missing million, until finally the bitter taste of frustration settled into his stomach and gave him an ulcer.

I suppose I'm reasonably happy with the way things turned out. My preference would have been for Destiny to inherit everything, but God saw fit to give her something a whole lot better—Charles. When I saw him swear that he'd love and cherish her for as long as he lived, I knew I didn't have to worry about Destiny anymore, she'd found what I'd spent a lifetime looking for. As for those bonds and what finally happened to them—well, that's another story.

# # #